getting warmer

For my parents,
Tom and Peggy Snow

acknowledgments

The transformation from manuscript to book is a long and mysterious process and one I won't even pretend to understand. For working their magic once again, I thank the talented team at Berkley, especially my editor, Cindy Hwang. Big thanks, also, to my too-wonderful-for-words agent, Stephanie Kip Rostan.

I am lucky to have so many friends who not only support my work but also cajole their neighbors, relatives, and neighbors' relatives into buying my books as well. An extra large thank-you goes to Holly Wert and Charlotte Bischel for sharing their time and considerable talents. Thank you, too, to Carrie Hosozawa for making valuable connections and for teaching me a thing or two about eye makeup. I had to learn sometime.

Melissa Karl Lam was kind enough to supply me with a wealth of school psychologist lingo for this book, while Kim Rueben provided enough early inspiration to fill several volumes. Just for the record, she is not really from Saturn. Perhaps most importantly, Maurine Tobin gave me an education in education back when I thought I might be something other than a writer. Make no mistake: teaching is a far more important job and about a million times more difficult.

Thanks to Kim Snow, as always, for her first-reader feedback, to Susy Sullivan for her stealth merchandising, and to Andrew Todhunter for pretty much everything else. And to Lucy and Philip: thanks for just being you.

prologue

It was Friday at the Happy Cactus, and we had a big decision to make. "Happy Cactus Hour" would end in five minutes and along with it our chance to order the two-for-one margaritas. As the cardboard cactus signs plastered around the room informed us, Happy Cactus Hour ended at 6:00 sharp. They meant it, too. A few days before, we'd placed an order at 6:03, only to be charged full price. We'd downed an extra basket of complimentary tortilla chips as a way of exacting revenge.

"I'm done," I said. "Gotta drive." I picked up my curvy glass and sucked on the straw, only to be rewarded with slightly sweet melted ice.

"But I'm getting another, so yours would be free. Besides, they're really weak." My friend outweighed me by a good sixty pounds. She wasn't fat so much as big-boned, not pretty so much as striking. In heels, she approached six feet tall. She could drink me under the table.

The waitress glanced around the mostly empty room, checking for impatient customers. In case you'd missed the spiky plants, lunar landscape and inhuman temperature outside, the restaurant décor let you know that you weren't in Kansas anymore—or in Spokane or Cleveland or wherever you had flown in from. Indian blankets and pastel canyon scenes covered the stucco walls. The waitstaff wore silver bolo ties shaped like geckos. Every few minutes, a blender whined loudly enough to drown out conversation. Welcome to Arizona.

Another customer waved, trying to call the waitress over. She held up her pen to let him know she'd seen him. "Should I just bring the check?" she chirped, tapping her pen on her pad.

"I'm done," I said.

"No, wait," my friend interrupted. "We can't go yet. It's a hundred and twelve degrees in the parking lot. In here, it's what?" She looked at the waitress. "Seventy?"

"I can ask the bartender to turn the AC down if you're cold. But right now I've really got to—"

"Maybe I can help you ladies out."

Here, then, was our knight in shining armor: mid-to-late thirties, average height, a rounded belly matched with incongruously skinny legs, a chubby face flushed from too much sun or alcohol or, most likely, both. His khaki shorts had a reddish stain in the middle of one thigh: salsa, probably. His white T-shirt read HOT, HOT, HOT.

"I couldn't help but hear you ladies talking. I was just thinking about ordering a margarita myself, and so . . ." He gestured with his beer bottle as he talked.

Once the margaritas had been successfully ordered, our new friend motioned to a chair at the empty table next to us. "You mind?"

He dragged the chair over and plopped himself down. "Whee-ew," he said. "All that talk about 'It's not the heat, it's the humidity.' What a load of bull! If you ladies will pardon my French." He took a draw on his beer. His eyes darted back and forth between us. Neither of us is beautiful, but I knew what he was thinking: blond or brunette? Big or small? Like he was choosing between a burger and a chicken salad, coleslaw or fries.

He wiped his mouth on the back of his hand and continued. "This morning I burned my hand getting into my rental car—like touching a hot iron." He held up his palm (which didn't look any redder than the rest of him), holding his beer bottle between his thumb and index finger. He took another swig of the beer before switching the bottle to his left hand and holding out his right. "I'm Darren, by the way."

"Pandora," I said, shaking his damp hand.

"Jo," said my friend, wisely choosing a finger wave over a soggy handshake.

"I'm in from Saint Louis for the fireplace convention. You hear about the fireplace convention? I'm with Bilco—you've probably heard of us, we make freestanding gas stoves, gas fireplaces and gas inserts." He drained his beer.

"You're in sales?" Jo asked.

"Yes, ma'am. Second biggest producer in the Midwest region this quarter."

"Does the first biggest producer get to come to Arizona in January instead of August?" I asked. Darren ignored me.

"And what do you ladies do for a living?" he asked, directing his attention now to Jo. "Professional models, perhaps?" He raised his eyebrows slightly, anticipating girlish giggles.

At this, the waitress showed up with the margaritas. "The bill," I mouthed. She nodded, understanding, and left to get our slip.

Jo left her full margarita glass on the table and poked idly at it with the straw. At the rate she was going, we'd be here all night.

"I'm a health care assistant," I said. I reached into my purse and pulled out a white pill. I put it on the table and slid it over to Jo. "You told me to remind you."

She held my gaze for a minute before giving in. She picked up the pill and downed it with a sip of margarita.

"You got a headache or something?" Darren asked.

"A headache? Oh, no." She stared off into the distance.

He giggled. It was not attractive. "Is that, like, speed, or something?"

I shifted in my chair, tilted up my chin. "We do *not* take illegal drugs."

"Oh, sorry, I—"

"This is strictly prescription-only."

"Antidepressants?" he guessed.

"Hardly," Jo said with a toss of her blond mane. "I have nothing to be depressed about. Not anymore."

"They're her . . . you know." I looked at Darren. He didn't know. "Her hormones." I checked his face: still confused. "Jo is a . . . you know."

Jo sipped her drink and gazed at the ceiling fans spinning lazily above us.

"I don't know," Darren said finally.

"A man!" I said. "At least for now." And then, turning to Jo: "Joseph, you're starting to pass!"

"It's Josephine now," Jo assured Darren in a voice that suddenly seemed lower. "Or, it will be once I get the papers filed. I'm counting down the days until the operation. Perhaps we can get together then?"

After Darren left—well, fled—Jo sat in silence for a while, grimly munching on slightly stale tortilla chips. "What?" I finally asked.

"Nobody would ever believe you're a man," she grumbled.

I shrugged. "You never know. People generally assume you're telling the truth." I reached into my purse and pulled out a little plastic box. "Tic Tac?"

o n e

Okay, before you jump to any conclusions—that I am a pathological liar, or an identity thief, or a nut—let me explain. My name is not Pandora, and I am not a healthcare assistant. My name is Natalie Quackenbush, but I can go days without being called Natalie. People call me Miss Quackenbush, Ms. Quackenbush, or Mrs. Quackenbush—no matter how many times I tell them that Mrs. Quackenbush is my mother. When they think I can't hear them, they call me The Quack or Quackers or, simply, The Duck. I teach English at Agave High School in Scottsdale, Arizona. Go, Roadrunners!

Here are some of the things I don't do: I don't shoplift, cheat on my taxes or sleep with married men. I don't pirate software or run red lights. I don't sneak thirteen items into the express lane at the grocery store.

So I lie a little. It's not like anyone gets hurt.

Besides, I don't lie during the day. During the day, I am a model of virtue. I watch my language. I wear knee-length skirts and high-necked shirts. I stick to my allotted thirty-five minutes for lunch (assuming I am not on lunch duty; on those days, I don't even get thirty-five minutes).

The day after the incident in the bar (just one of many incidents I've had in bars with "Jo" in the last six months or so; Jo's real name is Jill, by the way), I greeted the morning the way I always do: by hitting the snooze button three times more than is prudent. School starts at 7:30 A.M., even though every study that's ever been done says that teenagers need to sleep later than such a schedule allows. I'm going to go out on a limb and say that most adults need more sleep, too, especially if they've been flitting around bars pretending to dispense hormones the night before.

I gave myself a quick, cool rinse in the double-headed marble shower before yanking on a simple blue skirt and a simple blue shirt that would look better if I ironed them but would have to do. I accessorized with a new pair of dangly silver earrings and a luxurious silk scarf. These touches were unusual for me; I had a blind date after work, and while my hopes were low, I hadn't given up on miracles.

I waited till the last minute to put on my sandals. The house's Saltillo tiles felt cool and soothing on my feet. The effect was temporary. I'd start sweating during the drive to work; my Civic's AC just couldn't compete with Arizona in August, even this early in the morning. Downstairs in the kitchen, I opened the stainless steel refrigerator and grabbed a yogurt, an apple and a bottled Starbuck's frapuccino to drink in the car. I gazed out longingly at the boulder-rimmed Pebble Tec pool and spa in the backyard. If my date ended early enough, I'd take a dip, I silently vowed.

Oh, yeah, in case you haven't already concluded that I'm a total loser, here's another nugget: I live with my parents.

I got to my classroom at 7:31, a minute after the first bell had rung. It's a good thing the school custodians unlocked the classrooms at 7:15; otherwise I'd have had packs of students conspicuously waiting in the hallway at least once a week. Today the students were variously slumped in their seats or leaning on their friends' desks. "Seats, please," I said, clearing my throat. I did a quick scan of the room, praying that they were all on time, that I wouldn't have to choose between rule-bending and hypocrisy.

Rule-bending won. Robert Baumgartner strolled in four minutes after the bell. The yellow late slips sat prominently on my enormous brown laminate desk. It had been a mere two days since Agave High's faculty meeting had focused on the problem of tardiness and consistency. "We must declare our solidarity in this issue," intoned the principal, Dr. Florenzia White. "If a portion of the faculty looks the other way when students are tardy, the entire school suffers." She was right, of course. Dr. White was always right. "Final warning, Robert," I said with as much authority as I could muster. "Next time you get a slip."

"Sorry, Mrs. Quackenbush," he said, batting absurdly long eyelashes. "I had car trouble. It won't happen again, I swear." He settled his long, languid body in his chair. The girls in the class shot him worshipful looks.

"Mrs. Quackenbush is my mother," I said. "But let's move on. How many of you did the homework last night?" A scattering of hands rose in the air. I heard one voice say, "We had homework?"

Mistake number two: I had asked about the homework as if doing it had been an option. I should have said, "I assume you did the homework last night." Or, better yet, "Please pull out your homework." But this was twelfth grade "Adventures in English," otherwise known as, "The Slow Class." The first time I heard the

"Adventures" moniker, I envisioned a bunch of cape-clad adolescents soaring over the desert, Superman-style. A week and a half into the school year, I could tell that there would be very little soaring going on in this group. I had worried about behavior problems, but the fact was, there was almost no behavior at all.

Most of the kids weren't even slow. Some, like Robert, were of average or superior intelligence but afflicted with learning disabilities. Others spoke English as a second language (the first being Spanish, mostly). Still others just didn't give a damn. I mean a darn.

The one thing they had in common seemed to be a complete inability to grasp anything I taught them. When the bell rang, forty-three minutes later, it was clear that not one of the eighteen students knew how to use quotation marks.

Robert smiled at me on the way out. "I'll do my homework tonight. I promise."

"I'll remember you said that." I tried to sound like I believed him. Robert would probably end up in prison some day, which saddened me because I was already quite fond of him.

"You look nice today, Mrs. Quackenbush," he said. "I like the scarf."

"Why, thank you, Robert!"

"It's a nice change from your usual Secret Service look." And then he was gone.

At lunchtime, I went to the front office to find Jill. Jill is the school psychologist, a testament to the widely held belief that all shrinks are crazy. She was leaning over the tall counter that separates the secretaries from the students—ironic, considering that both secretaries had been students at Agave just a few years before. Dawna

("Mrs. Johnson") was twenty years old, already fat and married to a former Agave student with a baby named Chenille at home.

Nicolette ("Miss Badanski") was twenty-one and enmeshed in the process of choosing her bridal registry. Right now she was showing Jill a flier from Bed, Bath & Beyond. "I was totally set on that eggplant-colored duvet cover from Linens 'n Things—remember I showed you the picture last week? With the gold trim and the fringed throw pillows? But now I'm looking at this other one, it's—what do they call it?—claret-colored. Totally classy. But if I go this way, it means I'm going to have to change my towels. Macy's has me down for eggplant, but I'm thinking beige might be safer. But then I'm all—*beige*? Is that totally boring, or what?"

Jill studied the picture. "I'd stick to the eggplant. This one's a bit, I don't know. Too much."

"Miss Quackenbush? What do you think?" Nicolette asked.

I looked at the picture. Ick. "I'm with Jill. This one's a little overwhelming."

"Nicolette wants to go out with us sometime," Jill said to me. I glared up at her. We had never discussed enlarging our "circle" of two. Besides, Nicolette would get all the attention; she was blessed with the biggest breasts I'd ever seen on a thin person who had never undergone a boob job. (Hers were certified genuine; much of the staff had witnessed her girl-to-woman transformation during the spring of her freshman year. "Like she sprouted pillows overnight," was how one teacher described it.)

"Yeah," Nicolette said. "I've got to start meeting men. The guys around here are all losers." For all her registry talk, Nicolette was not only unengaged, she was unattached. She was weirdly rational about her burgeoning registry, which she had started the year before, following Dawna's marriage to Chad Johnson. Dawna had a brief (nine-day) engagement after discovering that "God had blessed her" with what was to become little Chenille. A scattering of high school friends (she had graduated the year before) and teachers had crowded in her parents' tiny backyard on a sweltering October day to hear Dawna and Chad pledge eternal devotion.

For all its shaky beginnings, the marriage seemed to be progressing smoothly. Chad took care of Chenille during the day; evenings he worked as a bellhop. Dawna took copious photos of their "family time," which took place between the hours of 3 and 5 P.M. When Chenille went to bed each evening Dawna posted the photos into scrapbook after scrapbook.

But Nicolette was unimpressed by Dawna's marriage. She focused exclusively on the wedding and what she considered a paltry take: a handful of gift cards (two for Wal-Mart), three salad bowls, two platters and too many candlesticks and vases to count. As documented in her scrapbooks, Dawna, Chad and little Chenille ate their four o'clock dinners off mismatched thrift store plates and drank their milk from plastic glasses. Their tablecloth was vinyl.

The lesson had not been lost on Nicolette. "I'm going to be ready," she said. "Even if I elope, I'll be prepared." She was currently registered at Linens 'n Things, Macy's, Robinsons-May, Target and The Great Indoors. She had gone so far as to get the registry form from Bed Bath & Beyond but was concerned that that might be overkill.

I let Jill have it when we sat down at our favorite corner of our favorite table in the teacher's dining room. "I can't believe you invited Pamela Anderson out with us."

"Not fair," Jill said, popping open her Diet Coke. "Nicolette's boobs are real."

"So are Pamela's. She had the implants removed. I read it in *People*."

"When do you have time to read *People*? Aren't you supposed to be reading *The Odyssey*?"

I sighed and pulled out my yogurt and apple. "I bought the *CliffsNotes*. I just couldn't keep up with those kids." That would be my ninth-grade honors class, which I'd inherited when the woman who had been teaching it since the seventies had a nervous breakdown on the second day of school.

"Would anyone believe Nicolette is a man?" Jill asked.

"Oh, God, is that what this is all about?" I peeled the foil off my yogurt. Jill unzipped her padded blue cooler and pulled out a hunk of French bread. "What is that?"

"Roast pork loin sandwich with roasted red peppers and goat cheese."

"Wanna trade? I won't complain about Nicolette anymore."

"Not a chance." She bit into her sandwich, and a look of bliss flickered across her face. "So what do you think? We try the transsexual routine with Nicolette, see if anyone falls for it."

"You don't look like a man," I said.

"Sure," she said. "You don't know what it's like to have every guy you've ever dated beg you to play volleyball for his company team."

The door to the dining room swung open. "It's Mr. Handsome," I whispered. He was carrying a plastic orange tray.

"Gay," Jill muttered.

"Is not."

"Just try not to look desperate."

I caught Lars's eye and waved. "Desperate," Jill hissed.

"Ssh."

Lars said hello to a couple of teachers and strode over to us. "Ms. Quackenbush. Ms. Green."

"Hello, Lars," I said in a decidedly casual, un-desperate way. Lars Hansen had flippy blond hair ("Too pretty," Jill said), a gym rat body ("Too vain"), and an easy sense of humor ("Too smooth"). He was twenty-six years old ("Too young"). Like me, he taught English, though he also had one drama class and responsibility for the school play ("Gay, gay, gay"). Lars was madly in love with me. He just didn't know it yet.

Lars put his tray on the table. Today's cafeteria lunch: a hunk of gray-brown meat, canned string beans, glutinous mashed potatoes. I could never be that hungry.

"Natalie has a date tonight," Jill announced.

"A blind date," I quickly clarified before wondering if I should have given him an opportunity to be jealous.

"Anyone I know?" Lars asked.

"*She* doesn't even know him. It's a blind date," Jill said in her teacher-talking-to-an-especially-dumb-student voice.

"Oh! Right! Well, good for you. I guess it's hard to meet men around here."

two

Three years ago, I swore off blind dates forever, but it turns out that forever was not as long as I'd expected. I'd been having one of those "crisis years," when everything in my life changed in rapid succession: my boyfriend, my apartment, my job.

My boyfriend's name was Ron, and while my mother still thinks I should have married him (her mantra: "Dartmouth undergrad, Harvard Business School, a promising career in investment banking—what more do you want?"), I have never regretted my decision to send him packing (well, to send myself packing; it was his apartment), though I occasionally wish I'd fought harder for the DVD player.

We were living in Boston. We'd been together almost four years, and everyone assumed we'd eventually marry. My parents had just sold their house in Newton and moved to Scottsdale. Their move hit me harder than I had expected. Suddenly, I had nowhere to go for Sunday dinner. Suddenly, Ron was my only "family"—and he didn't care about me enough to make me mashed potatoes and carrot cake.

It was more than that, though. While Ron obsessed over whether he'd be able to make his first million by the time he hit thirty (he was twenty-eight; I was twenty-six) or whether he had to wait till thirty-five (and if so whether he should adjust for inflation and raise his goal to 1.1 million), I was making my mark on the world by doing production work for a direct mail company, helping to create and distribute flyers for cabinet refacers, Chinese restaurants and cut-rate law firms.

My epiphany didn't come at once. Rather, it grew in my subconscious, kind of like when you get a glossy ad for a mattress and you throw it out, and then you get another mattress advertisement and you throw it out, and then you get another and you throw it out, and then one day you wake up at three o'clock in the morning, and you can't get back to sleep, and your spine hurts and your leg twitches, and it hits you like a ton of bricks: you need a new mattress!

But I didn't need a new mattress (well, not yet, anyway, though I would once I moved out). I needed a new boyfriend—or, failing that, I needed no boyfriend. And I needed a new career, preferably one in which I wouldn't profit from annoying people.

Teaching seemed perfect. I could indulge my love of literature while fulfilling my sense of service. Plus, I'd get to leave work at three o'clock every day and get summers off.

I didn't transform my life overnight, of course. There were applications to be filed, loans to acquire, new roommates to be found. There was a part-time waitressing job to endure, classes to attend, papers to write, a student teaching stint to complete.

While I remade my identity, Ron solidified his. A month after claiming he'd never be able to love or trust another woman, he hooked up with another Harvard Business School graduate four years his senior. Together, they bought a condo with views of the Charles River. I expected to be jealous. Sometimes it worried me that I wasn't, that there must be something wrong with me if I could care so little for a man I almost married.

My friends rallied. They assumed I was devastated and set to work hooking me up with every single man in Boston between the ages of twenty-five and thirty. After awhile, the men began to blur together. John had just returned from backpacking in Hungary. Steve was from California and missed the sun. Pete was doing a PhD in molecular biology. Chris had just broken up with his college sweetheart. And on, and on, and on.

They weren't all duds, but I was too tired to make much effort. When my friends called for the post-date play-by-play, I'd report back that, "He was nice, but . . ." John was too immature, Steve was too flaky, Pete was too nerdy, and Chris was still hung up on his ex-girlfriend.

Eventually, I exhausted the entire supply of my friends' unattached male friends. Or maybe my friends just got fed up with me. It didn't matter, anyway. When I failed to find a teaching job in the Boston area—the result of too many universities cranking out too many teachers—I heeded my parents' advice and applied for my Arizona teaching certification. After a round of interviews, I received several job offers in the booming, sprawling Phoenix Valley and accepted the one closest to my parents' house in North Scottsdale.

As I moved cardboard boxes into my new bedroom (which has cathedral ceilings, a walk-in closet and its own bathroom—though I still prefer my parents' double-headed shower in the master bath), my parents told me I was welcome to stay with them for now, "though you'll probably be wanting a place of your own soon." When I received my Fannie Mae student loan payment book and started to hyperventilate (I'd be almost fifty by the time I paid everything off), they suggested I go soak in the spa and said that of course I could stay until I got on firmer financial footing. Now that I've been here a year, we don't talk about me moving out. They simply remind me to water the plants when they leave town.

And they leave town a lot. Typically, Scottsdale's daily high temperatures start nudging toward one hundred in the middle of April. There are no spring showers. The average daily lows creep up gradually, peaking around eighty in July and August. Understand that "low" temperature hits at around four o'clock in the morning. Summer evenings rarely fall below ninety.

In June, just after I had finished up my classes for the year, my parents headed for higher elevations (while I headed for a mind-numbing summer job answering phones and filing permits in an architect's office). Their new best friends, Barbara and Stan Gillespie, have a cabin in Flagstaff, and my parents were able to secure a rental condo nearby. They came back for a couple of nights in July before flying East. My sister, Shelly, a graphic artist, a.k.a. "the creative one," lives in Rhode Island with her long-term, perpetual grad student boyfriend, Frederick, a.k.a. "he who will not commit." My aunts live in Connecticut and Pennsylvania. By mid-October, having exhausted their entire reserve of friends and family with nice guest rooms, my parents will fly back to their Spanish-tiled dream house—just in time to see the mercury plunge.

When people ask me where I live, I've taken to saying, "I'm house-sitting for my parents." I don't even like to admit to myself that I'm twenty-nine years old, unattached, mired in debt and dependent on my parents—not quite the idealistic save-the-world existence I'd envisioned. At least they have a killer pool.

And, yes, I've thrown myself back into a different kind of pool: that of eligible singles. Another English teacher, Mrs. Clausen, arranged tonight's rendezvous. Paul is a nice young aerospace engineer who works with her husband. Like me, he's from the East, so if we run out of conversation, we can always bitch about the weather and compare snake sightings. Mrs. Clausen met Paul at her husband's company picnic, got his number and, voila! I've got a date.

I arrived at Route 66, Scottsdale's coolest restaurant, at six o'clock—right on time. My blue shirt and skirt felt too English teacher-y, my dangling silver earrings too predictable. I looked like I could burst into a lecture on *Catcher in the Rye* at any minute.

I spotted Paul immediately. He was sitting alone at the neon-lit chrome bar, the only person in the place who looked even less trendy than I did. He was wearing a yellow golf shirt, khakis and brown cowboy boots.

"Paul?" I asked with a smile, thinking: maybe I can be out of here by eight.

He turned, looked momentarily confused, smiled back. His grin transformed his face, making him not handsome, exactly, but certainly appealing. His eyes were brown with little flecks of gold. They crinkled nicely at the corners. His hair was sandy and wavy, flecked here and there with gray. He looked older than I expected, maybe in his mid-thirties. His nose was sunburned and just starting to peel.

"I'm Natalie," I said. "I think our table is ready, if you want to eat now. Or we can have a drink first, if you'd like."

"I'd love to have dinner with you," he said. His voice was

warm, easy. Suddenly, unexpectedly, I looked forward to spending the evening with him.

"Okay, then." I smiled and started to walk toward the hostess stand.

"But I'm not Paul."

I stopped and turned around to stare. His brown eyes twinkled.

"Natalie?" said a voice right next to me. I spun around. This, then was Paul: medium brown hair, light eyes, average height, athletic build, around my age. He was interchangeable with at least five guys I'd been set up with before. He wore a black silk camp shirt, gray trousers and man sandals. He didn't look like an engineer. He looked like a Route 66 regular, only straight.

"Paul?" I asked. I wasn't going to embarrass myself again.

"Yes," he said. I smiled. He smiled back. Sort of.

"Our table's ready," I said. "You want to sit?"

"Okay . . ." he said.

We sat down at our shiny white table, which sat in the middle of the restaurant, leaving me feeling far too exposed. I pulled my napkin off the table and smoothed it across my lap. My palms were sweating.

"Is this your first time here?" I asked.

"Yes," he said.

"It's a fun place," I said. "The cocktails are good. And you've got to check out the bathrooms. The stalls are mirrored."

He was looking at me funny. I cleared my throat. "Not that I like to watch myself, you know. Using the, um, the restroom."

He was still staring at me. I tugged at my napkin. "And I'm sure the men's room has urinals, so if you don't like the whole mirror thing, you don't have to. You know. Use the stalls. Well!" I smiled at him. My face hurt. When you're in a hole, stop digging, I chided myself. *Stop digging!*

"You don't remember me," he said.

"Excuse me?"

"Michelle Stevens set us up a few years ago. In Boston."

I stared at him. So, he wasn't just interchangeable with other blind dates—he *was* one of my blind dates! I'd been set up so many times, I had run out of new men to meet. I was starting to recycle.

"Right! Ohmigod! How are you?" I was trying to place him. "How's Michelle? I feel so bad that I haven't called her."

"Michelle's good," he said evenly. "She has a new job—human resources for a nonprofit."

"That sounds great. This is so weird. Like, maybe it's fate or something." I'd written Paul off in Boston, but then, I'd written everyone off in Boston. As far as I could tell, he was an improvement over most of the men I'd met in Arizona. Maybe I'd give him a second chance.

Paul looked at me calmly. "You told Michelle that I spent the whole evening talking about myself."

"I said that? She told you I said that?"

"And that I had no sense of humor."

"That's—I'm sorry. That wasn't fair."

"And that all I cared about was running and I automatically assumed everyone else would be interested in hearing about training for the Boston Marathon."

The Marathon Guy! Now I remembered him!

"I'm sorry," I said with as much contrition as I could manage, though all I could think was: *Michelle! What a bitch!* "I was going through a rough time. It had nothing to do with you."

Paul stood up. "I'll tell Michelle you said hello."

"You're *leaving*?"

"I wouldn't want you to waste another evening on me," he spat. "And I have no desire to waste another on you." He turned and strode out of the restaurant.

My first impulse was to bolt. But I didn't want to run the risk of seeing Paul outside. I couldn't stay at my table; my sudden solitary status felt too conspicuous. So I headed for the bathroom and shut myself in a stall.

Mirrors. Given my inane ramblings merely moments before, you'd think I wouldn't have jumped when I closed the stall door only to see myself in front of myself and on either side of me. Four of me, all lit in pink neon—as if one wasn't enough.

I looked like shit. No, that's not true. If I was someone else looking at me, I wouldn't think I looked bad. I simply wouldn't notice me at all. In preparation for my teaching interviews, I'd chopped my long hair and kept it that way ever since. I tried to tell myself that the short hairdo looked chic, but really, it just looked short. My face wasn't pretty enough to pull off such a severe cut. I was tan—it was hard not to be around here—but after two weeks in the classroom, my skin was already getting that faded, sallow look. My blue clothes were even more wrinkled than they had been this morning. My scarf belonged on someone twenty years older. I looked like someone named Mrs. Quackenbush.

I exited the stall before I had to watch myself crying, flushing the unused toilet in case anyone was listening. I held back the tears by taking a few deep breaths and picturing a blank wall in my mind, a trick I used at least once a week at work, when I was so tired and frustrated and I just wanted to give some kid the finger and cry but

I couldn't. So at school I'd take a cleansing breath, hold it in, release and repeat. Then, when I'd finally regained my composure, I'd speak in an authoritarian tone and act like my feelings weren't hurt. Because everyone knows that teachers don't have feelings.

As I exited the ladies room, I was hit by a flash of yellow. The guy from the bar—the guy who was not Paul—was exiting the men's room at just the same moment. "Sorry," he said, grabbing my arm so I wouldn't fall over. "Oh, it's you." He was laughing a little.

"What's so funny?" I asked, sure he'd seen my date storming off.

"Oh, it's nothing. It's just—I guess I've never used the restroom here before. Are the stalls in the ladies room . . . ?"

"Mirrored," I said. "It's really funny when you're drunk. When you're sober—not so much."

"You mean Paul hasn't bought you a drink yet?"

"Paul? No." So he hadn't witnessed my humiliation. "Paul and I are no longer an item. Or a potential item. We're citing irreconcilable differences."

"That was fast."

"Yeah, it was kind of like speed-dating. Just without, you know, the other nineteen guys waiting to meet me."

"I'd like to meet you," he said, coloring slightly.

At that, a really, really, really tall woman with long black hair and a short black skirt said, "Excuse me?" We looked at her quizzically before realizing we were blocking the bathroom.

"Oh, sorry," the guy in yellow and I said at the same moment, clearing the way so she could waltz past us in her heels.

He turned back to me and said, "So, what do you think? Can I buy you a drink?"

"Only if you promise not to walk out on me after five minutes."

We made our way back to the bar. There was only one stool left; he let me have it. The guy sitting to my left was wearing eyeliner, I noticed. Even weirder, it looked good on him.

"What can I get you?" Jonathan asked. (We had traded names by now.)

"I don't know. Something colorful."

"Any color in particular?"

"Blue is nice. But maybe pink is safer."

"Oh, no. Let's go with the blue."

The drinks came quickly; Jonathan seemed to know the bartender. Great: a local alkie drinking alone at his favorite bar. Just when I was starting to like him, too.

Jonathan checked his watch. "We've reached a milestone. Six minutes."

"Things are looking up." I smiled and sipped (okay, gulped) my Blue Hawaiian.

"So, are you going to tell me why the guy walked out on you?"

"Did you see it? I got the impression you hadn't noticed." I looked over to Paul's and my table. It had been quickly filled by another couple who looked like they liked each other.

"I just happened to be glancing over," he said, not very convincingly. "If you don't want to talk about it . . ."

I didn't, but what could I say? I was about to tell the truth: kind of a funny story, really—except I'd come out like a total bitch for bad-mouthing Paul to my (former) friend. And I looked desperate for being set up so many times.

"There were just some things about me, about my life, that he couldn't deal with," I said cryptically. "My job and stuff."

"What do you do?"

"I'm a, uh, teacher." There. I said it.

"Why would that be a problem?"

Now what? If only Jill were here. I looked at my glass: empty already. I looked back up at Jonathan. I liked him. I liked talking to him. He had beautiful brown eyes. He spent his evenings drinking alone at bars. This was going nowhere.

I glanced at the man sitting next to me. He wore a shirt with wide, horizontal stripes.

"I teach prisoners to read," I said. "Out at the, you know. Prison." Whenever I drove to the nearest outlet mall, I passed signs that read, PRISON NEARBY; DO NOT PICK UP HITCHHIKERS. Besides, there were always chain gangs picking up garbage on Scottsdale Road.

"That's intense," he said. "What are they in for?"

"The prisoners? Oh, all kinds of things." I'd already started this thing. I might as well give it my all. "Drugs, violent crimes. There's some sex offenders, but I try to avoid them."

"Murderers?"

"Oh, sure. Murderers. Lots of murderers."

He sat back and sipped his Blue Hawaiian thoughtfully. "I can't believe that Paul guy walked out because of that."

He was criticizing Paul, I knew, but it made me feel that my story was somehow inadequate. "Then there's my living situation. I live with my parents."

He shrugged, looked puzzled as if to say: loser-ly, yes, but not worth such an abrupt exit.

"My mother's senile. Crazy. Alzheimer's. She howls at the moon and chases people. Sometimes she chases dogs."

"Oh, my God," he said.

"Yeah. My father is completely overwhelmed, so the caretaking all falls to me. So you can see why Paul left."

He shook his head. "Because he's a complete jerk."

I shrugged. "It's a lot to deal with. Most men can't."

"Maybe you've been meeting the wrong men."

"I won't argue with you there."

The bartender came over. "Jim called," he said to Jonathan. "Said to tell you he's had a family emergency and can't make it in tonight. Said you should call him tomorrow to set up another meeting. Or, if you want, you can wait around. Cherie will be here in about a half hour."

Jonathan paused. "Cherie Williamson?"

"Yeah. You know her? She used to work at that barbecue place around the corner. Anyway, drinks are on the house. You want another?"

"No, thanks. I'll just give Jim a call in the morning." Remembering his manners, he looked at me. "You want another drink?"

"No, thanks—I've got to drive," I said, even though I wasn't quite ready to say good-bye.

He pulled his wallet out of the back pocket of his khakis and extracted a generous tip for the bartender.

"You were waiting for someone?" I asked.

"The manager," he said. "I'm in restaurant supplies. Trying to drum up some new business." He looked up at me. His eyes twinkled. "What did you think? That I was a drunk on the prowl?"

"No!" I said, blinking furiously. "Of course not."

"I didn't think so. You wouldn't have been so honest about yourself if you had." He put his wallet back in his pocket and scanned the room. "Looks like the tables here are all taken. You want to go somewhere else and grab a bite to eat?"

three

I would have woken up smiling if I were the type; my evening with Jonathan had been the best I'd had since moving to Arizona. Instead I woke up swearing. "Gosh dang it!" I know: a pathetic excuse for an expletive. But I'd been scared straight. Last year, I'd knocked an enormous textbook onto my foot and started screaming my former favorite word, which, if you must know, begins with "s." The class stared at me, shocked. I was terrified they'd tell on me. They didn't, as far as I know. The incident made me realize, though, that I had to watch myself at all times; the goshes, darns and dangs had to be second nature so nothing R-rated would slip out. A couple of Mormon teachers recommended, "Oh, my heck" and, when utterly overwhelmed, upset and/or angry, "CHEESE and rice!" As yet, I hadn't fallen that far.

Anyway, I didn't wake up to a falling textbook but to the realization that the power had gone out in the middle of the night. My alarm clock was blinking. I had only ten minutes to get out of the house.

I made it. I was greasy and dirty and possibly even smelly, but I dropped my bag next to my desk with at least four seconds to spare.

The students were all on time and sitting in their seats, ready to learn. This was not Adventures in English, but freshman honors. We had a rotating schedule, which meant that every day I had a different first-period class. The rationale: students are more alert at certain times of the day. With a rotating schedule they'd be "optimally receptive to learning" in every class—at least some of the time. The reality was that I almost always had students from the wrong class wandering in, scrunching their noses and saying, "Am I here today? Is it Tuesday?" The schedule confounded me; I was immensely grateful to be able to stick with one classroom.

Cody Gold was sitting in the front row, as usual. "You look nice today, Miss Quackenbush," he squeaked, gazing up at me. I did not look nice. I looked like hell. Sorry. Like heck. But love is blind.

"Thank you, Cody," I said dutifully.

Next to Cody sat Claudia Pimpernel. (I referred to this as my "C" class: in addition to Cody and Claudia, we had Carlos, Callie, Candace, Christina, two Christophers and a Christian.) "Thank you for your comments on my essay," she said. "They are really helping me grow as a writer." Claudia was not in love with me. Claudia was in love with the image of herself starting Harvard in four years.

"I'm glad I could help, Claudia," I said. "Just remember: semicolons are not the same as commas." She nodded her enthusiastic assent and pulled out her Lisa Frank notebook so she could record my wisdom.

The first day of class, I had announced that students could choose their own seats. It seemed safe; honors kids almost never have behavior problems. Claudia secured her place in the front row early; Cody followed a couple of days later, when he mistook a sudden release of adolescent testosterone for love.

And then there was Jared. For Jared, I had no choice but to break my no-obscenity rule, at least in private, as he was, quite simply, a little shit. Before teaching, I had this absurd idea that my compassion and understanding could extend to anyone. Anyone! I discovered early that there were some students that I simply didn't care for. They were sullen, apathetic, rude—whatever. I looked forward to the last day of school and hoped I would not encounter these students again. At the same time, I congratulated myself for taking pains to set my feelings aside and grade fairly.

And then I met Jared. It wasn't his hyperactivity that made me despise him, though of course that didn't help. It wasn't that he had no business being in this class of bright-eyed overachievers; his parents had screamed at the principal and flashed some privately administered intelligence test scores until she finally relented. It was that, at his core, Jared was evil.

Jared sat in the front row—not by choice, of course. The first day of school he planted himself in the back, where he had no trouble convincing Carlos and one of the Christophers, two normally genial, placid boys, to throw spit balls. After four or five final warnings, I moved Jared to a seat next to the exemplary Sarah Levine. It worked for a day, and I congratulated myself on my problem-solving skills. Day two Jared had Sarah giggling and passing notes. Sarah teared up when I scolded them: "This is not the kind of behavior I expect from honors students." (Yeah, I know:

major gag.) Sarah stayed after class to apologize and had looked frightened in my presence ever since.

Finally, I had no choice but to place Jared front row center, displacing a heartbroken Cody. Now I spent every class trying to block out the sound of Jared's pen tapping and squeaky sneaker thumping. Since neither Cody nor Claudia had fallen prey to his charms, he talked to himself behind his palm, saying things that sounded an awful lot like, "This class sucks," and, "Who gives a fart."

Today, partly because I had asked Mrs. Clausen for advice on how to maximize class discussion and partly because I couldn't bear forty-five minutes of Jared staring at me with his rodent eyes, I had the kids move their desks into a circle. The discussion was pretty much the same as always (Sarah said something brilliant; Claudia interrupted her to say something inane; Cody thanked me for my insights), but at least the rearrangement killed three minutes (ninety seconds to put the desks into the circle, another ninety to put them back). Also, Jared wasn't quite so much in my face, and he even stopped tapping his pen for a few minutes.

Once the bell rang and the kids shuffled out, I straightened the desks. They were all mixed up, as I had told the kids to stick the desks back into rows before they left; I didn't say they had to return them to their original position. In the second row back, a desk on the end had new blue ballpoint graffiti: "Fuck the Duck."

Stupidly, I teared up. I doused the spot with some Comet that I kept in my desk. It left scratch marks on the beige laminate desk, but at least it obliterated the words. Thank God he hadn't had time to dig any deeper.

I fled to the English teachers' lounge. This was my prep period, but right now maintaining the caffeine level in my blood seemed like a more important priority than doing any actual work. Besides,

Jared's evil karma still hung over my classroom. I dropped a dime into the can next to the coffeepot and poured myself a mug that managed to be both bitter and tasteless at the same time. I added plenty of nondairy creamer to make sure I got my ten cents' worth.

The door swung open; Mrs. Clausen scurried in. "I need the Globe for my next class," she said breathlessly, grabbing the department's model of Shakespeare's theater. She looked immaculate, as always, in a tailored gray skirt, peach silk blouse and a thick gold chain. Her silver hair was short and expensively cut. "We're starting *Hamlet* today—the kids are so excited!" Mrs. Clausen is the kind of committed, innovative teacher I want to be, assuming I keep teaching and don't end up incarcerated for, say, sneaking poisonous oleander petals into Jared's peanut butter and jelly sandwiches. "How did it go last night?" she asked.

I suddenly brightened. "It was wonderful. I haven't had that much fun in ages."

"I'm so happy for you!" she said. "I just knew you and Paul would hit it off!" With a little wave of her pinky (she was holding the model, after all), she disappeared out the door. Oh, well. I could explain later—assuming Paul didn't explain first.

After guzzling my coffee, I made my way down to the counseling office, where I found Jill alone, relaxed and flipping through some paperwork. I swear: if I had it to do over, I would have gone the school psychology route. Yeah, sure, the job has its downsides: the Ritalin pushing, the suicide prevention, the STD talks. Last year Jill shared her file of syphilis photos with me; I haven't had sex since. But she is spared the nightly task of grading ninety-two homework papers. She never has to make sense of *The Odyssey*. Kids don't carve obscenities in her furniture. Genital warts just can't compete.

I closed her door behind me (the anorexics, suicidals and general delinquents would just have to wait) and settled myself in one of the two chairs across from her desk (typically, one is for a wayward student, the other for the parent responsible for bringing up such a thug). I grinned.

"So?" she said.

"I had a nice evening." I blushed. Behind Jill's desk, a poster showed a clean-cut boy in a varsity jacket chastely holding hands with a pretty girl. Above them, giant letters read: WAITING FOR MARRIAGE: IT'S THE RIGHT DECISION.

Jill leaned forward. "Oh, my God! Did you get laid?"

"No!" I said. "I just had a couple of drinks. Ate a burrito. Had a nice kiss." I blushed again.

"Who knew? Just when you were getting ready to swear off blind dates forever. I mean forever again."

"That's what's so funny—it wasn't the blind date guy!" I explained how Jonathan and I had met, the story I had told him. After chatting for a while at the bar, we'd gone for a walk out on the plaza to get away from the noise. Eventually, we got hungry, and Jonathan took me to this amazing hole-in-the-wall burrito place he knew of in Old Town Scottsdale. At this point, I regretted my lies, but I didn't want to ruin the evening. Instead, I steered the conversation around to the things about me that were true: my childhood in Massachusetts, college, grad school—pretty much everything up to the point when I took the job at the prison and my mother completely lost her mind.

Jonathan, in turn, told me that he was a Phoenix native. He loved the desert, loved the heat, could tell the good snakes from the bad. He loved the summer monsoons: the black wall of clouds that moves across the desert, its approach announced by a chain lightning marquis, and finally arrives to unleash apocalyptic rain and wall-shaking thunder.

"I'll come clean next time I see him," I told Jill. "We're going out on Friday. Hopefully, he won't think I'm too much of a jerk."

"Wow. Two dates in one week. You'll be having sex in no time."

"Would you stop?"

"I have some pamphlets if you want to refresh your memory," she said, opening her desk.

There was a knock on the door. "Damn," Jill said. "Just when it was getting good."

It was Nicolette. "Oh! Hi, Miss Quackenbush!"

"You can call me Natalie," I said, as patiently as I could.

"Right! Natalie! Anyways, did Jill tell you? That we're going out on Friday?" Without waiting for my reply, she plopped into the chair next to me (the parent chair) and babbled on. "I've got the funniest idea! For the story we make up? I say I was abducted by aliens! But like, they've let me come back. I mean, obviously. And Jill is from the FBI. And we're not supposed to tell anyone about it, and she keeps saying, like, *Shut up or we'll get in trouble!* And Miss Qua—Natalie? You're—you ready?—an *alien*! How funny is that?"

"It's funny," I said, not telling her the cardinal rule of bar lies: the story has to be at least minimally credible. "But I won't be able to make it. I've got a date." I tried not to look too smug, but when Nicolette asked for details, I simply told her the truth: "He's thirty-three, never married, runs his own business and owns a house." She gawked. Clearly, I'd found a man who was registry-worthy.

"We've only just met," I said, as casually as I could manage. "Who knows what will happen."

"Have you Googled him yet?" Nicolette asked.

"What? Of course not."

"I always Google my dates," Nicolette said. "One time, I went out with this guy who looked exactly like this other guy who was on *America's Most Wanted*."

"Was it the same guy?" Jill asked.

"No. But he did have two kids he'd forgotten to mention."

"You found that out online?" I asked.

"No, I found it out when I went to his apartment without calling first and there were two kids there. But I never would have checked up on him like that if I hadn't Googled him first and come across that picture."

The frightening thing about Nicolette is that she thinks she makes sense.

Jill checked the clock on the wall. "We don't have time now, but how about we meet in the Media Center at noon? We can Google Jonathan together."

"Okay!" Nicolette chirped. "See you then!" She left the room before I had a chance to answer.

I glared at Jill. "Jonathan has nothing to hide."

"You're probably right," she said. "Let's just hope he doesn't Google you."

The Media Center—what we used to call "the library" in the old days—was a large room in the middle of the school that was brightly but unflatteringly lit by fluorescents. One half—the empty half—held dusty books and outdated periodicals. Clearly, taxpayer dollars had all been spent on the other part of the room, which was filled by three rows of computers that were perpetually occupied by at least one and usually more like three students per monitor, most of whom had far superior machines at home. Parents, school boards and educators alike were committed to the importance of computer literacy. History teachers told their students to close their books and head down the hall to learn research skills. Math students took time off from pen-and-paper algebra to master Excel. The irony, of course, was that most of these kids knew how to navigate a computer long before they could read a book. They could create professional-looking report covers and bypass the most elaborate parental controls. So what if they never mastered punctuation and long division.

Jill and Nicolette were already waiting for me at the teachers' computer, which was located behind the librarian's desk. It was the only machine in the school without parental controls. As such, everyone joked about teachers using it to look at porn.

"What's his last name?" Nicolette asked. She had already typed "Johnathan" into the computer.

"There's no 'h' in Jonathan," I said.

"But Johnathan Garubo in the tenth grade spells it that way."

"That's just because his parents can't spell. His sister is named Gennifer with a 'G.' Let me do it." I took over the swivel chair. Nicolette leaned over me, her blond hair blocking the computer. She wore too much perfume, something flowery. I typed, "Jonathan Pomeroy," took a deep breath, and hit Enter.

"There," I said. I hadn't even realized I'd been holding my breath until I saw a heading marked "Pomeroy Restaurant Supply" and exhaled with relief. "He's just who he said he is."

"How do we know it's the same guy?" Nicolette asked, still holding out hope that Jonathan might be a fraud. She leaned over me, her bleached hair brushing my face and feeling like cobwebs. She clicked on the Web site, and sure enough, Jonathan was the company president, just as he'd said, and the company was located in Phoenix, just as he'd said. "What did you say he was? Thirty-three?" Nicolette asked, looking at Jonathan's picture on the home page. "He looks older."

"He's cuter in person. Guess I won't be joining you on Saturday," I said more nastily than I'd intended. Nicolette didn't seem to notice. She was clicking away at various other Google listings, squinting at descriptions of heating tables and pots before closing out and hitting another entry.

"What's this?" she asked, stopping at a news article. It detailed a recent charity function at the Arizona Biltmore.

"That's Jonathan in a tux," I said, leaning closer to admire him. "See? He is handsome."

"Yeah, but who's the babe standing next to him?" She was your basic blonde with big boobs, dressed in a sparkly gown with a plunging neckline. Her attire would have been more appropriate for the Oscars than for the Parkinson's Society benefit. She looked more or less the way Nicolette would in twenty years if Nicolette married well.

"Just some random bimbo," I said.

Nicolette double-clicked on the picture, and we all peered at the caption beneath: "Mr. and Mrs. Jonathan Pomeroy were among the many prominent businesspeople to show their support for stem cell research."

"Hi, Mrs. Quackenbush." I jerked my head up. It was Robert, leaning over the librarian's desk. He laughed. "Man, you guys are really into something. Is it true that the teachers use that computer to look at porn?"

four

Scottsdale has resorts the way Venice has gondolas. Actually, if you know where to look, you can even find gondolas at some of Scottsdale's splashier resorts. The pricey places have pricey drinks, however, so we went instead to the hotel bar at one of those cut-rate places that always looks so nice over the Internet. It was close to the Hyatt, which meant we could pop over for a gondola ride later.

I'd finally agreed to go out with Nicolette on the condition that she serve as designated driver. She wasn't pleased ("But I've only been twenty-one for two months! It's a big deal for me to use a real ID!") but we told her she was allowed one drink, which we'd pay for, and that next time she could get really sloshed. Besides, she thought that gondola rides sounded "awesome," and we convinced her that the experience would be "even more awesome" if she were sober.

Jill, Nicolette and I got to the bar a half hour before Jonathan was due to arrive. We'd already worked out that Jill was to be the prison warden and Nicolette a prisoner who had just completed her sentence for passing bad checks. I wasn't sure a half hour was enough time to get me buzzed enough to pull this off, but the alternative—to slink off feeling deceived and humiliated—was unthinkable. If anyone was going to be deceived and humiliated, it would be Jonathan.

Jill and I wore strappy sundresses. These were not sexy fashion statements, necessarily, but simply the type of garment that allowed for maximum airflow. Nicolette wore a low-cut, hot pink tank top that outlined her big boobies just so, a low-slung denim miniskirt that allowed glimpses of her thong (also pink) every time she bent over, and the kind of high-heeled sandals that keep podiatrists, chiropractors and orthopedists in business.

We'd barely made it through the door when a muscular guy with spiky hair appeared at Nicolette's side. And when I say muscular, I don't mean, "works out." I mean, "would have to pay a friend to pee in a cup if he ever wanted to compete in the Olympics."

"You're a breath of spring air," he said, his eyes flicking back and forth between Nicolette's eyes and breasts. She giggled. I inhaled and almost choked when I got a hit of his cologne. Nicolette tossed her hair, emitting her own dose of artificial pheromones with heavy floral tones and probably triggering allergy attacks as far away as Flagstaff.

"Can I buy you ladies a drink?" He glanced briefly at Jill and me before returning his attention to Nicolette. Jill and I declined, but Nicolette gushed, "Oh, I've been dying for a piña colada! Do you think they make them here?"

"Didn't you tell her the rule?" I whispered to Jill. The rule was: Never let a man buy you a drink unless he has already yapped about himself for at least twenty minutes, at which point he owes you.

Jill shrugged. "At least we don't have to buy it." She had a point.

Jill and I staked out a table. Really, I had no desire to play games with strangers, and I hoped Nicolette and Mr. Universe would find a place of their own. But after a quick trip to the bar, they popped over, Nicolette cradling an enormous frothy drink between her manicured hands. Once she'd settled it on the table, she pulled out the cherry and ate it in one bite, leaving a spot of piña colada by her lips. Her new friend took a cocktail napkin to blot away the mess. "Oh! Thank you!" she trilled.

This was excruciating.

The waitress came by. She wore a Hawaiian print sundress and sported a polyester hibiscus in her upswept brown hair. A tented card on the table tempted us to "Get Lei'd Every Tuesday," with half-price tropical drinks and free leis available from four till six. This being Friday, Jill and I ordered our usual margaritas, hers on the rocks, mine a frozen prickly pear.

"I'm Rodney," the muscle man said, holding out a thick hand. His grip was surprisingly weak. I've really got to start carrying some of that Purell stuff in my purse. "I just moved here from Denver. I'm in pool construction." He nodded approvingly at our surroundings. "Nice place, huh?" The bar had been done in a tropical theme, complete with Hawaiian florals and rattan furniture. Apparently, if you drank enough mai tais, you could forget that the nearest ocean was five hundred miles away.

"I'm Donatella," Jill said.

"I'm Hope," I said, ironically.

"And I've already met Chartreuse," Rodney said, smiling at Nicolette, who was sucking down the piña colada at an alarming pace. "You all tourists?"

Nicolette stopped sucking and leaned forward, her boobs a good two inches from popping out of her shirt. She held a finger up to her lips. "Shhh! You have to promise not to tell! But I was just abducted . . . by *aliens*!"

"I'm going to check on my drink," I said, standing up, heading for the bar, and probably ruining Nicolette's credibility.

"I'll come, too," Jill said.

"What happened to forgery?" I said, once we had settled on stools. "To prison? If she tells Jonathan I'm a UFO expert, I'll kill her."

"Actually, I'm the UFO expert," Jill said. "You're the alien."

Rodney appeared at the bar and ordered another piña colada. Jill and I hadn't even gotten our margaritas yet.

"That for you?" Jill asked. Rodney shook his head and grinned with unbearable enthusiasm.

"Chartreuse is supposed to stop at one drink," I said. "She's still adjusting to the earth's atmosphere."

He winked at me. "I'll make sure things don't get out of hand." He threw some bills on the bar, took the glass (which could double as a vase for a large bouquet) and left.

"I hate winkers," I said.

Jill waved at the bartender. He had unnaturally blond, spiky hair and the kind of tan you're not supposed to get anymore. "We ordered a couple of margaritas? From the waitress?"

He looked around, his mouth slightly open, and finally spotted the waitress delivering drinks to some businessmen on the far side of the room. "Yeah. She'll probably bring them soon." He picked up a glass and rubbed it with a white towel.

"So you've made the margaritas?" Jill asked.

He thought for a moment, then shook his head.

"Okay." Jill took a deep breath. "Can you just make us a couple, then?"

He scrunched up his orangey face (so maybe the tan wasn't natural) and shook his head. "I can't make your drinks till the waitress gives me the ticket."

Jonathan was early. He spotted me immediately, and he got this great big smile on his face that made his eyes crinkly. I smiled back and felt happy and sad and angry at the same time. At least I'd Googled him. Finding out about his wife would have been much worse later.

He was better dressed than last time: his polo shirt was a dusty green rather than that awful yellow, and his khakis were cut more stylishly. His cowboy boots, black this time, seemed dashing now that I knew he was from Arizona. I wondered if his wife had a matching pair. He leaned over to kiss me, and I jerked backward. He stepped away and blinked with alarm until he spotted Jill and softened, probably assuming I was uncomfortable showing affection in front of my colleague.

"Hi, I'm Jonathan." He held out his hand to Jill.

"Donatella," she said, shaking his hand firmly. "I'm the warden at the prison where Natalie so selflessly shines the light of literacy." Jill made a pretty convincing women's prison warden, though I knew better than to tell her that.

"Wow," Jonathan said. "And I thought my job was stressful."

"Prison work has its rewards," Jill said. "As when rehabilitation is successful and you help steer a wayward soul back on the proper path. Take our little Chartreuse over there." She pointed to Nicolette, who was snuggled up to Rodney, her piña colada glass empty on the table in front of her. "You'd never guess it, but twenty-four hours ago, she was wearing a jumpsuit."

"I don't think she'll ever wear stripes again," I said somberly.

Jonathan studied Nicolette, then turned back to us. "Prostitution?" he whispered.

I tried not to laugh. I failed. "No, no. Just a little forgery. Passing bad checks."

"But she's not going to do it anymore," Jill said.

"She promised," I added.

The bartender came over to take Jonathan's drink order. Jonathan turned to us. "Ladies?"

"They've got drinks coming," the bartender said.

"I'm not so sure," Jill said.

"The waitress is on her way over." Sure enough, she was headed in our general direction.

"I'll take a Sam Adams," Jonathan said. The bartender headed off to get the beer. The waitress breezed past us.

"Miss? Miss!" I used my sternest teacher voice, but it didn't stop her. I scurried off my stool and chased her to the other end of the bar. "My friend and I ordered margaritas," I told her.

She squinted at me. "Were you sitting at the table over there? Where that couple is?"

I was about to say no when I realized she meant Nicolette and Rodney, who did, in fact, look on the verge of coupling. "Right," I said.

"Oh. I thought you left."

"We didn't," I said as pleasantly as I could manage. "So you can just bring our drinks to the bar."

"If you're sitting at the bar, you have to order your drinks from the bartender."

When I rejoined Jonathan and Jill, his bottle of beer had arrived. The bartender was nowhere to be seen.

"Darn it!" I said. "Why is it so hard to get a drink in this place?" My eyes filled with hot tears, and my throat ached with the effort to withhold a sob.

Jonathan's eye's widened. "Are you all right?"

I nodded and started to speak but stopped because I was afraid my voice would crack. I took a couple of deep breaths and swallowed before I finally managed to squeak, "It's been a rough day."

It had been, too. Every time I turned my back on Jared, he made farting noises until I finally sent him down to Dr. White's office. My victory was short-lived. Eyes downcast, Jared told Dr. White that he was having "stomach problems" and that I had "totally embarrassed" him in front of the class. She decided not to punish him on the outside chance he was telling her the truth. Next, my Adventures Class had uniformly failed their commas test. And a kid in one of my college prep classes told me that *Catcher in the Rye* was "boring." That's me: the teacher who made Salinger dull.

"A prisoner escaped," Jill said evenly. "One of Natalie's favorites. We really thought she had changed." She lowered her voice and leaned toward Jonathan. "And then when Natalie went home after work, her mother didn't recognize her."

"She thought I was the dog," I said, feeling marginally better.

"They had a dog when Natalie was growing up," Jill said. "It was quite large, almost Natalie's size, in fact."

"A golden retriever," I said sadly. "We called her Bucky."

"Wow," Jonathan said, gazing at me with sympathy. "You really do need a drink."

"I don't know who you have to know to get one in this place, though," Jill said, relating our margarita quest.

When she finished the story, Jonathan looked up, caught the bartender's eye and motioned him over. I expected him to order the margaritas successfully. I braced myself to feel simultaneously annoyed that Jonathan would command more authority simply by being a man and relieved to be able to sit back and let him take over.

To my surprise, he said, "Hey, is Teresa here?"

"Teresa Levesque?" the bartender asked with complete and nervous attention.

"Yeah, we go way back." Jonathan smiled easily. "And what was your name?" He leaned forward to read the name tag pinned to the waiter's Hawaiian shirt. "Travis?"

"Travis. Right."

"Well, Travis." He looked at Jill and me, then back at the bartender. "My friends can't seem to get their drinks. I'll have to razz Teresa about that next time I see her."

The bartender's nostrils flared with fear, and he would have turned pale if his "tan" hadn't been applied so thickly. "Hey man, I'm really sorry about that. It was just, like, a misunderstanding. I'll get them right now. On the house." He scurried away out of earshot. We could see him pulling out a couple of chunky, blue-rimmed margarita glasses.

Jill stared at Jonathan with newfound respect. He took a long drink from his beer bottle and tried to look casual before he shot us side glances and broke into a grin.

"Who's Teresa?" Jill asked.

"The general manager."

"Are you close?"

"We, um, dated. A couple of years ago."

"And you're still friends?" Jill asked.

He scrunched up his nose for a moment, trying to find the right words. "Not exactly. We were never serious, but when I, you know, called things off, she snuck into my house and slashed my couch with a commercial grade knife. I call her The Slasher."

"What if she'd been here?" I asked.

"I'd have run like hell."

"Where'd she get the knife?" Jill asked.

"I'd sold it to her. Top of the line."

Travis, all effusion, returned with two really, really, really big frozen margaritas adorned with skewered pineapples. "Like I said, these are on the house. Sorry about the mix-up."

Jill squinted at her margarita. "Mine was supposed to be on the rocks."

Travis froze for a moment before whisking the offending drink away. "Back in a jiff," he said. "And again, please accept my apologies."

Nicolette came over, her smile wide, her face flushed. "Me and Rodney are gonna go check out the gondolas." Rodney stood behind her, a proprietary hand resting on the strip of exposed back that lay between her too-small shirt and too-short skirt.

"How long will that take?" I asked. The plan had been to spend just enough time with Jonathan to humiliate him and then leave abruptly.

"As long as an aria," Rodney cooed.

"Come right back when you're done," I instructed, as teacherly as possible. But they were already halfway to the door.

"How long was she in for?" Jonathan asked, watching Nicolette and Rodney leave.

"Who? Um, Chartreuse?" I licked my lips. "Two years."

"Wow," he said. "That seems kind of long for forgery."

"What she means is, it'll be two years when Chartreuse has finished her probation," Jill said. "She was only incarcerated for nine months. But let's talk about you. Natalie tells me you're in the restaurant business."

"Restaurant supplies," he said. "Pots, mats, cooking utensils, dinnerware, cutting boards."

"Knives," Jill added.

"Yes, knives. All very glamorous." He smiled.

I looked anxiously at the door, though it was far too early for Nicolette to return.

We settled in for the wait, moving to a table and ordering chicken quesadillas and another round of margaritas. A half hour passed. An hour. Jill grilled Jonathan, who said, as before, that he was thirty-three years old, never married, born and raised in Phoenix, a graduate of the University of Arizona. He had his story, and he was sticking to it.

We told Jonathan more about the prison: the battered wives who'd shot their husbands, the cafeteria brawls, the lesbian gangs. We dredged up every prison cliché and convict stereotype we could think of, and still, Nicolette did not appear. We ordered the nacho grande platter and Diet Cokes. Jonathan tried to hold my hand under the table. I didn't let him, even though he continued to be easygoing and funny and not like a philanderer at all.

Finally, I couldn't take it anymore. "I'm getting worried about Chartreuse," I said, thinking: I could kill that little tramp.

We left the bar and trudged out to the self-park lot; we were too poor to spring for a valet. Nicolette's car was gone. We hiked back to the hotel, where Jonathan handed a ticket to the valet, who magically produced a monstrous blue pickup truck.

"Wow. This is a big car for a single guy," Jill said as the valet opened her door.

"I need to haul a lot of stuff for work," Jonathan said casually, stepping up to the driver seat.

Jonathan drove us to the Hyatt. What a difference five minutes made. The place was all glass, slate, wood, soaring ceilings and warm lighting. I immediately felt like an imposter. The back wall was open, with misters cooling well-dressed guests like a field of tropical flowers. We stepped down into a bar full of comfy chairs clustered around candlelit tables, then walked across manicured lawns and past lit swimming pools until we reached the landing, where a gondolier from Fresno informed us that the girl with the blond hair and the guy with the big muscles had left at least a half an hour ago. "They seemed really in love," he added helpfully.

We tried Nicolette's cell phone, which, predictably, was turned off. We returned to the bar on the off chance that she had simply dropped Rodney at his hotel and returned to pick us up. She hadn't.

"You let her drive?" Jonathan asked. "I'm surprised she still has a car."

"It's her mother's," Jill said. "By letting her drive, we were trying to send the message that we trusted her."

"I'd be happy to drive you home," Jonathan said.

"We'll take cabs," I said, just as Jill chirped, "That'd be great!" She and I locked eyes. I blinked first. Jill and I lived in opposite directions, and neither of us lived near here. A cab would cost a fortune.

"If it's not too much trouble," I said.

As we left the resort and turned onto Scottsdale Road, the thoroughfare that divides Scottsdale and Phoenix, Jill casually asked, "So, Jonathan, do you live far from here?" I sat sandwiched between them on the bench seat.

When he said not really—ten or fifteen minutes—she said, "Why don't we go to your place for a cup of coffee, then?"

My face burned in the dark. I felt suddenly, hotly angry. I stared straight ahead at the taillights in front of us.

"Sure. I can make you cappuccinos." Jonathan sent me a brief smile before blinking in surprise when he saw my expression.

"We wouldn't be disturbing anyone?" Jill asked.

"Nope. I live alone. Don't even have any pets."

With a few exceptions, the Valley of the Sun has two basic house styles: Spanish and territorial. Spanish houses are white or beige stucco with peaked red roofs. Inside they have high ceilings, open floor plans, fancy kitchens and tiny bedrooms. Territorial houses look completely different from the outside, with flat roofs, wood beams and front courtyards. But inside? High ceilings, open floor plans, fancy kitchens and tiny bedrooms.

Jonathan's house was Spanish style. It looked like a Taco Bell. Well, a Taco Bell with a garage. So did the one on its right. And on its left. And across the street.

"How do you know which one is yours?" I asked.

He laughed. "It's the one with the cactus out front." Jonathan's cactus was a nicely formed saguaro, far superior to the saguaro across the street or the chollas and prickly pears on either side. A concrete driveway took up most of the front yard; the remainder was landscaped with gravel. Grass does not do well in the desert.

He clicked the garage door opener on the truck visor, and the beige door magically slid upward, revealing a tidy two-car garage lined with cabinets and a pegboard covered with hanging tools. He slid his truck into the center of the space and left the garage door open.

"I have to get either a smaller car or a bigger garage," he said. He was right: his truck stuck out a good foot beyond the door. "I just got a letter from the homeowner's association. I'm not allowed to leave my garage door open. But parking in the street is an even greater sin. Maybe if I parked diagonally . . ." He squinted at the wall.

My mind was whirring. On the way over, I'd decided the house probably belonged to a friend who was out of town. But if that were the case, would Jonathan really make up the stuff about the homeowner's association? How good a liar was he? Maybe this really was his house. He could be separated. Why would he tell me he'd never been married then? Of course, I had no right to object to a blurring of the facts. So he neglected to mention an ex-wife. So I told a colorful tale about life among the inmates. Perhaps some day we'd have a good laugh and live happily (and truthfully) ever after.

I was all set to be reassured by a standard-issue bachelor pad, complete with white walls, an enormous TV and recliners with drink holders when Jonathan let us into the kitchen. There were Indian pots and hanging ivy on the towering plant shelves. Custom-made cushions sat atop Mexican bar stools. Tailored valances hung from wrought iron curtain rods. A woman had been here.

"You've got quite an eye for decorating," Jill said. "What would you call that paint color? Mustard? Ochre?"

"I call it yellow," Jonathan said. "If I call it anything at all. My latest stepmother wants to switch careers from real estate to decorating. Once she finished my father's house, she moved on to mine. She keeps showing up to take more pictures for her portfolio." He rolled his eyes. "Whatever. It's better than anything I could have done."

I had a sudden image of his stepmother: the perfect silver hair, the trim figure, the tailored, sherbert-colored clothes and matching shoes. She would get her hair styled weekly, her manicure done twice a month. Her makeup would be flawless. I had seen his stepmother—well, others just like her—a thousand times since moving to Scottsdale.

"How many stepmothers have you had?" I asked.

"My mother was my father's second wife. There have been two since."

"So your father has made it down the aisle four times, and you haven't managed even once?" Jill asked.

He raised an eyebrow. "Think there could be a connection?"

I stared at him. If he was lying, he was frighteningly good at it. But what about the blond woman in the paper? Was she merely a date who had been misidentified by some champagne-guzzling society reporter?

Jonathan made cappuccinos from an enormous stainless steel model. "My post-adolescent rebellion against the stepmonster," he said. "She says the espresso maker dominates the space and that a sleek home model would be much more appropriate. But I like it."

His answering machine sat on the counter, the light blinking. "You have a message," I said.

"It can wait."

We took our cups into the great room, a high-ceilinged space open to the kitchen. It had a built-in entertainment center, built-in bookshelves, a ceiling fan and a gas fireplace. The couches were soft brown leather and strewn with Indian blankets and southwestern print pillows. The walls were a paler shade of the kitchen's ochre/mustard/yellow.

Jill stroked the leather couch. "Is this the couch the Slasher attacked?"

"No, that was beyond repair."

As I sipped my cappuccino (which was delicious, with just the perfect amount of froth), I noticed some framed snapshots over the television set (big screen, plasma). "Family photos?" I asked casually, wandering over.

"Yup," he said.

I spotted her immediately. It was a group shot. She was wearing khaki shorts and a sleeveless pink polo shirt, her blond hair pulled back in a ponytail. She looked more relaxed than in the newspaper photo. She looked prettier.

I rested my cup on the shelf and picked up the photo. I swallowed hard, more disappointed than angry. If only Nicolette hadn't taken off. If only I were in my own room now, flipping through a magazine or watching TV or even reading *The Odyssey*.

"Who's this?" I asked, as levelly as I could.

"Let me see." He walked casually across the room and leaned over my shoulder. He smelled good, like leather mixed with citrus. I tapped my finger against the glass.

"Oh, that," he said. "That is Mrs. Jonathan Pomeroy, Sr. My stepmother."

five

Jill couldn't understand why I was so upset.

"I like him," I told her on the phone the next day.

"He drives a pickup truck."

"It's for work."

"Yeah, sure, nice excuse. He could get a minivan."

"He's a single guy. Single guys don't drive minivans. God. You make it sound like he drives a Hummer."

"You know what we always say about guys who drive big cars," Jill said.

"Jonathan's different."

"C'mon. Say it with me."

"I'm not in the mood."

"C'mon. You know I'll just keep bugging you until you say it." She would, too. "On the count of three: one, two, three—"

"Big car, small penis," we chanted, though my heart wasn't in it. "He needs it for work," I said again.

"Did you see the size of his television? And that espresso machine? That guy's definitely compensating for something."

Jill was my best friend in Arizona; well, she was my only friend in Arizona. Still, there were times when I didn't like her very much.

I stared glumly out the window. The sky was a blinding blue. The pool shimmered. In the giant saguaro, a woodpecker tapped rhythmically. The thermometer read one hundred and eight degrees. "Do you think Jonathan would understand if I told him the truth? Do you think we could start over?"

She paused to consider. "He'd think you were deranged."

To make matters worse, Nicolette was in love. I stopped by the front office first thing Monday morning to make sure she hadn't been raped and mutilated, her body dumped way out in the desert to be devoured by coyotes and vultures. She was still alive, which was good because it meant I could hate her.

"It's like me and Rodney were made for each other," she proclaimed. "We spent the whole weekend together, and I never got sick of him."

"Rodney and I," I said reflexively. Teaching has turned me into a total dork. "Wait. Did you have *sex* with him?"

"Well, yeah." She pulled lazily at a lock of her long, blond hair. "I thought that was the whole point of going out and picking up guys."

"That is *not* the point."

She scrunched up her little nose. "Then what is the point?"

I blinked at her. "What's Rodney going to think when you tell him your real name? And that you made up that alien story just to trick him?"

"Oh, that." She made a little wave. "I told him my real name when we were in the gondola. And he never believed I was an alien, anyway. We laughed about it the whole weekend. It's, like, our first inside joke. Did you guys go on the gondola? It was totally awesome."

As I walked out of the office, I almost tripped over Cody Gold. Cody had a talent for showing up wherever I happened to be.

"Good Morning, Miss Quackenbush," he squeaked. Cody never called me Mrs. Quackenbush. Cody was the only student who cared whether or not I was married. "I finished *The Odyssey* over the weekend."

"You did? Well, good for you! Don't give the ending away to the others, though!"

Shoot. Cody had finished *The Odyssey*. I hadn't finished *The Odyssey*. I hadn't even finished the *CliffsNotes*. "Well, you'd better hurry to class. See you sixth period!"

"Third period," he said.

"Really?" I hated the rotating schedule even more than I hate Homer. "I mean—right! Well, then, I'll see you when I see you!"

First period turned out to be my Adventures class (I'd thought it would be, but I wasn't entirely sure). I had a big surprise for my students.

"For homework tonight"—I pressed my hands together and paused for dramatic effect—"I'm going to ask you all to watch television!"

Nothing. Not a, "Way to go, Ms. Q!" Not, "Hey! Are you serious?" Or, "How cool is that?"

Nothing.

A girl named Marisol sneezed. Someone mumbled, "God bless you."

"Now, don't get too excited," I said, hoping for a laugh but not getting one. When I was in high school, no teacher ever assigned television watching. No teacher was ever that cool. Maybe I should be assigning Nintendo playing or iPod downloading. Or shopping or drinking beer. Maybe that's what they were waiting for.

"Today we are starting a unit on marketing and advertising. And you all know what advertising is, right?" Nothing. "It's time or space that a company pays to expose its product. For homework, I want you to focus on television advertising, also known as . . . ?" Nothing. This was supposed to be the easy part. "Commercials. Right? Television advertising is usually done in the form of commercials." I wasn't even going to bother with a discussion of product placement.

For homework, I told them to each watch a half hour show. On a piece of paper, they were supposed to write down the name of the show. Then they had to write down every commercial that came on and who that commercial was aimed at. I moved on to the hard part.

"Who knows what marketing is?"

Nothing.

"Marisol?" She shrugged, sniffled and looked at the floor.

"Steven?" Steven straightened his gangly body in his chair. He was easily the slowest student in the class—no mean feat. But I didn't care. Steven was pure goodness: sweet and eager. He made me remember why I had gone into teaching in the first place, even as I proved utterly incapable of teaching him a single thing.

"Is marketing, like, when you go to the grocery store?" His eyes were wide, hopeful.

"You know, that's a good answer, Steven! Because a grocery

store is often called . . . what?" Nothing. "A supermarket? Right?" I
searched their faces for a hint of a nod or even a glimpse of understanding. "And what is the purpose of a supermarket? Robert?"

"They, um"—he looked around—"it's where your mother goes
when she has to get stuff for dinner."

"Right. So what does a supermarket do? Mandy?"

"They have, like, fruit and stuff. Bread and peanut butter
and stuff."

"Yes. Good. So if customers are *buying* the food, what is the
supermarket doing?"

"They have birthday cakes," Steven offered. "My mother always gets my birthday cake at Safeway."

"They have cakes. Yes. But do they just *give* the cakes away?"
Marisol raised her hand. Victory! "Marisol?"

"Last year, my mom got my birthday cake at Food 4 Less."

"I think Safeway's cakes are better," someone said.

Another voice piped in. "Last year? For my dad's birthday? I
made a cake from scratch. I used one of those mixes."

And another voice. "Betty Crocker mixes are really good."

And another. "My mom says Duncan Hines are the best."

"Okay!" I clapped my hands. "So let's move on." The class
gave me a look as if to say, "Do you mind? We're having an interesting discussion, for once."

"A supermarket doesn't just *give* the food away. Right?"
I chirped. "It *sells* the cakes and the cake mixes and the peanut butter. In a similar way, marketing is how companies present their
products in a way that makes us want to buy them."

Dead silence. And then, from Robert: "You mean, like when
they say, if you buy the right can of soda, you might win a million
dollars or something?"

"Yes!" I wanted to hug him. "And Cherie said something about Betty Crocker cake mixes. Why do you buy Betty Crocker and not, say, Pillsbury?"

"I like Duncan Hines. It was Raquel who liked Betty Crocker."

"Oh, right. And what is it about Duncan Hines that makes it so special?"

"Um, I don't know."

"Is it the packaging, maybe?"

She shrugged and stared at her desk.

"Okay. How about you, Raquel? Why do you like Betty Crocker instead of Duncan Hines?"

"Because I like chocolate."

I sighed. Looked at the clock. Only thirty-five more minutes to go.

"What *is* that?" I asked as Lars sank his teeth into a doughy hamburger bun dripping with orange goo.

He chewed carefully, swallowed and wiped his mouth daintily with a paper napkin. "Sloppy Joe. It's not bad, actually." Lars was perfectly groomed as always, his blond hair moussed just so, his white shirt tucked into his linen pants. I can't wear linen for five minutes without looking like I have slept in my clothes, but Lars pulled off the Ralph Lauren elegantly rumpled look with panache.

"Don't you ever worry about mad cow disease?" Jill asked.

"There's no mad cow in the United States," Lars countered, taking another bite.

Jill speared a chunk of chicken salad with grapes and tarragon. "I'm thinking maybe they imported some special for today's lunch."

I was eating—well, drinking—a yogurt smoothie that looked far more satisfying on television than it did in my insulated lunch bag. When I was done, I'd eat a not-quite-ripe banana. And then I'd be hungry for the rest of the day. I'd considered keeping cashews in my desk to stave off hunger pangs, but one of my students was dangerously allergic to nuts, and I feared leaving cashew residue on her corrected homework and sending her into anaphylactic shock.

There are some overweight teachers at school, but I don't know how they do it. At times I look at them with something approaching envy. Someone must be getting up early to pack them mayonnaise-laden sandwiches and homemade brownies—the same someone who cooks fried chicken or cheesy pasta for dinner while the teacher-spouse grades the never-ending pile of papers.

"I began my advertising and marketing unit today," I announced. Advertising and marketing was a required part of the senior curriculum, intended to stop teenagers from wasting their parents' hard-earned money on name-brand sneakers and flashy jeans. I described my television homework to Lars and Jill, feeling borderline clever, even if I hadn't gotten the initial response I'd hoped for.

"I'm having my kids create and market their own products," Lars said between sips of milk from his mini carton. "They'll design a marketing campaign and shoot thirty-second commercials. It got a terrific response last year—really made the kids look at the media world in a new way. I've got the whole thing spelled out on my Web site if you want to take a look at it." All of the teachers at Agave had Web sites. A handful even knew how to use them.

I tried to imagine my Adventures class creating marketing campaigns. I considered it a triumph if they handed in their homework on time. Or anytime.

"That reminds me," Lars said. "I've chosen the play for the autumn theater workshop. It's called *Romeo and Jules*—basically a contemporary version of *Romeo and Juliet*. A kid in my summer playwriting workshop wrote it, and I'm totally into the idea of producing an original work. At any rate, I could really use an assistant director, and you'd mentioned that you were interested in theater." He raised his eyebrows expectantly.

My interest in theater had fallen closely on the heels of my interest in Lars. I blinked at him, unsure of what I was agreeing to but nodding nevertheless.

six

I don't know what shocked me more: the sight of my mother standing in the kitchen or the envelope she held in her hand. "A young man stuck this in the front door, but he just kind of scurried away and waved when I called out to him." The envelope had my name scrawled on it. In the top left corner it said, "Pomeroy Restaurant Supply."

"What are you doing here?" I asked my mother. We hugged. "Where's Daddy?"

"I sent him to AJ's to pick up some food. Really, honey, you should keep the fridge better stocked." She put her hands on her hips. "You could look happier to see me."

"I am happy." I tried to look happy. "Just surprised."

"Didn't you get my messages?" I looked at the answering machine on the counter; the light was blinking. While I occasionally used my parents' phone for outgoing calls, my friends, colleagues, acquaintances and phantom dates all called me on my cell phone.

"Whoops," I said.

My mother rolled her eyes. "Well, anyway. Now you know. What do you think of my hair?" It was blondish when I'd last seen her. Now it was reddish.

"Nice."

"It looked fabulous in Rhode Island; I went to your sister's hairdresser. I thought it was the cut, but the minute I walked off the plane in Phoenix—" She shook her head. "This dry air is impossible."

In the past three years, my mother had abandoned the New England matron look in favor of Arizona glitz. She'd pierced her ears and started wearing eye shadow. Talbots was out; overpriced boutiques were in. She had a closet filled with drapey pastel pantsuits, espadrilles and southwestern print blazers. She wore visors and pink-tinted sunglasses.

"How is Shelly?" I asked.

She rolled her eyes. "That boyfriend."

"Still no ring?"

She pursed her lips and shook her head. "It's killing your father." My older sister started dating Frederick six years ago, when she was twenty-eight and he was twenty-five. Frederick was a big advocate of "taking it slow" and "making sure we're making the right decision." Now that they'd been living together for four years, my parents thought it was time to make a decision one way or another or, as my mother so eloquently put it, to "shit or get off the pot."

"Maybe for Christmas," I said lamely.

In the garage, I heard an engine purring, followed by a car door closing.

"The Lexus is still running smoothly," my father announced as he entered the kitchen. Unlike my mother, my father dressed exactly the same as always, in khakis, polo shirts and the occasional sport jacket. The Lexus was his one concession to Arizona flash. He worried that his last car, a Camry, stuck out at the AJ's parking lot. Whenever I bought groceries at AJ's (not often; I couldn't afford them), I parked my crappy Civic as far away from the other cars as possible. I didn't care about appearances; it was the possibility of scratching a BMW, Mercedes or, God forbid, a Bentley that terrified me. I'd never recover from the increased insurance premium.

"So, who's the stalker?" my father asked after putting down his paper grocery bags and giving me a hug.

"He's not a stalker. He's just . . . this guy."

"He ran like hell when your mother opened the door."

"Maybe he's shy," my mother said. I was twenty-nine years old. My mother was willing to overlook a little social awkwardness in my suitors. "Did you have any plans with him tonight?" she asked. "I mean, here at the house? Because your father and I could go out."

"We just got here!" he said, pulling a carton of lactose-free milk out of a paper bag. "Where does this go?"

My mother raised her eyebrows. "Where do you *think* it goes?"

"Refrigerator?" He paused a moment before opening the stainless steel door, putting the carton on an empty shelf and closing the door softly.

"If you've made plans, Natalie, we wouldn't want to be in the way." My mother smiled expectantly. If only she had been this accommodating when I was sixteen.

"I don't have any plans," I said. Her face fell, just a little. "And I am happy to see you. I'm just surprised, that's all. I thought you'd be in Connecticut about now."

"We went to Connecticut. Humid. Would you believe your aunt and uncle still don't have air-conditioning? They kept saying, 'There's only three or four days a year when we wish we had it.'"

"Unfortunately, we were there for those four days," my father interjected. "Does potato salad have to be refrigerated?"

"Only if you don't want botulism," I said.

"What did you buy potato salad for?" my mother asked.

"I like potato salad," he said. "Besides, we needed something to go with the soup."

"Soup?" I asked.

"It's too hot to cook," my mother said. "I told your father to pick up some soup for dinner."

If it's too hot to cook, it's too hot for soup, I thought, but I kept my mouth shut.

"Potato salad doesn't go with soup," my mother said, reaching into the brown bags my father had now abandoned and stacking the items on the counter.

"It does if you want it to," my father said.

"Why didn't you just go back to Rhode Island?" I asked.

"Our month with your sister turned into two weeks because I couldn't stand another minute with *that man*. Honestly, he did everything he could to avoid us. He spent most of his time in their bedroom with the television blaring."

"Isn't that a good thing?" I asked. "I mean, if you didn't have to talk to him?"

"No," my mother said, pouring a carton of fresh salsa into a little dish and opening a bag of tortilla chips. My parents eat a lot of salsa because they can feel southwestern and get their recommended intake of lycopene—at the same time!

"Your sister was tense. *Tense.* I try to hide my feelings about

Frederick, but she knows me so well that she can tell that I disap-
prove of their situation." Pretty much anyone within a hundred-mile
radius of my mother knows that she disapproves of their situation.

"And Pennsylvania?" I asked, still holding out hope that they'd
popped by to pick up a few tennis togs before catching a red-eye
out of Sky Harbor Airport. It's not that I don't love my parents or
enjoy spending time with them, but after two months alone in the
house, it felt like they were invading my space—and not the other
way around.

"Well, my sister-in-law called two nights ago—two nights
ago!" That would be my father's brother's wife, a.k.a. Aunt Mari-
lyn, a.k.a. The Hypochondriac. "She said she had a cold and didn't
want to get us sick." My mother took a supersize box of Cheerios
and stuck it in the pantry. "I said that was very considerate of her,
but we'd take our chances." She rolled her eyes. "And then, suddenly, it was more than a cold, it was probably pneumonia, and she
didn't feel up to entertaining. Well. I can take a hint. So I got on the
phone to Southwest. There's no penalty if you're over sixty." She
gazed around at the majestic kitchen. "Let me tell you, it's good to
be back in my own house."

"Yeah, it must be," I said.

I took Jonathan's note up to my room, shut the door and put on
a CD that one of my favorite kids from last year had burned for me
(she swore it was legal). Hiding out like this made me feel like a
teenager myself. Next thing you knew, I'd be instant messaging
Jonathan: *I can't w8 2 c u!* In truth, as much as I wanted to see him,
as much as I smiled every time I heard his voice on my voice mail,
I'd been avoiding him—or, more precisely, avoiding the inevitable
moment when I'd have to come clean.

He'd written his note on a simple white piece of copy paper:

Natalie,

I was in the neighborhood (okay, not really) and hoped to catch you since I haven't been able to reach you on your cell phone. (If I were not so supremely self-confident, I might think you didn't want to talk to me.) I hope I didn't upset your mother. I remember what you said about her chasing the UPS man with a paring knife because she thought he was a rapist.

Jonathan

Before I had time to talk myself out of it, I called him.

"I didn't expect to hear from you," he said.

"Why not?"

"Well . . . when a guy leaves three phone messages for a woman and she doesn't call back, he usually takes the hint."

"Then why did you come to my house?"

"Because I am especially persistent. Or especially dense. It was my last-ditch effort. I had a couple more planned in case that didn't work out."

"More last-ditch efforts?"

"Yup. A last, last-ditch effort. And a last, last, last-ditch effort." He paused. "Unless . . . are you calling to tell me to stop calling? If that's the case, let me know now before I humiliate myself further."

"That's not the case."

"Okay, then."

"Okay."

He asked me to have dinner with him. I couldn't, of course; I could hardly abandon my parents on their first day home. Besides, I had at least four hours' worth of grading and lesson planning to do. But I was free Saturday night, I told him—though maybe he could pick me up in a parking lot somewhere.

seven

Here is what I planned to say to Jonathan at dinner: "I hope that what I am about to tell you won't change the way you feel about me. The night we met, I was hating life and feeling bad about myself. I never thought I'd see you again. I had no idea how much I'd like you. I told you some lies, and then one lie built upon another. If you give me another chance, I promise I will never lie to you again."

Here is what I actually said to Jonathan: "I guess I thought it was just going to be the two of us at dinner."

"I know, I'm sorry. I'd completely forgotten that I was supposed to have dinner with my dad and Krista. I thought about calling them and saying I was sick, but I really hate to lie. I should have warned you. But I was afraid you'd back out."

I would have, but not for the reasons he thought.

He laughed. "Oh, God. First I leave notes at your house, now

I'm introducing you to my parents on our first real date. You're probably ready to take out a restraining order."

I bit my lip and looked out the window.

"Oh, sorry," he said, his smile fading. "Am I not supposed to make criminal jokes?"

I smiled—or tried to, anyway. "You can make all the criminal jokes you want. Really." I shifted uncomfortably on the bench seat of his gigantic truck.

He noticed my expression and pulled into a shopping center parking lot. He put the truck in park but left the engine running and the air-conditioning at full blast. "Look. If you want me to take you home, I will. I thought we had something going, but maybe I misread your signals." He shook his head. "Most of the women I meet are waitresses or bartenders. And it's not that they're not nice—a lot of them are. But . . . you're different. You're just so . . . real."

My throat ached with a pent-up wail. "My job—" I said, and then stopped.

I took a deep breath, but before I'd had a chance to form the right words (as if there were any right words), he said, "Your job is amazing. There aren't a lot of people who could do that day after day." We were quiet for a moment, and then he said, "Do you want me to take you home? I like you. I've made that embarrassingly obvious. But if you don't feel the same way, you don't have to keep pretending just to spare my feelings." He smiled wryly. "I'm a big boy. I can take it."

"I'm not pretending anything as far as my feelings go," I whispered. This was my moment to come clean, to fess up, to tell him what I *had* been pretending. But a funny thing happened. Jonathan leaned forward. And I leaned forward, too, at least until my seat belt snapped into place. I released it with a seductive click.

His lips were slightly rough, but the skin around them was smooth. He must have shaved right before he picked me up. He tasted of mint and smelled of lemons. My stomach grew warm.

When we parted, our faces still inches away from each other, he ran a finger along my cheek. "So you aren't just being nice?"

"I'm not as nice as you think I am," I whispered.

Even without humidity, Krista Pomeroy's blond hair looked fabulous: smooth yet buoyant. Her highlights looked so natural they had to be fake. She probably had salon expenses the way I have student loans. Her left hand glittered with the kind of gem never simply referred to as a diamond but rather, more bluntly, as "a rock"—though "boulder" might be more apt. She wore a simple coral-colored silk shift that set off her tan just so and delicate pearl earrings that coordinated with the strand around her neck.

I wore my navy blue skirt that should have been taken up an inch because it hit me at mid-calf, which any women's magazine will tell you is the most unflattering, leg-shortening length. Up until this moment, I hadn't cared.

We met Jonathan's father and stepmother at the door to Clarke's, which was located inside the intimate and ever-so-swishy Golden Palms Hotel. In Scottsdale, most good restaurants are located inside hotels, which unsettles me, as if the Phoenix Valley is just a nice place to visit and living here is a kind of extended vacation and not real life at all. Everything is geared toward visitors, as if the several million residents don't count. Still, I was excited to be eating here; my parents, in the process of working their way through Fodor's restaurant recommendations, had eaten here with the Gillespies, after which Mrs. Gillespie said to me, "It is so fabulous, you *must* get a date to take you there." I didn't know whether to feel insulted that Mrs. Gillespie didn't think I could afford to pay my own way or flattered that she'd think I could find a guy willing to spend that kind of money on me. Now I found myself wondering which guy was going to pick up the tab. I couldn't see Jonathan and his father splitting the bill.

As immaculate as she was, Krista looked older in person than in her pictures. She was forty-three, and she looked it—but in a "lived the good life" kind of way: countless mornings spent squinting at tennis and golf balls had left lines around her eyes, while afternoons at the pool had resulted in sun spots on her face and arms. I made a mental note to throw out my 4 SPF sunscreen and stick to the thirty. Krista's tan hands were flawless, though: long-fingered and perfectly manicured.

As for Krista's husband, there were many older husbands with younger wives in Scottsdale. Typically, they had full heads of silver hair, deep tans, toned physiques and self-satisfied, if slightly tired, smiles. But Jack Pomeroy looked like a man who had split his almost-seventy years between fine restaurants and expensive golf courses (where he wouldn't dream of walking between holes). Jonathan had described his father (whose name was also Jonathan, he informed me, as if I didn't know) as "a heart attack waiting to happen." For some reason—the young wife, I suppose—I had taken the description as an indication of a life led too quickly and filled with too much stress. As it turned out, Jack enjoyed his surf and his turf, preferably in large portions and doused with butter. His cheeks were mottled red and littered with sun spots. His navy blazer fit so well that it must have been custom-made to cover his girth. His scalp shone red through his sparse white hair.

Krista placed one of her delicate hands on Jack's elbow and said to me, "Is this your first time at Clarke's? It's Jack's absolute favorite place. We eat here at least once a week."

I said I had never had the pleasure but that my parents had recommended it. I caught myself and said quietly to Jonathan, "Though of course they haven't been able to come for several years."

Jonathan's father said, "Let's do a quick tour of the grounds, then." I smiled politely at him and his wife, trying not to gawk at their differences. I wondered if his previous three wives had been so attractive. What could all of those women have seen in him? And then it struck me: Jack Pomeroy was loaded.

"The Golden Palms was originally a private residence," Krista informed me as we walked under a Moroccan-style arch dripping with flowering vines and out onto a lawn flanked by orange and palm trees, their trunks painted white to protect them from the sun.

"You're probably hoping I'll build you a house like this," Jack said, squeezing his young wife around the shoulders.

She threw back her head and let out a musical laugh. "Maybe something a little bigger," she joked (I think she was joking), giving him a quick peck on the lips.

"Can't we just go eat?" Jonathan said in what sounded suspiciously like a whine. I swung my head to look at him, surprised by his tone. Neither Jack nor Krista seemed to notice.

"I just thought your friend would enjoy seeing the grounds," Jack said mildly.

Your friend. "Yes, thanks," I said. "It was really interesting. And I'm really looking forward to dinner." Every time I try to be diplomatic, I end up sounding like a weenie.

"You haven't seen the pool yet," Krista said.

"Aren't the reservations for seven?" Jonathan said. "It's five after."

"It's September," Jack said evenly. "They're half empty."

"You've got to see the pool," Krista said. "Jack and I had our rehearsal dinner next to it."

"Maybe after dinner," I said, finally taking sides. "I had an early lunch, and I'm starved." At that, Jonathan took my hand and squeezed.

The maître d' greeted Jack and Krista enthusiastically and ushered us to an outside table surrounded by bougainvillea and candlelight. A year ago, I would never have considered eating outside in ninety-degree heat, but my body had grown oddly accustomed to the ever-present warmth. The day's glaring sun still seared, of course, and waves of heat greeted me as I opened the door of my car when I left work, even if I'd managed to score a spot in the spindly shade of a paloverde tree. But I'd learned to love the warmth of a desert night.

I really wanted a margarita, but when the waitress took our drink orders, I ordered a glass of chardonnay because it seemed more sophisticated. Since I wasn't familiar with any of the chardonnays the waitress offered by the glass, I chose one at random, hoping it wasn't the most expensive. "Excellent choice," the waitress said. Damn. It had to be pricey.

Having a menu to peruse was a relief, as it provided a natural time-out from conversation. It wasn't that Jack or Krista were difficult to talk to; on the contrary, they had already shown themselves to be skilled conversationalists—so skilled, in fact, that the inevitable inquiry, "Tell us about your job," was just around the corner.

Eventually, I'd end up lying to them, I knew, but I could limit my sins. I wouldn't rack up too much of a dinner bill. I really wanted the arugula salad with mango and raspberries, but I vowed to make do with an entrée, no matter how hungry I was (and I was pretty hungry). I was trying to decide between the spit-roasted chicken and the barbequed salmon when the waitress glided over with our drinks (a beer for Jonathan, a Manhattan for Jack, and, for Krista, a sparkling water with lemon). My wine was delicious. I had definitely overreached.

"We have some additional specials tonight," the waitress said. She had strawberry blond hair and the kind of freckly skin that should never be exposed to the sun. She described a curried butternut squash bisque (I couldn't imagine eating soup in this heat, though it did sound good), a roasted goat cheese salad, and "miso-marinated sea bass served with baby green beans and roasted garlic mashed potatoes." Miso-marinated sea bass? I loved miso-marinated sea bass! The last time my parents took me out to dinner (last spring, before they fled the heat), we had gone to an Asian fusion place where I had foolishly ordered a sesame halibut, while my mother opted for, yes, miso-marinated sea bass. It was quite possibly the best thing I have ever tasted. She allowed me three bites before telling me I could order it next time and, "Eat your own food."

The chicken and salmon were both mid-range items. I hadn't even bothered to consider the lobster. "How much is the sea bass?" I inquired as discreetly as I could.

"Thirty-two fifty," the waitress said. Wow. Her tips must be impressive.

"I'll have the salmon," I said bravely.

"No, no, no, no, no!" Jack said.

"Have the sea bass," urged Jonathan.

"Don't worry about the cost!" Krista instructed. "Dinner's on us!"

"Oh, no, it's not that," I said. "I just—I'm really in a salmon-y mood. Is it good?" I asked the waitress.

"It's very popular," she said. "Anything to start?"

"No, thank you."

Krista touched my arm. "Get a salad!"

"I'm really not very hungry." I hoped no one had heard my stomach growling.

"Ten minutes ago you said you were starving," Jack said. "Try the mussels. They're fantastic."

"If I ate all that, I couldn't possibly eat my entrée. Just the salmon." I shut my menu with a snap and handed it to the waitress.

The waitress turned to face Krista. "And for you, miss?" I wondered whether she called all women "miss" or if she thought Jack and Krista couldn't possibly be married.

"I'll try the sea bass," Krista said. "With the arugula salad to start."

"Excellent choice," the waitress said.

I held in a whimper.

By the time the entrées arrived, I had eaten three pieces of bread with olive oil and wasn't really hungry anymore. My salmon was okay, certainly better than anything I would have eaten at home, but I was overcome with food envy. Krista put a delicate forkful of white fish in her mouth, closed her eyes and moaned. "Sweetheart, you've got to taste this." She forked off a chunk and transported it carefully onto Jack's plate.

He chewed and nodded with appreciation. "Fantastic."

"Natalie, would you like to try some? Jonathan?"

I was on the verge of saying yes when Jonathan said, "No, thank you."

"Thanks, but no," I said, glancing involuntarily at her plate.

Krista smiled at me. "So, Natalie, tell me about your job. Jonathan tells me you work out at the . . . prison?" Her eyes widened slightly.

"Well, I'm a teacher," I said, hoping I'd get eventual credit for speaking at least a shred of truth. "It's stressful but rewarding." I picked up my wineglass to take a drink before realizing it was empty. I placed it back on the table. "Do you have any children?" I asked, desperate to change the conversation. I was pretty sure she didn't, but maybe she'd talk about her sister's children or her neighbor's children or children she'd seen on *Oprah*. Honestly, I didn't care what we talked about as long as we didn't talk about my job.

My question stopped the conversation dead. Krista and Jack traded glances. Her lips twitched upward. She took the napkin from her lap and dabbed at the corners of her mouth.

"She doesn't have any," Jonathan said, looking up when the silence dragged on.

"Well . . ." Krista said. Jack took her hand under the table.

"We weren't going to tell anyone yet," Jack said, breaking into a grin. "But Jonathan, you're going to be a big brother!"

Krista laughed and flushed. Jonathan stared.

"Wow!" I said. "Congratulations! When are you due?"

"In thirty-six weeks. We've only just found out, but we've been hoping for a long, long time."

Jonathan still hadn't said anything.

"Well, son," Jack said. "What do you think?"

Jonathan looked at Krista. "Aren't you too old?"

She stopped smiling. I think she may have stopped breathing. I certainly did.

"Apparently not," she said quietly. She lifted her glass of sparkling water and took a long drink, staring over the rim at the candle that flickered in the middle of the table.

So it wasn't exactly the time to tell Jonathan that I'd lied about the prison thing and the mother thing.

He was quiet as we drove away from the restaurant. I don't know what had shocked me more: Jonathan's rudeness or his father's response. Jack had merely laughed (none too convincingly) and said, "And here I was thinking you considered Krista too young for me." From there, Jack turned the conversation to his favorite restaurants and his friends' favorite restaurants and managed to avoid any awkward silences or uncomfortable topics as we sprinted through our entrées. Jack ordered dessert and coffee. Krista stuck with water. Jonathan, without consulting me, said we'd better get going. I thanked Jack and Krista for the dinner with what I hoped was politeness that didn't cross the line into effusiveness and scurried after Jonathan, thinking, "He owes me a key lime tart."

When we left the restaurant, Jonathan started driving up Camelback Mountain. That would have been nice had I lived on Camelback Mountain—or even if he lived there. I considered asking why we were headed up the rust-colored, triple-humped formation, but I feared he might misinterpret a simple, "Where are we going?" He might think I was afraid that he had split personalities, that the good Jonathan had disappeared, leaving the bad Jonathan to rape and strangle me before bashing in my head with a jagged rock and throwing my lifeless body into a patch of creosote to be thrashed beyond recognition by coyotes, rattlers, hawks and all those prehistoric-looking bugs that I forever feared would take up residence in my shoes.

We wound up the mountain in silence. When we reached the top, Jonathan killed the engine. Below us, city lights sparkled. Outside the car, giant saguaros—those cactuses that come to mind when you hear the word "cactus," the ones they put on margarita glasses and Southwestern-themed Christmas cards—looked like malformed giants holding up their arms to worship an unseen god.

When Jonathan finally spoke, I expected him to blow: to explode with resentment at his father, hatred for his stepmother. Instead, he sighed and said, "Maybe we should have just gone to a movie."

I reached over and took his hand. "I don't know. There's nothing good out right now. And those concession stands are such a rip-off."

He squeezed my hand. His hands were warm, rough. "When I was a kid, my father used to drive me up here. All you could see was mountains and land, a few neighborhoods here and there. We'd come up to look at the sunset, and after the light faded, it was just dark—I mean, really pitch-black except for the little clumps of civilization here and there." Below us now, the Phoenix Valley glowed from the houses and shopping centers. Along the freeways, cars made trails of white and red. "My father bought land," he continued. "Anytime he had any money, he'd buy some new patch of desert. Whenever we'd come up here, he'd look over the valley and say, *Someday this will all be houses.*"

"He was right," I said.

"His first wife left because she thought he was throwing away their money. In the settlement, she got the house and the cash; he got the undeveloped land."

"Bad move," I said.

"Very bad move." He turned to face me. He smoothed my short hair and ran a finger along my chin. When he finally kissed me, it wasn't with the urgency he'd shown earlier, but rather with a sense of seeking. He trailed his kisses along my jawline, finally stopping at my ear. "I'm glad I met you," he murmured.

"Me, too," I murmured back, trying not to think too much about who he thought he had met.

eight

The following Monday, I was on time for school. Actually, I'd been on time every day since my parents had returned. They were "still on Eastern time" my mother announced brightly every morning at 6 A.M. when she brought me my coffee. It almost made up for losing out on my parents' double-headed shower. The one in my bathroom was a shower/bath combination, and the Waverly shower curtain, pretty though it was, was forever floating into my space and sticking to my wet legs. I know it's stupid to waste emotional energy on an inanimate object, but that shower curtain really pissed me off.

I stopped by the office to debrief Jill on my evening. She wasn't there, but Nicolette was—though it was hard to see her behind a wall of red roses.

"Two dozen," Nicolette informed me, looking up from a Ross-Simons catalogue. "I told Rodney they were my favorite. He must've dropped them off here on his way to work." She smiled dreamily and tilted her head back, revealing a stupendously large hicky just under her jaw.

"Sounds serious," I said.

Nicolette leaned forward. "Yesterday he said the 'L' word," she stage-whispered.

"Lesbian?"

"No—love! *Duh!*" She colored slightly. "I didn't mean to say 'duh.' Sorry, Miss Quackenbush."

"No offense taken. And, please. Call me Natalie."

My first class was eleventh-grade college prep. As far as I could tell, these students were preparing for college by perfecting expressions of desperate boredom and downloading prewritten essays from the Internet. One student, assigned to write about *Great Expectations*, handed in an essay entitled, "David Copperfield: A Colonial Dissemination of Self."

"Right author, wrong book," I informed him before scheduling a conference with his mother, stepfather, father, stepmother and Dr. White. "Though you did a first-rate job designing the title page."

Ten minutes into today's class, there was a knock on the door—an unusual formality. I opened the door to reveal a model-tall, model-thin girl with long, dyed black hair and improbably pale skin.

"I'm your new student? They told me I was in this class?" She clutched a loose-leaf binder to her chest and smiled shyly. She had beautiful teeth and clear, green eyes.

"Of course! Come in!" I had no idea who she was, but she looked so nervous that I didn't want to let on how unexpected her arrival was. I'd be getting new students all year long; Nicolette just couldn't keep up with the paperwork, and not just because she was too busy picking out silverware. The Valley of the Sun—a monstrous sprawl that encompassed not only Phoenix and Scottsdale but also a seemingly endless list of stuccoed cities including Mesa, Tempe, Gilbert, Chandler, and the improbably named Peoria—was growing so fast, it was a perpetual construction zone. Last I'd checked, the valley had almost four million people spread out over 14,000 seemingly uninhabitable square miles. With new jobs came families needing houses and children needing schools. That, in turn, brought in more jobs—in construction, real estate development, and, yes, teaching.

Agave High, built in 1996, was old for these parts. The main building was flanked by portable classrooms—a stopgap measure to accommodate the ever-increasing student enrollment. A mile down the road, another high school was being built to help ease the strain. I wondered how long it would take before that, too, burst at the seams.

I ushered the new girl in. "We're out of desks. Here, take my seat." I pulled my chair from behind the big teacher desk and set it at the end of the front row.

"Class," I announced. "We have a new student." She was the third student added to this class in the few weeks since school had begun, making for a total of thirty-three. School policy called for capping classes at thirty-two—hence the missing desk—but we could always squeeze in one more. Or two. Or five.

"Would you mind introducing yourself?" I said, not wanting to admit that I didn't know her name.

"Certainly," she said. She stood up and turned to face the class. "My name is Katerina Carboni. My family just moved here from Michigan." Her voice was clear and musical, her bearing erect.

"I guess it's a little hotter here than Michigan," I quipped, realizing too late that I'd made the same joke when the other two students joined the class. ("I guess it's a little hotter here than Ohio." "I guess it's a little hotter here than New Jersey.")

Still, Katerina smiled warmly, while the other students more or less ignored me. "A little," she said.

Katerina lingered after class. "Do you know where room P-eleven is?" she asked. "I'm supposed to go there for study hall."

"It's one of the portables," I said. "That's what the 'P' stands for."

"Portables?"

"Those things that look like trailer homes."

"I wondered what those were."

I asked her what she thought of Arizona.

"It's okay, I guess." She shrugged her tiny shoulders. "I mean, we've got a pool, and that's cool." She stopped. "Well, actually, it's warm." Her laughter brought color to her pale cheeks.

My Adventures students were beginning to file in. "It must have been tough to leave your friends in Michigan," I said.

"Yeah." Her smile faded. "I did drama, and I had this really close group of friends. We were doing *Othello* this year, and I was really hoping I'd get to be Desdemona." She shrugged. "Oh, well. My dad got this totally great job, and this is the best thing for the family. That's what my mom says, anyway."

The bell rang. I scanned the crowd slowly settling into their swing-arm chairs. It looked like everyone was here . . . except . . . Robert. What a surprise.

"Guess I'd better get to study hall," Katerina said, sounding a little regretful.

"Wait," I said. "We're doing a play this fall and I'm helping. Auditions are next week. Will you try out?"

Her face brightened. "Yeah, definitely! What's the play?"

At that, Robert made his entrance, armed with his heart-stopping smile. "Sorry, I'm late, Miss Q."

I gave him The Look. They teach you The Look in grad school. The Look is intended to silence a chattering class or chasten a rude student. The Look says, "Watch it, buddy, or you're in for trouble."

I'm an utter failure at The Look. I really need to practice more, to glare into my mirror at home while silently counting to five.

To my astonishment, Robert froze. His eyes grew wide. "The Look worked!" I thought to myself.

"Did you do your homework?" I asked, drunk with newfound power. But he didn't respond. "Robert? Homework?"

"Huh?" It was then that I realized Robert wasn't responding to The Look at all. He was responding to Katerina.

He blinked at me. "Did we have homework?"

My parents were in the kitchen when I came in.

"We were hoping you were the bug guy," my mother said from her perch on one of the carved Mexican stools that lined the granite island.

"Sorry, just your youngest child."

"He was supposed to be here an hour and a half ago," my father said from his own bar stool. Like my mother, his feet were pulled as high off the ground as possible.

"There's a scorpion in our bathroom," my mother said, momentarily squeezing her eyes shut as if to block out the memory.

I plucked a handful of grapes out of the fruit bowl. The central air hummed around us. "Why didn't you just step on it?"

"It's poisonous!" my mother hissed.

"Not if it's dead." I popped a fat green grape into my mouth. "The scorpions aren't so bad. It's the millipedes that freak me out."

"You mean, you've seen scorpions before? In the house?"

I looked up at the ceiling, counting. "This would be the third this summer. No, wait—the fourth. But one was dead. There's something about the heat that brings them out." I shrugged.

The doorbell rang. I answered it, as my parents looked too frightened to leave their stools.

"Hey, Steve," I said to the bleached blond man at the door. He wore a bright yellow uniform that said, "The Bug Guy."

"Hey, Natalie, how are you, your mom called, or maybe it was your dad, they said you've had some kind of an infestation of scorpions, so, anyway, sorry I'm late, I was up in Carefree, big ant problem up there this summer, probably because of all the rains, and I got held up by the construction—you know the work they're doing up there—anyway, I'm here now, so why don't you tell me what's been going on."

Steve should really lay off the pesticide.

"It's not an infestation," I said. "It was one scorpion."

"It was enormous," my mother called from the kitchen.

Steve nodded rapidly. "Okay, then, I was wondering why you'd have so many when I was just here last month for your quarterly service, and so you're not due for your regular service till, let's see, November, but as you know, anytime there's a problem, we're always happy to come out, no extra charge, so I'm happy to take care of these pests for you."

"Pest," I said under my breath. "There's just one."

Steve headed upstairs (after almost four years of regular treatments, he knew the layout). I went back into the kitchen, where my parents remained glued to their island stools. "You could go out-side if you're worried about bugs in the house."

"It's too hot."

"So turn on the misters."

"They're clogged. Hard water deposits. Water here is hard as a rock—no wonder my hair looks so awful. I told your father we should get a softener."

"So go swimming," I said.

"The water's too cold." (It was, actually. In September, the nights get so chilly that the pool becomes unusable long before the days cool down.)

We heard footsteps coming down the stairs. Steve appeared in the kitchen. He had a little twitch under one eye. "I looked all over the bathroom—you did say the master, right?—but I didn't see any sign of a scorpion, probably it ran away, they don't like the light, mostly come out at night, they like to hide in dark corners or un-der furniture. Hope you're checking your shoes before you slip them on in the morning. Or it could be up in the vents, they love the vents. Tell you what I can do, I can sprinkle silicone crystals around all your doorways and the other entry points to the house, you know, the outlets, the dishwasher, any place a pest might find a way in, and what those silicone crystals do is, they cut a bug up as it crawls over your entryway, kills it before it ever gets into the house."

It was quiet. Dead quiet. My parents stared at Steve. Finally, my mother spoke. "The scorpion was *gone*?"

"Yes, ma'am. No sign of 'em. Could be anywhere."

"You should have stepped on it." I opened the shiny fridge and pulled out a Diet Dr Pepper. I smiled warmly at my mom, the buyer of the Diet Dr Pepper, the only person in the world who knew which foods I loved best. "Next time, call me. I'll step on it." I popped open the soda. "Really, it's not so bad. It's not like you found a rattlesnake in your bathroom."

"You seen any rattlers?" Steve asked.

"Not yet." I took a drag of my soda.

"They're good fried," he said. "With catsup."

nine

Twenty-four hours later, I had the house—and the double-headed shower—to myself. My parents had spent the night on the pull-out couch in the bonus room because the guest room (the one other than the one I slept in) shared a wall with the master bath.

"But if the scorpion is in the vents, it doesn't matter how close you are to the bathroom," I said calmly. "It could blow out anywhere."

By the time I got home from work, my parents had wrangled an invitation out of the Gillespies and were packed for an extended visit at their cabin. Flagstaff has scorpions, too, but I didn't tell my parents. I didn't want to upset them. And I had really missed that shower.

"I've pulled your bed away from the wall," my mother said. "So you're not sleeping under a vent anymore."

I rolled my eyes, though I had to admit the thought of a scorpion popping out of a vent did freak me out a little.

Jill was thrilled. "Party at Natalie's!" she said after school the next day as we stood sweating in the faculty parking lot. Our car engines were running, all doors open, air conditioners at full blast. The interiors wouldn't get truly cool, but in a few minutes they'd be bearable.

"Glad to see you're in touch with your inner adolescent," I said. "I don't even know enough people for a party. Besides, I'm supposed to be starting a unit on *Our Town* tomorrow, and I haven't even read it yet."

Jill fanned her face with her hand. "Small town in New Hampshire. Boy meets girl. Boy gets girl. Girl dies. That's really all you need to know."

Lars walked out of the school and headed for his Prius, a rarity in a parking lot filled with tired-looking Civics, Escorts and Saturns. It was easy to tell the faculty lot from the students'. The students' cars were much nicer.

"Hey, Lars!" Jill held up her arm and waved. "You wanna go over to Natalie's house later? Her parents are out of town."

"Jill's coming," I said as he got closer, just to make sure he didn't get the wrong idea. How ironic if I finally got a shot at Lars now that I was no longer interested. After all, I was dating Jonathan. Or, someone who looked just like me was dating Jonathan, at any rate.

Lars approached, twisting open a water bottle. "Actually, Natalie, I was hoping we could go over some audition stuff, anyway." He poured some of the water onto his cupped hand and splashed the back of his neck. He did it again, dousing his forehead this time.

"It can't go too late," I told Lars. "I've got to put together my first *Our Town* lesson for college prep."

"Just assign parts and have the kids read it out loud," Lars said.

"But they've already read it," I said. "I assigned it for homework."

Lars raised his eyebrows. Mentally, I ran through the kids in my college prep classes. "Well, some of them read it. Two, maybe."

Jill took Lars's bottle and splashed her own face. "Okay, then. I'll bring the food. Lars, you bring the booze. We like margaritas. Six o'clock work for everyone?" She handed the bottle back to Lars. He took a swig.

"And what about me?" I asked, eyeing the water bottle. I wanted some to dump on my own sweaty face, but taking it would seem oddly intimate now that it had touched Lars's lips. "What should I bring?"

"You just sit there and look pretty," Jill said. Then she took the bottle and drained it, returning the empty container to Lars.

Jill, hauling a brown bag, got to the house first. "Where's Lover Boy?"

"Oh, please. Lars is just a friend. Besides, I'm seeing Jonathan now."

She strode into the kitchen and put the bag on the counter. "Oh? And who does Jonathan think he's seeing?" When I glared at her, she laughed. "Just tell him. He'll probably think it's funny."

"I'm not so sure," I said.

"Would it be such a great loss?"

I blinked at her. "I like him."

She shrugged. "Okay." She reached into the bag and pulled out a bag of sushi rice. "You got a rice cooker?"

"Yes. Except in this house, we call it a pot. So—what? You don't like Jonathan?"

"Of course I like him. What is there not to like?"

"Meaning?"

"He's just a bit, you know. Sedate. And he has absolutely no sense of style." She retrieved more items from the bag: baby zucchini, ginger root, bagged lettuce, brownies, and a package wrapped in white butcher paper. "Ahi," she informed me. "You do have a grill, don't you? I'm making seared ahi."

"Of course we have a grill. Stainless steel, enormous. You could roast a turkey on that thing." I folded up the paper bag and stuck it on the shelf of the walk-in pantry specially designed to hold brown paper bags. "Lars has style, and you think it makes him look gay."

"I don't really think Lars is gay. Confused, maybe." The doorbell rang. "Speak of the devil."

"I brought margaritas," Lars said, holding up a giant yellow bottle. He gazed up at the ceiling fans whirring high above us. "Wow. Nice place." He wore linen Bermuda shorts and a silk floral shirt that looked Tommy Bahama—but surely a teacher didn't spend that kind of money on clothes. I wore shorts and an old tank top, almost deliberately underdressing, as if to prove that I was over—so over—Lars, while Jill wore a billowy black skirt and a strappy shirt from Target.

Jill took the yellow bottle. "Premixed? Lars, you philistine."

"You should have asked for martinis. Those I know how to make." He trailed Jill into the kitchen. "Granite counters. Nice."

After I poured the second-rate margaritas, Jill said, "I'll make dinner. You kids go work on your play."

I smirked. "Yes, Ms. Green."

Lars and I spent the next hour discussing *Romeo and Jules* and enumerating the qualities necessary in our leads. For Julia Smythe (Jules) we needed someone "beautiful, vulnerable—just plain sexy," Lars said. And Romeo Flores? "Charismatic, maybe a little dark, intense." I deferred to Lars's opinion because I hadn't actually read the script yet, though I didn't want to admit it. It had been sitting on my nightstand for a week now. But when I wasn't grading papers I was planning lessons or slogging through *The Odyssey* (okay, through *The Odyssey CliffsNotes*). I kept promising myself a night off, an evening spent slack-jawed in front of the television, but even that was more than I could fit into my schedule. Still, I told Lars I knew a girl, a new student, who might be perfect for the role of Jules.

By the time Jill called us to dinner, I was on my third margarita (the glasses were very, very small) and making statements like, "Shakespeare's work stands alone for its timeless understanding of the human condition."

Jill had set the table on the covered patio outside the kitchen. Above the stucco walls that rimmed the yard, the sky was turning all the colors of a Southwest sunset: powder blue and grayish purple and baby girl pink. It was hot outside, but not a midday, unbearable heat.

"How do you turn on the misters?" Jill asked.

"You don't. They're clogged."

"You can get a water softener to help with that," Lars added helpfully.

After some debate, we decided to eat outside despite the heat. We'd polished off the margarita bottle (not so terrible when you considered it was premixed and therefore largely juice). Lars took the opportunity to show off his skills with a martini shaker. My parents' liquor fridge was well-stocked (not to mention maintained at an ideal temperature of sixty-five degrees). I took careful notes as Lars poured Grey Goose vodka, vowing to replace whatever we took and wishing my parents stocked cheaper booze.

"You could just fill the bottles up with water," Jill suggested. "It's what the kids at school do."

"Do their parents notice?"

"Why do you think those kids end up in my office?"

Dinner was far better than anything I could make or that my parents could buy at the takeout counter: seared, blackened ahi tuna, sushi rice, grilled vegetables. The only harsh note was the martini, which burned my throat. I considered raiding my parents' wine fridge (which sat next to the liquor fridge, with matching see-through doors), but they mostly bought the good stuff, and I didn't want to shell out the money to replace it. I found myself annoyed at Lars. He was supposed to supply the booze, after all. I got myself a glass of water. Lars and Jill stuck to their martinis.

By the time we hit the brownies, I was starting to get that dull, thirsty, cranky feeling you get when you stop drinking too soon (or too late, depending on one's perspective). Lars and Jill had moved on to Irish coffees (note to self: restock the Irish whiskey). I stuck to water. Sweat dripped down my back; the thought of a hot drink was utterly unappealing.

The heat, the coffee and, of course, the liquor all conspired to turn Lars's face bright red and shiny. It made his Nordic hair look oddly yellow in contrast. Even his usually flippy hairdo had grown limp. "Shoulda passed on the coffee," he murmured. "Man! I'm hot! I think I'm gonna have to jump in that pool."

"Did you bring a bathing suit?" I asked.

"Bathing suit?"

"Yes. A bathing suit. It's what we call the garment you wear for swimming."

Jill raised her eyebrows. I wasn't normally snide to Lars. I wasn't normally snide to anyone. But I was tired and cranky and I just wanted them to leave.

"Do pool regulations require proper bathing attire?" Lars asked in an almost Shakespearean diction.

"What. Ever." I rolled my eyes, channeling my inner adolescent. I certainly had enough role models. "You can borrow one of my Dad's, I guess." Lying to Jonathan was one thing. Letting another man swim naked in my parents' pool was a far greater sin.

"Underwear's pretty much the same thing as a bathing suit," Jill announced. "Don't be so inhibited." And with that, she stood up and yanked off her tank top, revealing a big strapless black bra with substantial underwires. She pulled at the sides of her pouffy skirt and let it fall to the ground. Her underpants were a faded blue. The elastic on one side was coming unraveled. Her thighs were strong and shapely, but her belly was mushy. As if recognizing her imperfections, she scurried over to the edge of the pool with uncharacteristically tiny steps and jumped in, creating a huge splash. She came up screaming.

"Holy crap, it's cold!" She treaded water, gulping down air. "C'mon, Lars! You're the one who started this. Get in!"

Lars fumbled with the buttons on his tropical print shirt. "You want a hanger for that?" I asked, smirking.

He missed the sarcasm. "If you have one, that'd be great." He beamed his Mr. Handsome smile.

Inside, I did a quick change into my most flattering bathing suit (boy shorts and a bikini top) and returned with a wooden hanger for Lars. His shirt lay crumpled on his chair, label exposed: it was a Tommy Bahama, after all. I picked it up and slid it onto the hanger, then hung the whole thing from the back of the wrought iron chair.

Jill and Lars were in the spa, bubbles brewing. "Is the water warm?" I asked. I hadn't turned it on, and the air temperature was falling by the minute.

"No, but it's better than the pool," Lars said, teeth chattering dramatically.

"Lars is a pussy," Jill said. "You pussy!" She splashed him. He laughed and splashed back.

I went over to the pool equipment and hit a switch. "It'll warm up in a minute." I padded over to the spa. The Arizona flagstones were warm under my feet, still clinging to the heat of the day.

"Join us!" Lars said before submerging briefly. When he reemerged, his hair was slicked off his face. He had a very high forehead. He rubbed the water out of his eyes. "It feels good once you get used to it."

"Bullshit!" Jill said. "It's fucking freezing!" It was odd to hear Jill swearing—like she was the Chess Club president trying to sound cool.

"I'll wait till it warms up." I sat on the edge of the spa and stuck my feet into the frothy water, right at the spot where the warm water gushed out. The bubbles obscured the bodies underneath. "You are wearing underwear, aren't you, Lars?"

"Yes, ma'am!" He popped up. "Calvin Klein's finest." They

were black and form fitting and revealed the smallest beginnings of an erection. I looked away.

"They're boxer briefs," Jill said. "Or brief boxers. I told Lars they demonstrated a fear of commitment. You know the old question—boxers or briefs? Well, for Lars, it's neither!"

"Or both!" he piped in, lowering himself back into the froth. "It's getting warmer."

"I feel like we're on *Elimidate*," I said. They both cackled furiously. I am very funny when other people are drunk.

I heard a faint whirring from inside the house. "The phone," I announced, pulling my legs out of the water.

The answering machine had picked up by the time I reached the kitchen.

"We're in Flagstaff," my mother's voice informed me, in case I'd forgotten. In the background, a woman's voice chirped, "Hello from me!"

"Mrs. Gillespie says to tell you hi," my mother continued. "Anyway, we're just checking to make sure everything is okay and that you haven't seen any more scorpions." More murmuring in the background. "And Mrs. Gillespie says to tell you that her daughter Celia is engaged. You remember Celia." More murmuring. "And she says to remind you to shake out your shoes before you put them on in the morning."

I just stood there looking at the machine until my mother said her good-byes. ("Anyway, hope you're out doing something fun. Maybe on a date.") What was I supposed to say? That I'd chosen the first possible moment after my parents' departure to fill their hot tub with half-naked educators?

My cell phone lay on the counter next to the kitchen phone.

I checked my messages; Jonathan had called. I looked out the window. Lars lounged in the spa, his arms stretched around the edges like a bird's wings. Jill sat half in, half out of the water, exposing her black bra (which, I was happy to see, appeared to be holding up).

I dialed Jonathan.

He answered on the second ring. "Hey." There were voices in the background. Laughter.

"Hey, yourself. Did you go out to dinner without me?" Oops: too possessive?

"Nope. I'm at my father's. They're having a dinner party." His voice was low. The background noises faded as he spoke, then disappeared entirely. I heard a click. "Okay. I'm inside. I would have invited you, but, well, I like you."

I laughed. "I liked your father. Krista, too."

"Yeah, I know. Everybody does. I'm just not sure you'll like me when I'm around them. What are you up to?"

I looked out the window. Jill was back up to her neck in bubbles, while Lars's hairless chest shone in the moonlight. Did he wax his chest, or was it naturally that smooth? "Just hanging out at the house with a couple of friends from work."

There was a brief pause. "Guards?"

"No, um, I don't really, we don't really mix. There's my friend you met, the, uh, warden. Plus another teacher."

"And your mother, she's not upset?"

My mother. Oh, crap. "She's not here, actually. My dad took her up to Flagstaff for a little while. The heat was bothering her."

"Can he handle her on his own?" Oh, right. That's why I lived with my parents: to help with my mother.

"Her doctor put her on some new medication. Something

experimental. We're not sure what it is, but so far, it's working wonders." I suddenly wished I hadn't called Jonathan. Every time we spoke, I dug farther into the mess I had created. Mercifully, he changed the subject.

"So, are we still on for Saturday night?"

"Definitely," I said. And I'd come clean to him, I suddenly vowed. It was time to make things right.

ten

Saturday morning I graded papers, making a point to write at least one line on each to prove I had read it. "Excellent insights!" "Watch comma usage!" "Use exclamation points more sparingly!"

When I'd exhausted my pile, I moved on to my jam-packed e-mail in-box. Every teacher at Agave had an e-mail address; mine, regrettably, was *natquack@agavesecondary.edu*. The school e-mail system was intended to make teachers more accessible and more efficient. It certainly made us more accessible. A sampling:

To: natquack@agavesecondary.edu
From: Lynette Pimpernel
Re: Re: Grading on a Curve

Dear Mrs. Quackenbush:
Thank you for your reply to my recent e-mail regarding grading on a

curve as it relates to recent events in my daughter, Claudia's, class, freshman honors English. Your points regarding punctuation mastery are well-taken, and I can appreciate why you believe it was fair to award Claudia, who has always been a straight-A student, a B on the recent apostrophe test, corresponding, as you said, to her 86% mark. I hope you understand, however, why we would have expected her to receive an A given that over four-fifths of her honors classmates scored lower than 80% on the same exercise. It is my sincerest hope that in the future you will resist punishing Claudia and her classmates by assigning low grades for material that, evidently, they were not given an adequate opportunity to master.

Sincerely,

Lynette Pimpernel (Claudia's mom)

To: Lynette Pimpernel
From: natquack@agavesecondary.edu
Re: Re: Re: Grading on a Curve

Dear Mrs. Pimpernel:

It is always encouraging to have a parent take an interest in her child's education. Claudia is an excellent student, and I have no doubt that she will go far in life. She cannot run before she can walk, however, and she cannot write a groundbreaking dissertation, novel or Supreme Court decision until she has mastered the difference between "its" and "it's." I will be retesting the students on Tuesday. Perhaps Claudia can use the weekend to review chapter 5 in her vocabulary book.

Regards,

Natalie Quackenbush

To: natquack@agavesecondary.edu
From: codycoyote@freenet.com
Re: Have a nice weekend

Dear Miss Quackenbush,
I just wanted to say thanks for working so hard to teach us The Odyssey. (See? I even remembered to underline the title, just like you taught us!) I hope you have a really excellent weekend. I am going to use my free time to read some books I just got out from the library and to listen to some new music. Well, that is all for now. Have a nice day.
Your friend,
Cody Gold

To: codycoyote@freenet.com
From: natquack@agavesecondary.edu
Re: Re: Have a nice weekend

Dear Cody,
It is good to hear that you are spending your free time reading! If you liked The Odyssey, you may want to try The Iliad, which, regrettably, I will not have time to teach this year.
See you on Monday.
Ms. Quackenbush

Jonathan took me to dinner at a restaurant perched on top of a craggy mountain, suspended above a million city lights. We sat out on the deck for cocktails, scoring a table next to a stainless steel propane heater. Jonathan ordered a bottle of pinot noir. As we clinked glasses, I vowed to come clean to him before the bottle was finished.

"Fodor's named this place the most romantic in Phoenix," I told him.

He smiled. "You're going to start thinking I like you or something."

"Have you ever been here before?" I asked, turning around to look at the restaurant and imagining Jonathan sharing a dinner with Jack and Krista.

He didn't answer right away. "Not recently," he said finally.

"Oh," I chirped, forcing a smile. "You take your dates to nice places." I drank my wine and waited for him to disagree, to say he hardly ever dated. He didn't say anything. "Do you come here often?" I asked.

"No," he said.

"Ah." And then, before I had a chance to think about it, I asked, "Who was on your answering machine?"

"What?" He looked genuinely confused.

"The night I was at your house. With . . . my friend. Your answering machine was blinking."

"Ah."

I took a deep breath and tried to sound convincing: "I mean, if you're dating other people, that's okay. I mean, not entirely okay, but certainly allowed. It's not like we're, you know. Intimate." I gulped. What a ridiculous word. "I mean, I'm not dating anyone else. But if you are, it doesn't need to be some big secret." I drank my wine to keep myself from saying anything more.

Jonathan put down his glass, leaned over the table and took my free hand. He looked me in the eye. "I'm not seeing anyone else. I don't want to see anyone else."

"Okay." I exhaled.

"The message on my machine—it was from someone I used to go out with. It's been over a long time, almost a year, but she still . . . for a long time she kept holding out hope. And calling. Pretty much every day. And stopping by unannounced."

"Was this The Slasher?"

"No, The Slasher was a couple of years ago. This was The Stalker."

I felt an odd sense of relief. Compared to these women, I was downright normal.

Funny thing about alcohol: it makes you lose your resolve. When we finished the bottle of wine—we were inside and enjoying our salad course at this point—I still hadn't told Jonathan that I was a high school English teacher. In my defense, though, I hadn't told him any new lies, which was a warped kind of progress.

"So what about your mother?" I asked him. "Did she ever re-marry?"

"Nope. After my father left her for another woman—"

"Younger?"

"Naturally. After that, my mother became a certified man-hater. I can't count how many times she's said to me, 'All men are ass-holes. Except you, of course.' She did all right financially, though. When my father left, he didn't have a lot of liquid assets, so she had to settle for land. In the nineties, she sold it all and bought herself a nice spread in Santa Fe."

"And what about your father's third wife?"

"Evil." He grimaced. "Thought my father had a lot more money than he did because he lived in a huge house that he'd bought for next to nothing. She was always whining about want-ing to take a cruise, then after they'd get back from the cruise, she'd whine that they should have taken a better cruise line. She hated me, of course. The way she saw it, money spent on my food and housing could have been put to better use at Saks."

"Did he go right from her to Krista?"

He shook his head. "No, there was a big gap. Let's see . . . Janelle and my dad divorced the year I turned nineteen. He left her right before he was set to make a small fortune selling a big parcel in Chandler. After that, he was single for more than ten years. Single-ish, anyway. He had a lot of girlfriends. A couple even moved in with him for a while. But no one got a ring until Krista."

"And you're not that crazy about Krista."

He shrugged. "She's okay. Could have been worse."

The waitress came and picked up our empty wine bottle. "Can I get you another?"

We said no and asked for more water. When I finished my water, I'd tell Jonathan the truth.

I never even touched the glass.

eleven

Audition notices went up on Tuesday. They were supposed to go up on Monday. My first duty as assistant director was to design and post them, a task that sounded simpler than it was. Creating the flyer was easy: I sat down at the English department computer and typed up the time and place of the auditions. I named the play and listed the available roles.

But when it came time to print, the computer froze up. I had to reboot (which, to me, means "turn it off and turn it back on again"), and by then the document had vanished. I typed it again, saving it on the hard disk this time. I congratulated myself on my foresight when the machine crashed again. I didn't have to reenter the document. I did, however, have to hunt down a blank CD, finally begging one off Neil Weinrich, the pompous math department head, after assuring him that I would bring in a new, blank disk the next morning. By this time, I had to teach a class.

At lunch, I took the disk to the Media Center, where I successfully managed to send the document to the printer—only to discover that the printer was out of paper. Actually, the whole Media Center was out of the "right kind" of paper, and the Media Center Specialist (what we called "a librarian" in the old days) refused to allow the "wrong kind" of paper into the printer, even though I assured her it wouldn't do any damage. Lunch was almost over by then, anyway.

In the end, I took some of the "wrong" paper into my classroom and wrote the information out multiple times while my college prep students wrote an in-class essay, the main difference between in-class essays and out-of-class essays being that in-class essays actually got written.

The class, with the exception of Katerina, scurried out the minute the bell rang. She lingered by my desk, talking about *Romeo and Jules*.

"I read it over the weekend," she said. "It was totally amazing."

"It's powerful," I concurred. (I still hadn't read it.)

"Hey, what's that?" Robert asked, appearing breathlessly at my desk a full two minutes before the bell. Ever since Katerina had shown up, Robert had been remarkably punctual. For her part, Katerina always hung around my desk until the last possible moment. I wondered whether her chronic lingering should be attributed to her fondness for me or her attraction to Robert. I suspected the latter and felt oddly jealous.

"Audition notices," I said. "You ever think about acting, Robert?"

He looked at Katerina. "I've thought about it," he said. "It looks fun."

"Maybe you should audition," I said.

"Maybe I will," he said, smiling at Katerina.

"I think I've got a Romeo for you," I told Lars at lunch.

"No way," Lars said when I named Robert. "I had that kid last year. Totally unreliable."

"He's changed," I said, unconvincingly. He had yet to turn in a single homework assignment, but at least he'd become punctual.

"He's a good-looking kid, I'll give him that." Lars shrugged. "Let's see how his reading goes."

On Wednesday, I invited Jonathan to dinner at my house, a move I immediately regretted: my parents' home did not look like an invalid's house. Besides, I can't actually cook.

"No problem," Jill said when I told her. "I have some cold Asian pork salad in my fridge. It's got ginger, sesame seeds—really tasty. You can have it. Buy some good bread, a bag of salad, and you're in business."

"What about salad dressing?"

"I'll whip some up for you." Jill had finally stopped making fun of Jonathan's cowboy boots and pickup truck. "You deserve to be happy," she'd said.

When he first arrived at the house, he asked for a tour. I couldn't say no (though I considered it), but I found myself wishing I had hit a medical supplies store on the way home from work. A safety seat in the bathtub would have been a nice touch.

"I call it 'Boston meets *Bonanza*,'" I said of the décor. In an effort to be Southwestern, my mother had filled her Spanish-style
house with Mexican dishes, terra-cotta planters and dried-chili
wreaths. Still, she couldn't bring herself to part with the furniture
she had either inherited from her parents or discovered on antique
hunts in Maine: the mahogany dining room set, the camelback
sofa, the grandfather clock, the Hummels. The overall effect wasn't
eclectic so much as ambivalent.

As we walked up the stairs, Jonathan took my hand. My heart
began to beat faster. I've seen enough Lifetime Channel movies to
know what it means when a man takes a woman's hand as they
head for the bedroom—except on Lifetime, the scene usually cuts
to a Tampax commercial the moment they reach the bedroom
door.

It was our fourth date, and everyone knows what that means.
Okay, in case you aren't "anyone," I'll tell you: after four dates, if
you really, really like someone, you can sleep with him without being what my more streetwise students would affectionately term
"a ho."

However, while Jonathan made my skin tingle and my stomach
grow warm, I didn't think we should sleep together until he knew
who I was—assuming he'd still want to, of course.

So, when we reached my bedroom, I halted at the door. "This is
where I sleep. Not too exciting."

He peered beyond the door. "No foreign doll collection? No
teddy bears?"

"I had a shelf of ceramic animals. My mother gave them to
Goodwill before they moved. I'm still not ready to talk about it."

Still holding his hand, I guided him down the hall to my parents' bedroom. "The master suite," I announced. The walls were

burnt orange, a tone my mother chose after Mrs. Gillespie encouraged her to "make a bold statement." It was bold, all right, but my mother said she felt like she was waking up in a pumpkin every morning.

"My mother's been asking my father to repaint this room for two years, but he keeps putting it off. She says he secretly likes the color, but mostly I think he just doesn't want to cut into his golf time."

"It's good that she's so aware, though." Jonathan put his arm around me. "That she remembers having asked before."

"Come this way," I said, leading him below an arch. "I like a bathroom big enough to hold a dinner party in. Check out the double-headed shower." I blushed, realizing what I seemed to be suggesting—and realizing that I liked the idea.

"Actually, I, um . . ."

"Yes?" My face was burning.

"I need to use the, uh . . ."

"Oh! Right." I showed him the toilet, which was off by itself in a tiny, dark closet. "I'm going to get dinner going—meet me back in the kitchen."

Of course, "getting dinner going" meant taking the cold sesame pork out of Jill's Rubbermaid containers and arranging it artfully in one of my mother's Mexican bowls. I did the same for the bagged salad. The bread I wrapped in foil and stuck in the oven to warm.

"It looks wonderful," Jonathan said when he came down a few minutes later. "Where are the dishes? I'll set the table."

As he headed for the patio with the dishes, silverware and napkins I'd given him, he said, "There was a scorpion in the bathroom. But don't worry—I stepped on it."

"Good thing my mother isn't here. Scorpions really freak her out."

A few minutes later, I walked outside to the patio, holding a tray filled with the various bowls. When I saw the table Jonathan had set, I burst out laughing. "Napkin swans?"

"I spend a lot of time in restaurants, remember." He bowed slightly and pulled out a chair. "Mademoiselle . . ."

A bottle of Riesling sat uncorked on the table. Still standing, Jonathan poured a splash into my glass. I picked it up and sipped. "Fruity, with oaky undertones. Hints of ginger and fig."

He broke into a grin. "A wine connoisseur. I had no idea."

"Not really. I'm just good at pretending." At this, I felt myself flush. I looked down at my glass as Jonathan filled it. Between us, a candle, half-buried in sand, flickered in a glass hurricane. Jonathan sat down and filled his own glass. He swirled the amber liquid around and took a sip, which he held briefly in his mouth before swallowing. "I would have said apricot overtones. Though I agree with you about the fig."

"Are you faking, too, or do you know what you're talking about?"

He shrugged. "Professional hazard."

I touched my swan napkin. "How did you do this, anyway?"

He picked up his own napkin with two fingers. With a flick, it was a napkin again. "The napkin has to be square," he said. "The thick commercial ones are best."

With some regret, I unfolded my perfect swan and laid the napkin flat on the table. I followed Jonathan as he folded, twisted and fluffed. My final product looked nothing like his. "Mine looks more like a pigeon. An old, fat pigeon."

He laughed and then reached for the bowls, serving me first. "So, what's happening in the American justice system?"

"Huh?" At first I thought he was referring to some news story. Then I realized he was asking about my job. "Oh, you know. The usual." I picked up my pigeon napkin and spread it out on my lap. "We're doing a play. *Romeo and Jules*. I'm the assistant director."

"Cool." He speared some pork with his fork. "How are you going to do it with just women?" He put the pork in his mouth, and an expression of bliss flickered across his face. "This is wonderful."

I stopped mid-chew, then forced myself to swallow. The pork felt lodged in my throat. I gulped some wine. "We're joining forces with the men's prison," I said, making prison sound like an exclusive boarding school. "How's Krista feeling?"

After all the quizzing I'd done on our last date, Jonathan probably didn't want to talk about his stepmother—but it beat having me yap about my prison production.

"Krista? Let's see. She nauseous, she can't stop urinating, and her breasts are enlarged and tender." He wrinkled his nose.

"Too much information?"

"You have no idea. This was over cocktails, no less. When she started talking about her enhanced libido, I had to leave the room."

"Eew," I said. "Are you okay now, though? I mean, about the baby?"

He shrugged. "I still think it was a terrible idea. My father's going to be too old to play catch with the kid, to teach him to swim and all that. But maybe I can help out, be a kind of favorite uncle. I always wanted a brother or sister when I was growing up. Better late than never, right?"

I stuck a forkful of salad in my mouth before I had a chance to say any of the things I was thinking: that if he were a kind of favorite uncle, maybe I could be a kind of favorite aunt. That being a favorite uncle is a great warm-up to being a favorite dad.

We gazed at each other over the candlelight. His eyes crinkled. He knew darn well what I was thinking.

twelve

An outdoor amphitheater probably seemed like a good idea when the school planners walked the site on a winter day. In mid-September, it was unbearable.

"Maybe we could move the auditions into the multi-purpose room?" I suggested.

Lars pushed his blond hair out of his face. "Girls basketball has dibs."

"Why don't they just use the gym?"

"Boys soccer is in there."

"Since when is soccer an indoor sport?"

"Since soccer moved to Scottsdale."

Around us, students were starting to gather. They gazed listlessly at the concrete tiers, searching futilely for shade.

"What about your classroom?" I asked.

"Maybe. If there aren't too many kids."

"I think there's going to be a good turnout," I said, perking up. "Did you see those audition notices? Really eye-catching." He looked unimpressed.

A lot of students showed up—almost sixty—but we wound up in Lars's classroom, anyway, instructing the stragglers to wait in the hall. Katerina was there, of course, with Robert at her side.

I hadn't been in Lars's classroom this year; we generally saw each other in either the English office or the lunchroom. I had assumed it would look pretty much like mine, with vanilla-colored cinderblock walls hung with Shakespeare quotes, an oversized calendar and a "Great Moments in Literature" timeline.

But Lars's room was different. First of all, it was a Mediterranean blue, a color that Lars had picked, paid for and painted himself the week before classes began. In a back corner, five computers and a printer sat under a banner that read, IDEA LAB.

"You have a printer! Do you know how much time I wasted trying to print those audition notices on Monday? How'd you swing the computers, anyway? I thought only the math department had them."

Lars picked up a stack of photocopied scenes (copied by me, of course; at least the Xerox machine was working) and started passing them out. "There's this foundation that collects and refurbishes old computers for schools. I wrote them a grant proposal last spring—and voila."

"You know how to write grant proposals?" I took a bunch of the scripts for the kids in the hall.

"It's a good thing to know if you're going to stay in education."

"That's a big if," I muttered, heading to the door.

Next we passed out "audition cards," which were printed on yellow half-slips of paper. On them, the kids had to write their name, graduating year, acting experience, desired role(s) and—my favorite—their cell phone numbers.

An angular blond girl raised her hand. "Where you ask for the cell number? What if we have two cells? Do we put both numbers?"

I squinted at her. "Um, just put whichever one you use most."

She nodded. "Okay, that would be the one that takes pictures."

My next duty as assistant director was to collect the cards and divide them into two piles: boys and girls. (And to think that I'd worried that I wouldn't be up to this job.) A quick glance revealed that all of the boys—tall, short, old enough to shave or not—dreamed of playing dark, intense, hunky Romeo. And all of the girls—gangly, chunky, cute or acne-prone—had set their sights on ethereal Jules. Nobody wanted to be a friend (Romeo and Jules each had two) or a parent (one apiece).

In the end, we called the students up in the random order of their collected audition cards, a boy and a girl at a time, and had them read one page of a *Romeo and Jules* scene.

Cody and Claudia, having secured their usual front row seats, read first. Claudia, perhaps not surprisingly, showed a dramatic flair, while Cody, who had only discovered an interest in theater after learning I was involved, read his lines clearly but without emotion. I glanced at his card. If he didn't get a part, he wanted to help haul sets. I looked at his skinny frame. Maybe he could do props.

After the fifth or sixth reading, the kids began to blur into one another. Cody's flat delivery was fairly typical, I discovered. A couple of students showed potential, but in the interest of time, Lars cut them all off after a page. For the standouts, there would be time for further consideration during callbacks. Good and bad, they all looked so eager, so hopeful. I was glad that Lars would be deciding their fates and not me. We were still in the educational age of self-esteem, and the thought of rejecting any of these kids filled me with dread.

When I pulled Robert's name out, I cheated, flipping through the girl cards until I got to Katerina. I called their names out casually, as if I weren't playing Cupid. I shot Lars a smile as if to say, "See? Robert showed."

Katerina wore a flowy turquoise skirt, a white eyelet shirt and black leather flip-flops. Robert wore a sleeveless Nike T-shirt, basketball shorts and high tops, yet somehow he and Katerina looked perfect together. Robert loped to the front of the room a step behind Katerina, gazing at her from behind his long lashes, while all of the girls in the crowded classroom stared at Robert, pleased to have the opportunity to examine him openly.

Katerina held her script out in front of her. She put a hand on her hip and shook her filmy black hair out of her face. Robert eased himself onto a wooden desk chair and lounged back, immediately displaying the stage presence I'd promised Lars.

The entire room was silent. Finally, Robert spoke without looking at the script. (We'd all heard the scene a good twelve or fifteen times already.) "People talk about love all the time. Until now, I didn't know what they were talking about. I thought love was just a way for Britney Spears to sell CDs or for the Gap to sell jeans."

Katerina tossed her hair. "Sometimes I think you just love me because you're not supposed to."

"You know that's not true," Robert replied, his eyes boring into her. "I love you because I can't help it. From the first time I saw you, standing across from me at the Starbucks, there was no one else in the world."

It was clear Katerina had been on a stage before. She stood erect and spoke clearly, more to the audience than to Robert. A few lines in, she softened. Robert's charisma was palpable. I stole a glance at Lars. His eyes were wide, thrilled. He bit his lip, trying to control his excitement.

"Your friends think I'm stuck up because I carry a Dooney and Bourke purse," Katerina said.

"Your friends think I'm trash because I'm a barista," Robert countered.

She strode toward him and covered his lips with two fingers. "Don't say that word."

Robert took her hand. "I don't feel like trash with you," Robert said. "With you, I feel like Gucci."

When they finished the page, Robert popped up from his chair and grinned at Katerina. She grinned back.

"No—keep going," Lars said.

Robert stared at him. "You didn't like it?"

"I did. I want to hear more. I think we all do. Go on to the next page."

Robert sunk back onto the chair. Katerina flipped her script to the next page. Robert followed suit. The next line was hers. She cleared her throat and read: "You matter more to me than my family. Than my friends. I would die for you."

And then: silence. Robert looked at Katerina. He looked back at the script. He turned a page. "Where are we, again?" He seemed to shrink into himself.

"Page thirty-two. Second line," Lars said.

Katerina took a step over and pointed to the spot on Robert's script. She read her line again: "You matter more to me than my family. Than my friends. I would die for you."

Robert began to read—or, rather, to sound out. "Whaa . . . wha. Wha . . . air. Where? Aah. Are . . ." The room was still. I had stopped breathing.

"Where are you going after this," I said.

"Oh, right." He rubbed his eyes. "Where are you going after this?" he said, almost, but not quite, inhabiting Romeo again.

"To the Rock 'n Roll Sushi at the mall," Katerina responded. "My mother said to meet her there. She made me promise not to see you anymore."

Silence. I prompted Robert: "Why does your mother hate my father so?"

"Why does your mother hate my father so?" he echoed, his voice wavering. He wasn't even looking at his script.

Katerina leaned toward Robert and put a hand on his arm. "It is because they both wanted to buy the same Mercedes dealership. And even though my father got it, and we're rich because of it, she thinks that my father had a heart attack because of the stress."

Robert licked his lips. He squinted at the paper in his hand. "I wuh . . . I wuh-ih. I wiss. Wish." He stopped. He looked up at Katerina, desperate. She looked confused.

Robert dropped the script on the floor. "I can't do this." He looked up, focusing on no one. "I gotta get out of here," he mumbled. He sprang up from his chair and rushed out of the room, leaving a baffled Katerina at the front of the classroom.

"Okay," Lars said finally. "Thank you, Katerina. Ms. Quackenbush, who's next?"

I thrust him two yellow slips of paper. "I gotta go." I ran out the door and toward the student parking lot.

"Wait!" I shouted once I reached the far side of the lot.

He stood next to his little orange car, the front doors open to air it out. Robert's car could have belonged to a teacher: it was that crappy.

I hurried across the lot. Heat radiated from the dark surface. A bead of sweat slid down my back.

"Why didn't you tell me?" I asked when I finally reached him.

"Tell you what? That I'm too stupid to read?"

"You're not stupid," I said gently. "You have a learning disability."

"Yeah, I know, I've been hearing that since I was seven. Once I might have even believed it."

"Robert, there are people who can help you. There's Miss Baker, the reading specialist. I can set up a time for you to meet with her."

"I've met her," he said slowly. "You see what good it did?"

"Well, maybe there's someone else."

"Like Mr. Garcia? He was the reading specialist in junior high. Nice guy—he used to give me LifeSavers. But he couldn't teach me to read. Neither could Mrs. Boroski or Mrs. Schmidt. They were the special ed teachers in elementary school. Don't you see? It's hopeless. I'm hopeless."

"You're not. You just haven't had the right kind of help. I'll ask around, I'll find someone who—"

"Does this mean you're going to fail me?" Robert interrupted. I stared at him. "If you fail me, I won't graduate."

I blinked at him. "How did you get this far? There are tests. All those stupid standardized tests. Why didn't they catch this? I've seen your scores. They weren't great, but they were good enough to pass."

He smiled wryly. "So seat me next to a smart kid next year. My scores will go up."

We were quiet for a moment. His question about failing hung between us. I had no answer.

"See you around," he finally mumbled. He slid his tall, lanky frame into the little car and drove off without looking back.

I almost skipped callbacks the next day, but Lars said he needed my input. I phoned Robert's home number: no answer. I tried his cell phone and was rewarded with a, "Yo! This is Rob! Leave a mess!" I smiled. It was the old Robert, the slick Robert, the Robert who everyone assumed could read.

In the end, Katerina got the part of Jules. I didn't even have to push. Claudia was cast as her bitchy best friend, while Cody was named assistant stage manager. An overgrown, chunky kid named Ralph got the role of Romeo. He couldn't hold a candle to Robert.

thirteen

Jonathan knew something was wrong. He called on Friday to firm up plans for Saturday. We'd talked about seeing a movie, going to the mall—anything to get out of the heat.

"What's wrong?" he asked when I told him how glad I was that the week was over.

"Nothing. Everything. Maybe it's just the heat. It's almost October, for God's sake, and it's still a hundred degrees."

He called me Saturday morning a couple of hours before he was due to arrive. "What are you wearing?"

I looked down at the oversized, faded T-shirt I had slept in. "Uh, a lacy black thong and a bustier?"

He burst out laughing. "Actually, I meant what are you planning to wear later. Though what you've got on sounds okay."

I smiled. "I hadn't really thought about it. Just something nice-casual, I guess." Hadn't thought about it? I was so full of crap.

I had an above-the-knee white skirt, a pale green cotton blouse and silver jewelry already laid out on my bed upstairs.

"Wear something casual and comfortable," he said. "Do you have hiking boots?"

"Um, no."

"Sneakers are okay, then."

"Where are we going?"

"It's a surprise."

"Sounds like we're going hiking." I tried to sound enthusiastic. Hiking: terrific! Snakes, blisters, heat exhaustion—what could be better?

"Wear thick socks," he advised.

He showed up at eleven o'clock, as planned. I was wearing the green blouse but had traded the white skirt for a pair of white jean shorts.

"You look nice," he said, after kissing me hello.

"Thanks."

"You might want to change into long pants, though." I looked at his clothes. He was wearing tan cargo pants, bulky green and brown hiking boots, and a blue polo shirt.

"I don't like to be hot," I said as matter-of-factly and non-whiny as possible.

"Being hot is better than scraping your legs."

That did it. I'd been stuck with cactus prickers before. Everyone in Arizona had. You didn't have to rub up next to a jumping cholla to get poked; prickers blew onto pool decks, just waiting to skewer a soft, bare foot. They snuck into the house on pool towels, the better to stab an exposed back. To make it worse, they weren't simple needles; they were little barbed spears that hurt at least as much coming out as they did going in, leaving behind a spot that remained tender and furiously itchy for hours.

Upstairs in my room, I retrieved a storage box from under my bed and rifled through the trousers that I hadn't worn or thought about since last winter. My work pants were too dressy; my casual pants were too worn. Still determined to stick with my original look, I tried a pair of white pants only to remember why I never wore them: they were so thin that my underpants showed through. I thought I'd hit the jackpot with a comfortable old pair of khakis. Then I looked in the mirror and realized just how unflattering high-waisted, pleated-front pants really are.

I finally settled on jeans. I might drop dead from the heat, but at least I'd make a reasonably fashionable corpse.

As I checked myself one last time in the mirror, I grimaced with annoyance at the change in plans, and then I felt oddly freed. I'd been lying to Jonathan for so long for fear of losing him. But maybe he wasn't so great, after all. What kind of nut would go hiking in this heat? Had living in the desert all his life permanently messed up his internal thermostat? Or was he simply too cheap to buy me lunch?

Fine, I thought. If the heat gets too bad and I just can't stand it anymore, I'll tell him the truth. If he says, just one more hill, just another half hour till the next water break, let's see what's up around the next bend, I will stop dead in my tracks, cross my arms over my chest and say, "Jonathan, there's something I've been meaning to tell you."

There was a lightness in my step as I traipsed down the stairs. But then the weirdest thing happened. I looked at Jonathan sitting on the couch, one booted foot resting on the opposite knee, his head bent over one of my mother's *Sunset* magazines. When he heard me on the stairs, he looked up and smiled, and it was like the bottom fell out of my stomach, like suddenly my feet couldn't move fast enough and I couldn't hold him soon enough.

He dropped the magazine on the coffee table and strode over to the foot of the stairs. I stopped on the bottom step, which left me at eye level with him. I put my arms around his neck, and he pulled me gently toward him.

He tasted like peppermint toothpaste and smelled of Coppertone. I buried my face in his neck and breathed deeply before returning to his lips. Our bodies relaxed into each other. After a minute or so, we stopped kissing and held each other tight. "We should get going," he murmured.

"If you say so." I looked into his eyes, and the bottom dropped out of my stomach again, as much from fear as desire. I would do anything for this man, I suddenly realized. Even climb a mountain in a hundred degrees. Even wear uncomfortable clothes. Even pretend to be someone else.

We headed north to Cave Creek. It was a bit cooler there, maybe ninety-five degrees to Scottsdale's one hundred. Then Jonathan turned his car west, and I brightened further: maybe we were going to the outlets?

We were heading away from civilization, but civilization had a way of hanging on. Just as the houses grew farther apart, the open stretches more plentiful, bam! We'd come across another crowded cluster of red-roofed houses, another stucco strip mall under construction. How many Targets does a population need? How many Linens 'n Things, how many Best Buys? Well, a lot, I realized. All the brand-new Spanish houses were filled with brand-new beds in need of sheets and multiple bathrooms in need of towels. Their sitting rooms had fireplaces topped with entertainment nooks just waiting for televisions, stereos, DVD players and TiVo boxes.

"I bet you've driven this route a few times," Jonathan said.

"More than I should," I laughed, thinking he was referring to the outlets. Not that shopping was much fun these days: all those flat shoes and modest skirts. Just then, I spied the infamous DO NOT PICK UP HITCHHIKERS sign. We were approaching the prison.

"I mean, sometimes it feels like all I do is work," I continued, lamely.

"Do you ever get nervous?" Jonathan asked. "I mean, in your job."

I considered carefully. Would it frighten me to enter a prison every day? To spend my hours locked inside with drug addicts, child abusers, thieves and murderers? Heck, yeah.

"The population I deal with is generally nonviolent," I said carefully. "There are some substance abuse issues, a few chronic liars, but I've never worried that anyone would hurt me. What really gets me is that I'm not sure that I'm making a difference." I swallowed hard. "I don't think I'm a very good teacher."

"You can't believe that."

"It's true."

"It's not."

"How do you know?"

"I just do."

His eyes still on the road, he reached over and took my hand. I closed my eyes and relaxed so much that I didn't even notice when we passed the outlets.

For most of my life, I've been an insomniac. To get any sleep at all, conditions had to be perfect: cool air, complete darkness, a fluffy pillow. Even then, I often had to resort to relaxation exercises, warm baths, some Benadryl. I tried herbal teas, herbal supplements—anything to ease me into unconsciousness.

Then I started teaching, and the cure for insomnia presented itself like a bat to the head: sleep deprivation. I bring work home every night. Should I weaken enough to go out on a school night—or even spend too long at the grocery store or flip on the TV—I'll be working until eleven or sometimes midnight. I'm due at the school at 7 A.M. (not that I typically make it); my alarm goes off at 5:45. I am running a constant sleep deficit. I no longer need a soft-yet-supportive bed to fall asleep. I have stopped popping melatonin (which never worked, anyway). Give me one uninterrupted minute with my eyes closed, and I will drop off like a narcoleptic.

When I opened my eyes again, the landscape startled me: the craggy mountains had given way to a seemingly endless progression of plateaus. "How long was I asleep?"

Jonathan shot me a sideways grin. "It's been days."

I checked the clock: I'd been out for almost an hour. "Is this where we're going hiking?" If we got lost out here, no one would ever find us, I thought.

"Let's see." Jonathan squinted at his dashboard. "Eighty-three degrees. How about if we shoot for under eighty?"

"Are we going to Flagstaff?"

"Sedona."

"Sedona! I've been wanting to go there since I moved here!"

"You've never been?" he asked incredulously.

It was kind of surprising, I guess. Sedona was only two hours away, and everyone gushed about its beauty. "I've just never found the right person to go with," I said truthfully.

A short time later, Sedona loomed in the distance, its red rocks rising from the desert floor like something from a Hollywood western. As we drove toward them, the red cliffs got bigger and bigger until they engulfed us, towering in unreal shades of brick and red and orange. As we entered the town, Jonathan began naming the rock formations: Coffee Pot Rock, Bell Rock, Snoopy Rock, Thunder Mountain. "Isn't that a ride at Disneyland?" I asked. And, indeed, the outcroppings did seem Disney-esque, popping up against the bright blue sky.

"Are you hungry?" Jonathan asked as we neared the end of the main drag.

"Starving," I admitted. I brought my eyes down to ground level and was disappointed. What nature had made, man had ruined— or tried to, anyway, with fast food joints, strip malls and shop after shop hawking Kokopelli T-shirts, gecko magnets and bottles filled with colored sand. "I've seen a Taco Bell, a Taco Maker and a Del Taco. Perhaps that's a sign."

"I think we can do a little better than that."

Ten minutes later, we were still driving. My stomach grumbled. A seven-layer burrito was actually starting to sound pretty good.

Civilization dwindled, then disappeared. Along the road, hikers parked their cars and strapped water bottles to their waists. The beauty was overwhelming, the red cliffs so close they seemed to embrace us, but I was so hungry I'd swap it all for a Burger King. "Uh, are you sure there's a restaurant out this way?"

"I thought we'd just keep driving until we came across something nice."

Just then, a gate house came into sight. Jonathan stopped the car and opened his window. I felt a hint of cool air.

"We have lunch reservations," Jonathan told the gate house guard. "Last name is Pomeroy."

The guard scanned a clipboard and then smiled warmly at

Jonathan. "Of course, Mr. Pomeroy. Enjoy your lunch." With that, the iron gates in front of us swung magically open.

A resort lay ahead of us. For once, man had gotten it right. The clusters of pueblo-like stucco casitas were the same red as the mountains. The landscaping was lush without looking artificial. "I think I'm underdressed," I said.

"You look perfect." Jonathan put a hand on my knee. "So, what do you think?"

"I think this is the most beautiful place I've ever seen."

Boynton Canyon rose around us, with layers of red and orange rock. Evergreen trees that dotted the landscape saved the canyon from the look of barren desolation that I'd grown to associate with the desert. This wasn't stark beauty or an acquired taste. It was awe-inspiring, what would have once been called awesome before the word was hijacked by sixteen-year-olds in low-rise jeans.

We ate lunch outside on a deck overlooking the canyon. The sun felt warm and soothing on my face and arms.

"I thought we were going hiking in Phoenix," I admitted as the waitress brought us fruity iced teas.

"I only do that to the girls I don't like," he said.

"Easier than just breaking up with them?"

"Quicker."

"I'll remember that." I forced a smile.

"I can't imagine you'll have to." He reached across the table and took my hand. He grinned. "I mean, unless you have some deep, dark secret I don't know about."

I must have looked startled (I was startled) because Jonathan stopped smiling. "What's wrong?"

Here it was: the perfect lead-in to my long-overdue confession. And ruin the most perfect day of my life? Not a chance.

"I was just thinking," I said. "About work. But it doesn't seem to matter so much now. Here."

"Did something happen?"

I picked up my iced tea glass and took a long drink, stalling for time. "Remember that play production I told you about?"

"Romeo and Juliet?"

"Well, *Romeo and Jules.* It's basically the love story Shakespeare would have written if he were alive today. Well, if he were alive and he had no talent and he spent all of his time at the mall. But, anyway, my student, Robert . . . I thought I was making progress with him, I thought acting would be a great experience for him. But when he got up to read, well, it turns out he can't read."

Jonathan nodded. "Is that really surprising, though? I mean, maybe that's why he turned for crime in the first place. It's not your fault."

"But I should have recognized it earlier. I should have been working with him."

"Have you talked to him since then?"

"I haven't been able to get ahold of him," I said before catching myself. "I mean, he ran away—to his cell block."

Jonathan squinted. "Don't the men live in a different building?"

"Oh, right. Yes, of course they do." I hoped they did. "What I mean is, he didn't run away literally so much as metaphorically. He buzzed the guard, and the guard took him back to the men's prison, and then he told the guard to tell me that he didn't want to do the play anymore. And he hasn't been showing up for class, either."

"What's he in for, anyway?"

There was condensation on my glass. I stroked it with my index finger and left a trail. "Identity theft," I said.

For lunch, I ate a southwestern chicken salad. Jonathan warned me not to order anything too heavy. "The hiking line wasn't just a trick to get you to have lunch with me."

One look at Jonathan's boots, and I knew he could scale some serious mountains. Out of consideration for me and my Nikes, however, he stuck to a tame route. First we hiked up to a rock that Jonathan told me was called Kachina Woman. "See? It looks like an old woman huddled under a blanket."

"It looks like a chimney or a—what do you call it—chiminea. They should have called it Chimney Rock."

"There's already a Chimney Rock."

"So they should have called this 'The Other Chimney Rock.'"

As we approached the formation, we saw a woman—a real one—sitting cross-legged underneath it, her eyes closed, her hands resting on her thighs. "This is a vortex," Jonathan whispered.

"What's a vortex?" I whispered back.

"A spiritual, magnetic energy center. Or something."

"But something good."

"Something very good."

We worked our way back down and then walked for a while on a flat wooded path before Jonathan started heading up another rock face. It was fairly steep but surprisingly easy to climb. The rock was flaky in spots, reminding me incongruously of a Napolean pastry.

"How high are we going?" I asked.

"Just over there."

I looked up and blinked. In the rock face I could see . . . windows? Yes, windows. And doorways and walls. "Is this . . ."

"Indian ruins. Anasazi."

"Wow." I gazed in wonder. Something tugged at my brain. "Didn't the Anasazi, you know. Eat people?"

Jonathan chewed on his lip for a moment. "Only when they were very, very hungry."

We climbed as high as we could but stopped when the slope became too steep. We sat on the warm rocks and gazed at the ruins. Finally, Jonathan looked at his watch. "We should get going."

"Right." I tried to keep the disappointment from my voice. Having gotten a taste of Sedona, I was greedy for more.

Jonathan climbed down just ahead of me and held out his hand to keep me from slipping. Back on flat ground, we didn't talk much as we walked along the trail back to the resort, but the silence felt soothing.

When we reached the resort, I expected Jonathan to turn off toward the parking lot, but he kept walking until we reached a low building.

"Now I'm confused," I said.

He smiled sheepishly. "I've booked us a couple's massage. I hope that's okay."

Thirty minutes later, I was facedown on a massage table, clad only in fluffy white towels and a pair of panties (which a less inhibited person would have removed). A twenty-two-year-old named Marcus rubbed rosemary and lavender oils down my spine, coming just a little too close to my crack for comfort.

On the table next to me, similarly prone and clad (or un-clad, as the case may be) lay Jonathan. His masseuse was named Rona. Rona was one of those post-menopausal women who refuses to go down without a fight. Her gray hair hung down her back in a heavy, steely braid. Her forearms were so sinewy, she could probably break bricks with her bare hands. I wouldn't want to piss Rona off.

Jonathan's face was relaxed, his eyes closed. He looked utterly at ease under Rona's hands, at one with the eastern-influenced New Age music that plinked in the background. On the counter, a tabletop fountain tinkled over rocks and bamboo.

All that tinkling made me have to—well, you know. I cursed myself for drinking so much cucumber water while waiting in the pre-treatment lounge and tried to focus on the scent of sandalwood that drifted through the room.

Marcus repositioned my towel and started kneading my upper thigh. Together, his muscular hands, the oil, and my not-so-muscular thighs created an embarrassing squishing noise. I tensed a bit.

"Is that too hard?" Marcus asked, truly concerned.

"No, no, it's fine," I said neutrally, as if a waiter had just asked if my coffee was too hot. I shifted my weight in a futile attempt to relieve the pressure on my bladder.

After squishing away at my other thigh for a bit, Marcus murmured, "Would it be okay if I rubbed your abdomen?"

"Um, sure, that would be fine," I said—because, really, how are you supposed to answer such a question?

Marcus held my towels in place while I hauled myself over. I caught Jonathan's eye as I settled down onto my back. He smiled slyly, clearly hoping my towel would slip. I checked the wall clock: only twenty-five more minutes left in our hour-long massage. That wasn't so long. I could hold it.

Marcus adjusted the towels around my chest and hips and poured some more warm oil onto his hands. Behind me, the fountain tinkled relentlessly.

Marcus placed a slippery warm hand on my stomach and pressed. I yelped.

"Does something hurt?" he asked, a note of fear creeping into his normally placid voice.

"I just—I, um, I have to use the restroom." I swallowed.

"Oh, of course! I wish you had said something. We'd never want you to be uncomfortable." Was he kidding? I'd never been more uncomfortable in my life. My bladder was the least of it.

"You know where it is?" he asked. I nodded. "We'll leave the room for a moment so you can put your robe on." Marcus and Rona slipped out the door, closing it soundlessly behind them.

Jonathan was still lying on his stomach. He raised his head and propped it up on one hand, resting on his elbow. His shoulders were muscled, I could see, and he had the perfect amount of hair on his chest: enough to be masculine but not so much as to evoke any zoo animal images. "Too much cucumber water?" he asked.

"Way too much." I sat up awkwardly, clutching the towel to my chest. My white terry robe hung on a hook on the door, where Marcus had left it. I'd gotten myself onto the massage table by lying facedown in my robe, pulling a towel over my butt and then wriggling out of the robe and chucking it onto the floor.

I slid off the table clutching the top towel to my breasts with one arm, the bottom towel with the other. As soon as I stood up, the bottom towel started slipping, and I hunched over to hold it in place before realizing how ridiculous I must look. Jonathan watched me intently.

Slowly, I straightened. I let the top towel fall away. I moved my other hand to my side, and the bottom towel slid down my legs and landed in a pile at my feet.

Jonathan drew in a breath. "Damn," he whispered. "You kept your panties on."

* * *

It took all of my self-control not to sigh audibly as we passed through the resort gates on the way out. I was unused to luxury. I mean, I'd actually been pretty excited by the idea of going to a movie theater: at nine dollars a pop, I almost always waited for the DVD. And, while I found the whole massage experience a little icky, I loved the fluffy robes, the firm showers, the Jacuzzi tub and all those complimentary lotions and potions.

"That was nice," I said, inadequately.

"I thought about booking us a room," Jonathan said. "But I didn't want to be presumptuous." He shot me a look to check my reaction. I gave the most mysterious half-smile I could muster.

The sun had fallen low in the sky as we drove back through town, lending the rocks an almost surreal glow.

"Do you need to get back?" Jonathan asked. "Or can I show you one last thing?"

We turned onto a steep road, passing signs for the Sedona Airport, and winding up, up and up some more.

"Are we going on one of those little airplanes?" I asked, trying to keep the fear out of my voice.

"No flying," he said. "Sorry."

Relief flooded me, followed by the tiniest twinge of regret: no fatal airplane crash meant no easy way out of my predicament.

We parked along the side of the dusty road, joining a mass of cars. Jonathan pulled a folded Mexican blanket from the back. We crossed the street, and I caught my first glimpse of the main attraction: sweeping, vertigo-inducing views of Sedona.

"This is amazing," I said.

"This is nothing." Jonathan glanced at his watch. "Give it another twenty minutes, and you'll get amazing."

Sedona sunsets are a staple of southwest calendar manufacturers and postcard producers, but nothing prepared me for the light show that lay ahead. Like a hot new Broadway show, there was competition for the best seat in the house. We secured a spot by a boulder. Jonathan spread out the blanket and settled himself against the rock. I planted myself between his legs, using his torso as a backrest.

Around us, a crowd of maybe fifty tourists, clad in T-shirts and shorts, milled around, waiting for the show, while stocky Native American women hawked silver jewelry spread out on colorful blankets.

As the sky began to turn, the crowd quieted and stilled. The sky seemed on fire, the clouds flaring orange and red, while the rocks glowed like piles of burning coals. Jonathan held me tightly, his breath gently touching my cheek, his heart thudding against my back. The clouds changed, growing more pink than orange. Tourists took pictures. The Indian women kneeled in front of their blankets, their backs to the view.

A hush hung over the crowd until the great orange ball finally slipped below a mountain, a fiery sliver seeming to burn the top of the cliff for a shining moment before being snuffed out entirely. We were quiet for one last instant before the crowd broke into applause, giving Mother Nature a well-deserved ovation. Women began drifting over to the Indian blankets, bending over to see the silver Kokopellis as the sky turned to a mellow pink and a soothing purple.

I twisted my head to look at Jonathan's face. "That was something."

He leaned around and kissed me. I shifted in the dirt until I was facing him. I put my arms around his neck and combed his hair with my fingers. As we sat there, lip-locked in the fading sunset, I thought of the halls of Agave High, lined between classes with students locked in hungry embraces, without a thought of how they looked to everyone around them. Then Jonathan kissed me some more, and I forgot about everything but him.

When we finally pulled apart, my heart was pounding, my face hot. "It would have been okay if you had booked a room," I whispered.

The only available room at the resort had a kitchen, a dining room, a sitting area and a beehive fireplace.

"This can't be cheap," I said tactlessly.

I picked up an apple from a bowl on the counter (that's how nice this place was; they had free fruit) and tossed it up lightly before catching it. "You must really want to get me into bed," I said, congratulating myself on my boldness even as I felt a blush bloom on my cheeks.

Jonathan smiled. He reached over for the apple and took a bite before returning it to my hand. "You're on to me."

I wandered into the main room. "Speaking of beds, um, there aren't any."

"There are Murphy beds. The maid will pull them down later."

"So, you've . . . stayed here before?"

"The guy at the front desk told me about the beds."

"So you haven't stayed here before."

He was quiet for a moment. "I didn't say that."

"You're being evasive."

"I am?"

I looked him straight in the eyes and raised my eyebrows. "Well?"

He put his arms loosely around my waist. "Let's just say I've never been this happy to be here before."

I smirked at him.

"What?" He broke into a grin. "I thought that was a pretty smooth answer." He kissed me, effectively ending the inquisition. Suddenly, I felt nervous. "Do you want to get something to eat?"

He looked at his watch. "We could. Are you hungry?"

"Not really."

"I'm not really hungry, either." He walked over to the fireplace and hit a switch. The fire blazed to life over a cluster of artificial logs. "Is this too smooth?"

"No," I said. "That's perfectly smooth."

He took me in his arms and covered my mouth with his. We stood there kissing, standing in front of the fireplace at first and then shuffling over gradually until we settled onto the overstuffed couch. We stayed like that—kissing mouths, nibbling ears, licking necks—for what seemed like ages until I felt his hand fiddling with the buttons of my green blouse. I cursed myself for not wearing sexier underwear, for not owning sexier underwear, but my doubts fell away when he gently pushed the blouse from my shoulders and sat back to gaze at me. A small smile played on his lips as he reached for the front of my bra (which sports a highly unsexy front closure) and eased it open. He looked at me—well, okay, at my breasts—for a moment before slowly reaching forward to stroke them. A groan escaped from my lips.

He leaned forward and placed his mouth on my neck, kissing me gently as he worked his way down my throat.

There was a pounding on the door. "Housekeeping!"

"Oh, shit!" I yelped, surprising myself with the epithet. I bolted up from the couch and grabbed my bra and blouse.

"Just a minute," Jonathan called out in a strangled voice.

I scurried across the enormous, high-ceilinged room and shut myself in the bathroom, hastily refastening my bra and buttoning up the blouse. I caught a glimpse of myself in the mirror and was startled. My cheeks were pink, my eyes, shiny. My tousled hair was still too short, but it was starting to grow out and had stopped looking so severe. I looked—was it possible? Yes. I looked pretty.

I looked like I was in love.

I blinked at my reflection, then suddenly laughed. I covered my mouth, though of course no one could see me.

When Jonathan knocked on the bathroom door, I was sitting on the closed toilet, my knees clasped against my chest. The sudden knowledge that I was in love was followed by the frightening realization that I had more to lose.

"We have beds," Jonathan said when I opened the door.

"We were actually doing okay without them."

"Shall we unpack?" He held up two Kmart bags. We had stopped off on the way back from the sunset. While I allowed Jonathan to buy me lunch, a massage and a night in the nicest hotel room I had ever seen, I had insisted on buying my own toothbrush and underwear (cotton Hanes, in a three-pack). I had even sprung for the communal toothpaste. I am nothing if not independent.

I took my bag over to a set of drawers and slid the package of undies inside before Jonathan could see how boring they were. I'd considered leopard polyester, but I knew I'd feel—and probably look—ridiculous in them.

"I bought you a present," Jonathan said, walking over with his bag.

"Oh, you didn't have to buy me anything," I said, suddenly feeling like too much of a taker. "But thank you."

"Don't thank me before you see it." He reached into the bag and pulled out a pink shirt with Southwestern lettering that read SEDONA.

He handed it over. It was ugly and borderline tacky, but it made me absurdly happy.

He reached back into the bag. "I got myself one, too. We'll match." His was bright yellow with identical lettering. "Think they'll let us into the restaurant wearing these?"

"Maybe we should just order room service."

"An excellent idea." He put his arms around me. "Did you like the massage today? You looked kind of uncomfortable."

I bit my lip. "I loved the spa. And I loved spending time with you. I just, well . . . I don't really like strangers touching me."

"And me?"

"Oh, you can touch me anytime."

"Perhaps I should give you a massage, then." He ran his hands down my back.

"That would be okay."

"Okay?"

"Nice."

"*Nice?*"

I looked up at him. "That would me amazing. Incredible. Heavenly. A dream come true."

"Well, then." He stepped back. "Let's get you set up." He went into the bathroom and came back with a fluffy towel. "Get yourself ready—I'll wait in here." He went back into the bathroom and shut the door softly.

My heart pounding, I scurried over to the bed and pulled down the bedspread. I unbuttoned my shirt. My hands were shaking. I dropped my clothes on the floor and wrapped a towel around me. I walked over to my drawers and put my dirty clothes in with my new underpants and T-shirt. Then I dove back to the bed and lay facedown, the towel covering my bottom half.

I lay there for a moment, wondering whether I should call out to Jonathan. But the bathroom door opened softly. "Are you ready?" he asked quietly.

"Mm-hm," I said, trying to keep my breathing under control.

He had put on a white terry robe. He had a tiny bottle of the hotel's moisturizer in his hand. He sat next to me and popped open the top of the lotion. He squeezed some into his palm, and then rubbed his hands together to warm it. He put his hands on my shoulders and rubbed in circular motions. Then he moved up to my neck, and down each vertebrae. My breathing slowed and my body relaxed. He put more lotion on his hands and then worked his way down one arm and then the other, taking time to stroke each finger. He put his hands back on my lower back and pressed gently.

"Would you mind if I massaged your abdomen?" he whispered.

"Not at all."

"Then roll over."

fourteen

When we pulled up to my parents' house and saw that the blinds were open—I was certain I had left them closed—my first thought was that the house had been robbed.

If only I had been so lucky.

My mother came hobbling out of the house on crutches just as I stepped out of Jonathan's car, heat blasting up from the driveway. She was wearing turquoise track pants, one tennis shoe, an Ace bandage, and a white T-shirt emblazoned with brightly colored hibiscus. Her hair looked grayish.

I stood frozen to my spot on the driveway, my mind whirring but not coming up with any solutions to the crisis that lay ahead.

"Oh, I'm so relieved!" my mother said breathlessly when she reached us. She leaned on the crutches, her shoulders pointing up to her ears. "We got home yesterday afternoon, and when you weren't here, I figured, well, she's probably just out shopping. And when you didn't come home for dinner, I thought, well, she probably has plans with her friends. But then it got to be eight o'clock, nine o'clock—midnight! And I really, really started to think something awful had happened." She looked at Jonathan, standing there in his yellow T-shirt, and she brightened immediately. "Oh, hello!"

I couldn't look Jonathan in the eye. My heart was racing. My mother did not sound disoriented. She sounded agitated, though. And the crutches were a nice touch.

"We went to Sedona," I said. "It got late, and we stayed over."

"Sedona's a town north of here," Jonathan said gently. "It's known for its red rocks."

"Oh, I know Sedona," my mother said. "Natalie's father and I visited last year. Beautiful place. Beautiful! We stayed at that place up by the airport. Oh, look—you bought T-shirts! Where did you stay?" Jonathan told her. Her eyes widened. "I've heard that's magnificent." She turned to me and mouthed, "*Expensive.*" Then she shot Jonathan one more enormous grin before saying to me, "Aren't you going to ask what happened to my ankle?"

"What happened to your ankle?"

"I sprained it. Walking down the Gillespies' ridiculous stone steps." She turned to Jonathan and rolled her eyes. "The Gillespies had a log cabin built. Understand, these are people from Long Island. *Long Island.*"

She turned back to me. "You know what Barbara Gillespie's reaction was? To my sprained ankle? What she said to me before I'd even taken an ibuprofen? *'I hope this doesn't mean you'll have to miss shopping this afternoon.'* And when I said it would, that my ankle hurt like the devil and I couldn't possibly leave the couch, she said, 'Well, then, would you mind if I went on my own? I really need to get those soapstone coasters.' Coasters!"

"You should probably sit down," I said, trying to will my mother back into the house.

She shifted on the crutches. "I know, I know. I'm supposed to keep the foot iced and elevated. That's what the doctor in Flagstaff told me. We had to wait four hours in the emergency room, and it wasn't even covered on our health plan." She perked up. "Jonathan? It's Jonathan, right?"

He blinked. "Yes. It is."

"Won't you join us for lunch? We were just about to sit down."

"You've probably got stuff to do," I said to him.

"Uh . . ." He looked really confused. "I don't really, but, um, if you want me to go . . ."

"No," I said. "Of course not."

"We're having soup," my mother said as she hobbled back toward the house.

Jonathan stared at me. We were silent until my mother made it back into the house. "She gets like this sometimes," I said, once the door had closed. "Coherent. For a day or two at a time. Once it lasted a week. It's—it's like a gift."

It was almost chilly inside the house. "What do you have the air conditioner set to?" I asked my father.

"Seventy-five." The ceiling fan whirred above the kitchen table, ruffling his thinning silver hair. He had a fresh sunburn on his nose.

"You're supposed to keep it at eighty," I said. "From an energy conservation standpoint."

My father slurped his soup to cool it down. "It was eighty when we got back yesterday. Too hot. Your mother said it made her ankle swell."

"Swell even more," she interjected.

My father rolled his eyes.

"It might help to drink ice water," I said, my innards glowing from the soup. "Maybe take a dip in the pool."

I was babbling. In truth, I didn't care how hot or how cold my parents kept the house. In fact, coming home to seventy-five degrees would be like heaven if only it didn't mean introducing Jonathan to my lucid (if whiny) mother. My goal was to get through lunch without blowing my cover, which meant steering the conversation away from my job and my mother's mental health.

"I can't swim with my ankle like this," my mother said, as I'd known she would. "I can't even take a shower, for God's sake. This morning your father had to help me in the bath." I shuddered. It doesn't matter how old you are: the thought of your parents naked—especially together—is just icky.

Jonathan kept as quiet as he could, even as my mother grilled him.

"Did you and Natalie meet at work?"

"No, um—at a restaurant, actually."

"It was a bar," I interjected. "He picked me up at a bar."

"So, you're not a teacher?" I stiffened, but it was okay. As I'd explained to Jonathan, my mother would be upset to hear that I worked at a prison (a true statement), so I'd just told her that I was a teacher (another true statement).

"No," Jonathan said. "Nothing so worthwhile." He shot me a warm smile. "Just to make it clear, I was working the night I met Natalie."

"You're a bartender?" my father asked, his soup spoon clanging against his bowl.

"No, I own my own business. Restaurant supplies."

The phone rang—to my great relief—but as my father started to stand, my mother barked, "The machine can get it! We're enjoying our lunch." She smiled at my father, but the gesture was clearly for Jonathan's benefit. Of course, we stopped enjoying our lunch as we sat through the rings. On the fifth, the machine picked up.

It was Shelly. "Mom? Dad? I've been calling for days, and I keep getting the machine, but I haven't—you didn't return my messages." Her voice cracked. The answering machine was turned up so loud, it hurt my ears.

"Shelly called?" my mother said.

"Oh, yeah," I muttered. "I meant to tell you, but—"

"Shhh!" my mother hushed.

"Frederick left me," Shelly continued, letting out a sob. "I really need to talk to you, and—"

Without thinking, my mother sprang out of her chair in the direction of the phone, collapsing the instant her full weight hit her ankle.

"Shit!" She sprawled on the ground. My father pushed out of his chair, making a loud squeak on the ceramic floor. "Get the phone!" my mother shrieked as he reached down to her. "Get the goddamned phone!"

My father grabbed the receiver just as Shelly was whimpering her good-byes.

"Shelly? It's your father," he said, as if she wouldn't know. The answering machine continued to broadcast at an ear-wounding volume.

"Oh, Dad!" Then Shelly really let loose with her crying. I glanced at Jonathan. He looked alarmed, like: she told me her mother was nuts, but her sister, too? Is it genetic?

Finally, Shelly composed herself long enough to wail, "Why didn't you answer the phone?"

"We were eating soup," my father said.

"For the past four days?"

"Do you want to talk to your mother?" my father asked.

"Frederick left me!" Shelly burst into sobs anew.

"I'm sorry to hear that, honey. I'm really sorry." He glanced nervously at my mother, who was making her way across the floor on all fours. Jonathan leaped out of his chair to help her up. She held out her hand for the phone as my father scurried across the room to pass it over. Jonathan continued to hold her up. "Maybe it's for the best," my father said as a way of closing the conversation. "Your mother never thought Frederick was right for you."

"We both thought it!" my mother yelled, taking the portable phone and holding it out between them. "You said he was irresponsible and selfish! You said it!"

Blinking nervously, Jonathan helped ease her back over and into her chair.

My mother put the phone to her ear. "Tell me what happened, sweetheart. Just tell me."

"Frederick left me," Shelly said for the third time. And then, the kicker: "Because I'm going to have a buh-buh . . . *baby*!"

"Ohmigod!" My mother's voice grew high and breathy. "A baby! You're going to have a baby!" She dropped an octave. "And he left you? When you needed him most? Just left you?" Back up an octave. "But—a baby! I'm going to be a *grandmother*!" At that, she broke down, her sobs mixing with Shelly's. Together, they sounded like a pack of coyotes that had just caught a bunny.

fifteen

I couldn't believe my luck. I didn't have to convince Jonathan that my mother was losing her mind; she did all the work for me. He left shortly after my mother got off the phone, thanking my parents for their hospitality and tactfully saying that we probably needed some time alone as a family right now.

That night I went online to check out the Arizona Department of Corrections. They were hiring, though not English teachers, specifically. Well, not any teachers. But if I could get a job there—just something part-time, temporary and not overtly life-threatening—I could honestly tell Jonathan that I worked at the prison. And then I could quit the prison job, claiming burnout, and begin work at Agave High School.

And we could begin anew. And I would never, ever lie to him again. I mean, after my mother had a miraculous recovery from Alzheimer's—which, as it would turn out, wasn't Alzheimer's at all but merely an allergic reaction to black mold encountered in a cut-rate motel room at the Grand Canyon.

I was feeling high on life's possibilities when I walked into my Adventures class on Monday and saw Robert's seat empty. That wasn't necessarily significant; until Katerina came along, Robert rarely made it to class on time, and never on Monday. I dove into my marketing lesson and tried not to glance at the clock.

Over the weekend, I had assigned the kids, once again, to watch television commercials and identify the target market. The first time I'd tried, it had been hopeless.

"What was the commercial for?" I'd asked Marisol.

"A Volkswagen."

"Which model?"

"What do you mean?"

"I mean, is it a Passat? Or a Beetle? What kind?"

A pause. "I didn't know we were supposed to write that down."

"That's okay—no big deal. It was a Volkswagen. Good enough. And what was the television show you were watching?"

Another pause. "I forget."

"Did you . . . write it down?"

She hunched over her desk, her hair falling in her face. "I didn't know we were supposed to."

This time, I'd created a worksheet: program name, program time, network, product advertised, and, the grand finale, the target market. (Or, as I'd put on the sheet, "Who do they think/hope is watching the show?")

First, I called on Cherie. "I couldn't do the homework," she shrugged. "We have TiVo, so I always just, like, skip the commercials."

"Couldn't you have *not* skipped the commercials?"

She looked genuinely surprised. "I didn't think of that."

Next, I tried Racquel, who had actually completed the assignment. She had watched *The Real World* on MTV at one o'clock in the morning.

"What were you doing watching television at one A.M.?" I asked.

She shrugged. "My brother wouldn't let me use the Xbox."

The product advertised? Red Bull (presumably to help kids stay up until three o'clock).

"Okay," I said, ready to drive home the point. "MTV is showing *The Real World* at one o'clock in the morning. Red Bull pays for air time. Who do they think is watching, Racquel? Who is their target market?"

She looked at me with rare confidence. "People who watch TV," she said.

Next, after giving Racquel a self-esteem boost—"Yes, very good, because if no one was watching, no one would see the ad, right?"—I asked, "But to take it even further, who do they think is watching? Do they think your parents are watching?" The kids snickered. "Do they think I'm watching?" They snickered again, which made me feel really, really old. "No, they think *you're* watching. And you, and you, and you. And how old are you? Are you sixty?" And so on.

I glanced at the clock (ten minutes in, and still no Robert), and moved on to the other students. The last one I called on, when the class was almost over (and still no Robert), was Steven, who, dear boy, had watched the news with his grandmother: six o'clock on NBC. Between stories about a convenience store robbery in Gilbert (family-owned business, family didn't speak much English, came from a country that started with a "V") and an arson incident in

Carefree (really big, expensive house under construction, neighbor next door smelled smoke, called 911 but it was too late, the house had already burned beyond repair, neighbor said it was really sad when you couldn't feel safe in your neighborhood anymore), Steven had watched a commercial for Viagra.

I should have seen this one coming. I expected laughter. There was none. Shock? None. I took a deep breath. "And what's the target market for . . . this product? Who did they hope was watching?"

Steven wrinkled his nose. "People who like to take baths outside?"

That was as good a time as any to wrap things up and assign the next day's homework. Which left us with four more minutes to spare. Every great teacher knows that class time is precious and you shouldn't waste an instant.

"I guess you can just start on your homework," I said.

At least this way they'd do their homework, or at least some of it.

"Has anyone seen Robert since last week?" I asked as casually as I could. They looked at me blankly. A few kids shook their heads.

"I heard he couldn't read," Marisol said. "That he went out for that play and he didn't know what the paper said."

The kids stopped rummaging in their backpacks. Their heads shot up.

"Oh, *please*," I said, rolling my eyes for effect. "This is how rumors get started. Robert tripped over a couple of lines because he was nervous. Stage fright. I guess he's just sick or something." I bent my head down to look at some papers. The kids went back to their backpacks. I pretended to believe they were looking for paper and pencils and not their cell phones.

When I had a free period, I went down to the office to tell Jill about my weekend. She was standing next to Nicolette's desk, leaning on her elbows. Nicolette looked pale and tired. Her hair was lank. A hangover, I assumed.

Jill stood up when she saw me. "Nicolette and Rodney went to Vegas this weekend."

"Really? I went to Sedona. With Jonathan."

"You're not getting it," Jill said. "Nicolette and Rodney *went to Vegas*."

"I get it. Casinos. Cigarette smoke. Hookers. Vegas." I smiled suggestively. "Sedona was incredible."

Jill rolled her eyes. "Show her your hand, Nic."

Nicolette held out her left hand and forced a smile.

It took me a minute. "You didn't." The band was white gold and speckled with diamond chips. "You did?" I looked back at her face. I realized why she looked so drawn. She wasn't hungover; she had simply neglected to apply makeup this morning. "But you wanted a big wedding. The bridesmaids were going to wear teal."

Nicolette began to twist the ring around her finger. "All that really matters is that me and Rodney love each other. And I'd changed my mind about the bridesmaids' dresses. They were going to wear ice blue." She burst into tears.

Jill squatted down and assumed her professional tone of voice. "You acted impulsively. You can get the marriage annulled."

"You mean, like, divorced? No! I love Rodney!"

Jill took her hand. "Why are you so unhappy, then?"

Nicolette paused to take a scratchy institutional tissue from the brown and tan box on her desk. She blew her nose, dabbing into the nostrils to make sure she hadn't left any residual snot. She threw the used tissue into her metal wastebasket and took Jill's hand. Jill, to her credit, didn't flinch.

Finally, Nicolette spoke, almost inaudibly. "Nordstrom."

"What?"

"I was gonna register at Nordstrom this week. Now it's too late."

In her office, Jill filled me in on the details. Rodney had planned the whole thing. In front of the Bellagio, while the fountains swayed to "Singing in the Rain," he had fallen on one knee and whipped out a little velvet box. He said he'd never loved anyone like this before, not even his second wife. He had already booked the chapel, ordered the flowers: everything. He even took Nicolette to a boutique at Caesar's Palace, where he bought her a $2,400 dress. The service was tasteful: no Elvis impersonators or show-girls. The flowers were genuine silk.

When Nicolette told her parents, she expected them to be happy. More to the point, she expected them to spring for a reception. But her mother kept saying, "I didn't get to see my oldest daughter get married!" And her father kept saying, "At least we didn't have to pay for it."

"She could send out announcements," I said. "She'd probably score some gifts."

"I know, I said that. But all she kept saying was, 'I want my fucking wedding!'"

"Oh, my gosh. Did Dr. White hear her?"

"No, just the president of the computer club. He'd stopped by to drop off a form."

"It's probably good for him."

"That's what I was thinking."

s i x t e e n

When I got home after school, I found my mother sitting on the couch, her bandaged foot on the coffee table, propped up on Southwestern print pillows. She was reading. I leaned over to check the title: *What to Expect When You're Expecting*.

"Oh, Mommy, are you going to give me a little sister?"

"Funny." She glanced up without smiling. "Would you believe your sister hasn't even started taking folic acid?"

I shrugged.

"I can understand why she didn't take it before she knew she was pregnant. It wasn't like she was anticipating a baby. But now . . . tsk." She shook her head and went back to reading.

I wandered over to the kitchen and surveyed the overflowing fruit bowl. After pressing the flesh of a still-firm nectarine, I chose a pluot, which is a cross between a plum and an apricot. My mother buys fruit—or sends my father to buy fruit—that nobody has ever heard of. In the summer, it's: "That's not a plum, that's a pluot." In the winter: "Anybody can see that's a tangelo. It's got a little bumpy thing on the end. Oranges don't have that."

I bit into the fruit. It was sweet and juicy. I was eating a lot better now that my parents were home. I wandered back to the sitting area. "Isn't Shelly the one who should be reading that book?"

"We just sent her a copy from Amazon. She should get it Friday."

"And the folic acid?"

She turned the page. "I had your father FedEx a bottle today."

"They do have stores in Rhode Island, you know."

She pursed her lips at something she had just read. "Do you think your sister knows enough not to eat sushi?"

"If Shelly doesn't know enough not to get pregnant, she probably doesn't know enough not to eat sushi."

My mother put down the book and let out a giant sigh. "What Shelly needs—what Shelly has always needed—is a man who will take care of her." She shook her head in disgust. "Instead she's wasted the best years of her life—*the best years*—with that immature, self-centered, self-righteous . . ." Here she mumbled something that sounded an awful lot like "son of a bitch."

Here is all you really need to know about Frederick. He is thirty-one, three years younger than my sister. My mother thinks that's significant. "Maybe if she'd find someone her own age, she wouldn't always have to be the adult in the relationship." He's a bit on the short side and not fat, really, but soft and pale, utterly lacking in muscle tone. He has a pleasant enough face; if he took to jogging in the sun every day, he might approach attractive.

But the only thing that truly matters about Frederick, the reason Shelly has devoted six years of her life to him, is this: Frederick is brilliant. Frederick is working on his second PhD, in biostatistics and epidemiology. (I am so not-brilliant that I don't even know what that means.) His first PhD was in molecular biology. I'm not entirely sure what that is, either, but at least I can pronounce it.

Shelly thinks Frederick will cure cancer some day. Pretty much everybody else thinks Frederick will just stay in school until he runs out of biology graduate programs, at which point he will retire to the basement and devote the rest of his life to reading back issues of *The New Yorker*.

"Your sister wants you to call her."

I looked at the bulging tote I had hauled home from school. "I've got a lot of work to do."

My mother glared at me. "Your sister needs our support right now."

She answered on the third ring.

"Hi, Shelly."

"Hi."

I waited for her to talk. She didn't. "Mom said you wanted me to call you." That didn't come out quite right.

"I never said that." She cleared her throat. "But, um, it's nice that you did."

"So . . ." I said.

"So . . ."

"How are you?"

She snorted. "Well, let's see. The man I thought I loved is a fucking asshole. I feel like I'm going to puke, like, twenty-two hours a day. And I have no idea how I'm going to support a baby on my crap-ass income."

"But other than that, Mrs. Lincoln, how did you like the play?"

She didn't laugh. "I never even thought I'd be able to get

pregnant. My periods were so irregular, every doctor I went to see said my hormones were out of balance." That was news to me, though it did explain a lot. "And that piece-of-shit Frederick, he thinks I did this to trap him. That's what he said. 'You're trying to trap me.' Fucking, piece-of-shit asshole." She blew her nose.

"Like he's such a prize," I said.

She was quiet. And, then, a whisper: "He's really brilliant, you know."

seventeen

Robert lived in a one-car garage townhome in the Sonora Sunset town houses. The complex was about as far as you could get from Agave High and still be within the required limits. An unarmed octogenarian in a security uniform manned a tiny gatehouse.

"I'm here to see Robert Baumgartner," I told him. "Unit B seventy-six." He gave me directions without calling Robert or checking my identification, more Wal-Mart greeter than gate-keeper. Still, his presence allowed Sonora Sunset's residents to boast that they lived in a gated community, which mattered at least as much as personal safety.

The townhomes, rather predictably, were white stucco with red roofs, their garages like row after row of great, yawning mouths. Here and there, silver-haired seniors in pastel track suits strode by, fulfilling their daily power walk requirements before the sun got too hot. Mostly, though, the complex was quiet, even by Arizona standards. Unit B seventy-six was a middle unit, near the back of the development. A tidy white car sat in the driveway, the garage door closed. Robert's clunker was nowhere to be seen.

I didn't really expect him to open the door; it was early, after all, not yet 7 A.M. I'd stopped by on the way to school, hoping I could encourage Robert to return to class. If he was here, he'd probably be sleeping. Still, it was worth a shot.

He opened the door almost immediately. He was even dressed, in gym shorts and a Nike T-shirt, although maybe that's what he'd slept in. Comforting smells wafted out from behind him.

"Did I wake you?" I asked after a moment's silence.

"No," he said. "I was just cleaning up from breakfast." He blinked at me. His eyes were brown and round, fringed with thick, black lashes. Standing in the doorway, he looked both younger and older than at school: younger because he seemed less cocky, more forthright; older because he was so clearly in charge of his household.

"Can I come in?"

He stepped aside. I was prepared for dimmed lights, a big screen television with a game cube or Nintendo or Xbox or possibly all three.

The walls were Southwestern mauve, the furniture blond wood. There was a television, of course, but it was small and neatly stacked on a freestanding glass-and-bamboo bookshelf, between a potted jade plant and Robert's framed high school picture.

"Are your parents home?"

"My mother's sleeping," he said.

"Oh," I said, silently disapproving.

"She's a nurse," he said, scratching his arm. "Works the night shift. She takes care of premature babies."

"Oh," I said, feeling chastened for the flash I'd had of his mother as a crack addict. "And your father?"

"Left when I was three."

I nodded and waited for him to say more. He didn't. "Does your mother know that you haven't been going to school?"

He paused, looked down at the carpet for a minute, then back up at me. "Do you know I'm eighteen? 'Cause that means I'm responsible for myself."

"I know that you're eighteen," I said. "And I'm not trying to get you into trouble. I just want you to come back to school."

"Why?" he said. "What's the point?"

"How do you expect to get a job without a high school diploma?"

He ignored my question and wandered into the tiny kitchen. "You hungry?"

I started to say no and then realized I was starving. I hadn't had time to eat before leaving the house, and my mother, now that she was injured, had stopped serving me breakfast in bed.

"The omelet's all gone, but this is pretty good." He handed me a blueberry muffin. So that's what smelled so good.

"Your mother bakes after working all night?"

"No." He smiled. "I'm the cook of the house."

I cupped the muffin in my hand so I wouldn't get crumbs on the tan linoleum floor and took a bite. "You made this?" It was simultaneously lighter and creamier than the usual blueberry muffin. I took another bite. "What's in here?"

"The usual stuff, plus sour cream and cream cheese. A little lemon rind."

"This is amazing." I looked at him. "I never would have taken you for a baker."

"You're not going to tell anyone, are you?" he asked, half smiling. "It wouldn't do much for my rep."

"Your secret is safe with me." I took another bite. The kitchen was quiet except for the hum of the air conditioner. "You never answered my question. About how you're going to get a job without a high school diploma."

He took a muffin for himself and placed it on a napkin on the glass-topped kitchen table. "I already have a job. At the hospital laundry." He settled himself into a chair, his long legs spread wide and braced on the floor, as if for stability.

I sat down in the chair across from him. "And that's what you want to be doing twenty years from now?" I put the remainder of the muffin in my mouth and chewed slowly.

"I'll work my way up. There's this guy I know, works in the hospital kitchen, says he might be able to get me a job in there."

"Is that what your mother wants for you?"

He sighed. "Listen. My mother has done everything for me. Everything. She's tired, like, all the time. She could live in a bigger place than this, a nicer place, without so many old people, but she wanted to make sure I was in a good school district. But I just . . . I can't do it." He poked at his muffin but didn't eat it. I thought, what a waste.

He popped up from the table, leaving his muffin. He strode over to the fridge, pulled out a carton of orange juice and poured it directly into his mouth.

"I'd always heard teenage boys did that, but I didn't really believe it," I said.

He grinned and wiped his mouth with his forearm. "You want some?"

I laughed. "Thanks. I think I'll pass."

He put the juice back in the refrigerator and shut the door. "So, what's the deal with the play? Who won?" He leaned against the refrigerator, his arms crossed in front of him.

"Who won? You mean, who got the parts?"

"Yeah, whatever."

"Katerina got the lead," I said.

His smile faded. He nodded. "I figured."

"You talk to her?" I asked.

He shook his head.

"Ralph Herrera got your part," I said. "I mean, the part I thought you'd be good for."

"Ralph? You gotta be kidding me. Kid's a total dweeb."

"He's not bad," I said. "But you would have been better."

"Whatever," he mumbled. He looked up. "I wouldn't have been able to do it anyway," he said. "Even if I'd pulled off the audition."

"We would have worked something out," I said. "I could have helped you run lines."

"I don't mean that." He rolled his eyes, as if his illiteracy were insignificant. "I'm talking about my work schedule. Four to eleven, five days a week. I called in sick that day."

"Four to eleven? My gosh. When do you have time for homework?"

He raised his eyebrows and looked at me expectantly.

"Oh, right. I forgot." No wonder he was always so late for school.

We heard shuffling down the hall. A slightly hoarse woman's voice called, "Robert? There someone in the kitchen with you?"

"Just a friend, Mama," he said anxiously, heading for the hall. "Go back to sleep."

"You should have left for school by now," the woman said, clearly getting closer.

Robert whirled around to look at me, his eyes panicked. "You can't tell her!" he pleaded. "Please don't tell her!"

"Robert, I'm not going to lie to her," I said.

"I'll go back to school! I'll meet with the special ed teachers or come in for extra help—I promise! *Just don't tell her*!"

She appeared in the doorway, wearing a faded blue terry bathrobe. She was surprisingly short and curvy, in contrast to her tall, lanky son. She had curly black hair, olive skin, and Robert's big brown eyes. "Hello?" She blinked at me, clearly expecting to encounter a nubile sixteen-year-old.

"Hello, Mrs. Baumgartner," I said. "I'm Natalie Quackenbush, Robert's English teacher."

"Please, call me Lupe." She smiled, but she looked troubled. "Is there a problem?"

I glanced at Robert. He was staring at me, pleading.

I swallowed. "I, um, no. No problem." There it was: another lie I couldn't take back, though hopefully this was for a good cause. "I'm helping with the school play, and I just . . . Robert said he might be able to help behind the scenes. Build sets and whatnot. But I guess, with his school and work schedule, it's not really going to work out."

She looked up at her son. "You should do it, Robbie. You can cut back your hours for a couple months." She turned her gaze to me. "He doesn't get to have enough fun."

I nodded, thinking: and here I had always assumed that Robert suffered from having too much fun.

As I sat in my Civic, Robert moved his mother's white car out of the driveway and onto the street, opened the garage, backed out and parked his orange clunker, returned to the white car and drove it into the garage. I heard the car door slam. He appeared from the darkness, hitting a button on his way out. The garage door slid back into place. His mother could have saved him a lot of time by simply parking her car on the street, but this was Scottsdale, and on-street parking was not allowed.

He walked over to my car. I rolled down the window.

"You don't have to babysit me," he said. "I'll see you at school."

I smiled and drove away. Then I pulled into the first shopping plaza I came to and waited until Robert's car passed me. I let a few cars get behind him before sneaking my car into the traffic and following him all the way to Agave.

I had to walk quickly through the corridors to make it to my classroom before the bell rang, but there was a lightness in my step today, a new sense of purpose in my heart.

I walked into the classroom just as the bell rang. A quick glance showed me that my Honors English students were all in their seats, pencils on their otherwise empty desks.

I strode over to my desk, dropped my bag and said, "Good morning, class. I hope you studied last night, because, as you know, today I'm going to have you write an in-class *Odyssey* essay."

A figure in the corner caught my eye. I looked over.

It was Jonathan. He was completely still, his arms crossed in front of his chest. "Good morning, Miss Quackenbush," he said at last.

eighteen

I left Claudia in charge. "These are the essay questions," I said, thrusting a piece of paper at her. "Write them on the board." I yanked open a desk drawer and pulled out some blue test books. "One per student." I dropped them on the desks.

"What if someone fills up all the space?" Claudia asked.

"Then give them another book."

"Ms. Quackenbush?"

"Yes?"

"Shouldn't it be 'Give *him or her* another book?'"

We stood in the hallway outside my classroom, our silence echoing down the corridor. Farther down, a dark, hulking boy in oversized nylon shorts embraced a too-thin girl in too-tight jeans, their arms clinging to each other's necks, their faces and bodies smushed together, their legs entwined. I was supposed to stop them. I was supposed to check them for hall passes. I was supposed to report them to the office.

I turned to Jonathan. I looked at his face. Unable to bear his expression, I looked at my sensible, rubber-soled shoes. My heart thudded all the way down to my stomach.

Finally, he spoke. "Why don't you just have them do their essays at home?" he asked quietly.

"Because their parents will write them. Or some of their parents. And it's not fair to the kids who do their own work."

He nodded.

"I was going to tell you," I said.

"Mm," he said.

"I've actually . . . I've actually looked into getting a job at the prison. To make it up to you."

He squinted in a way that let me know I'd just said something ridiculous.

"How did you find out?" I asked.

"I Googled you. Nice Web site, by the way."

"Every teacher has one. I don't actually know how to use it."

"It didn't have a picture," he said. "Up until the moment you walked into class I thought maybe, just maybe, there was another Natalie Quackenbush in town."

"My mother doesn't have Alzheimer's," I said.

"I kind of got that," he said.

"I was going to tell you."

"Did I ever tell you that my mother has Alzheimer's, too?" he asked.

"No," I said, aghast.

He waited a beat. "That's because she doesn't." He turned and began to walk down the hall.

"Jonathan! Wait!" I scurried after him. The necking couple paused to look at us and then slunk around the corner.

He stopped, but his expression was stony. "Can we get together later?" I asked. "To talk?"

He stood frozen for a moment. And then he shook his head.

"So this is it?" I asked. "You're just going to walk away?"

He didn't answer.

"We have something good going," I said. "We have a connection." I searched for yet another hackneyed expression and came up with: "You can't just walk away from this."

"Watch me," he whispered.

"Oh, yeah? Like you walked away from all the others?" I said, suddenly angry. "And what little nickname will you give to me?"

He narrowed his eyes and tightened his mouth. "The Big Letdown."

And then he left.

My day went from crappy to crappier. After Jonathan disappeared around the corner, I ran off to the faculty bathroom in a vain attempt to compose myself before returning to class.

After taking a few deep breaths and splashing cold water on my face, I headed back to my classroom and to what I assumed would be the hushed concentration of a room full of overachievers spewing forth intricate sentences peppered with multi-syllabic words. (The uninspired essay topic: "Is Odysseus a classic hero? Explain.") Instead, I heard squeals of laughter upon approaching the classroom. I opened the door and stood there, frozen for a moment. Jared stood in front of the class, one hand on his hip, the other gesturing dramatically. He warbled in a high-pitched voice, "Okay, Class, that's a good concrete example, but, Class, I need you to use your *higher level thinking skills*." The students were red-faced with mirth. It took me a moment to realize that Jared wasn't just being randomly obnoxious. He was doing a full-on impersonation of me—and, judging from the reaction, a pretty good one.

"*That's enough*," I said. They quieted immediately, staring at me with wide-eyed remorse. "Class, I need you to focus on your work. Jared—" Here I stopped to shoot him evil death rays. He glared right back at me with a sociopath's self-assurance. "Jared, go to the office. *Now*."

Once he was gone, I sat down at my desk, shaking, thankful that the kids had a task to focus on, that for once I didn't have to perform. I should make in-class essays a regular thing. Once a week, maybe. And the kids could do in-class presentations on another day. That left only three days a week for actually teaching—and surely I could shave that time away, too.

I was crying. I didn't even realize it until a big, fat tear plopped on my desk, landing on a stack of *Odyssey* chapter summaries.

I fled to the faculty bathroom without leaving any instructions. Without Jared around, the class would be fine.

I shut myself into one of the two stalls and let loose. Good thing I hadn't had time for eye makeup before rushing out of the house. When I heard the outer door swing open, I muffled my sobs as best I could. Eventually, I flushed the unused toilet and opened the stall door slowly.

Mrs. Clausen stood by the sinks, looking concerned. "Natalie! Is everything okay?"

"Not really," I sniffled. "It's just . . . it's been a rough day. I'll be okay."

"The first couple years of teaching are the hardest," she said. "Everyone cries."

I nodded. I couldn't imagine Mrs. Clausen crying. I couldn't imagine her being anything but perfectly groomed and perfectly composed.

She unrolled some brown industrial-grade, super-rough paper towel and handed me a piece. "Do you want to talk about it?"

"Later." I blotted my eyes with the paper towel. "Right now I've got to get back to class."

I called Jonathan before my next class started. No answer. I tried him again when it ended. Nothing.

Robert showed up for Adventures, but he seemed different, more subdued, like a spark had gone out of him, like he was just another Adventures student.

I called Jonathan after Adventures. He didn't answer.

At lunch, Mrs. Clausen sat next to me. Sweet, but I'd really wanted to spend the twenty-five minutes wailing to Jill about Jonathan. Instead, I described my encounter with Jared, who had been given detention (big whoop). Then I told her about Robert.

"Have you talked to the Special Ed department?"

"Yeah. They're going to see him twice a week. The thing is, he's been in Special Ed most of his life, and it hasn't worked."

I called Jonathan after lunch. I was so surprised when he answered that I didn't even know what to say.

"You've got to stop calling me," he said after a moment's silence.

"How do you know I've been calling? I never even left a message."

"My phone tells me every time I've missed a call."

"Maybe you need a new phone." Silence. Perhaps this wasn't the time to be funny. "I should have told you sooner." Silence. "I'd like to start over." Silence. I took a deep breath. "I hope it's not too late."

Finally, he spoke. "It started off too late."

"I don't want to lose you," I whispered.

"You lost me at hello."

Later, during play practice, Jill slid into the seat next to me while I pretended to pay attention to the kids running their lines.

"I heard you lost it during your honors class," she whispered.

I looked at her aghast. "Did Mrs. Clausen tell you?"

"No, of course not. I heard it from Claudia."

"Since when does Claudia need counseling?"

"She doesn't really. She just likes an opportunity to talk about herself."

I told her about Jonathan. "'*You lost me at hello*?' That's pretty funny, actually. I didn't think he had it in him." She snickered. I scowled and told her that I was devastated. Heartbroken. As low as I could go.

"It was kind of inevitable, though, wasn't it?" she said. When I looked pained, she added, "At least you got to have sex first."

And this from a woman who got paid to be sympathetic.

Play practice ran until five o'clock. "Is it always going to be this late?" I asked Lars.

"Sometimes it'll be later." He shot me one of his trademark Mr. Handsome smiles. "Why? You got someplace better to be?"

Going home meant finding my mother moping on the living room sofa, her foot propped up on pillows, the television flickering in the background. "I cleaned the bathrooms this morning. Now I'm paying for it." She readjusted her foot on the pillows.

"Doesn't Molly Maids come next week?"

"I couldn't wait another week. The bathrooms were disgusting. And the laundry was out of control."

"You didn't do my laundry, did you?"

"I was doing a load anyway. Well, three loads."

"I can do my own laundry."

"You were almost out of underwear."

I hauled my tote bag stuffed with *Odyssey* essays, comma quizzes and *Our Town* worksheets upstairs, shut myself in my room and crawled into bed.

nineteen

The thermostat plunged without warning. We traded daily high temperatures hovering just under a hundred for crisp mornings and sunny, breezy afternoons.

I had never been so cold in my life.

I piled on layers and tried not to shiver, even as I told myself that sixty-five degrees wasn't cold. The thing is, after five months of heat that ranged from stifling to suffocating, my inner thermostat was completely out of whack.

"This is why we moved to Arizona!" my father proclaimed each morning and evening, stepping out on the covered patio to survey his gravel-and-cactus domain. Well, at least until my mother declared that "Shelly needs us right now" and "the goddamned cactuses will still be here when we get back." As soon as she was back on her feet, she and my father walked out the door, bound for Sky Harbor Airport.

And so I got the house to myself again.

I tried a couple more times to explain myself to Jonathan. My prepared speech wasn't bad, I thought:

Jonathan. You have every right to be angry at me. What I did was wrong. The evening we met, I'd been hurt and rejected. Being someone else seemed like a good idea, even for a night. It was childish to make up that story—even more childish to keep it going. But I never lied about my feelings, not once. I would have told you the truth sooner, but I was afraid of losing you.

The actual conversations went something like this:

"Jonathan. You have every right to be angry with me."

"I'm not angry with you."

"Really? That's . . . that's wonderful."

"I have to go now."

"But . . . I thought you weren't angry with me."

"I'm not angry. I'm disappointed. I had feelings for a person who, it turned out, didn't exist."

I edited my speech for the next phone call:

"Jonathan. You have every right to be disappointed in me. It was childish to make up that story, even more childish to keep it going. I never lied about my feelings for you. And I think your feelings for me were real, too."

"The person I had feelings for would never do what you did. And, if you'll excuse me, I have to get back to work now."

The whole thing would have been enough to cause sleepless nights if I actually had time to go to bed. Play rehearsals meant staying up until the early morning to grade papers. To make my sleep deprivation even more severe, I was getting up almost an hour

earlier than before, meeting Robert in my classroom forty-five minutes before the first bell. I brought the Starbucks; he brought the
baked goods. Robert wasn't completely illiterate, it turned out, just
lacking in fluency. Had he spent half as much time with reading spe-
cialists as he'd led me to believe, he probably would have been reading long ago. But he had switched schools so many times, both
because of moves (there had been three) and redistricting (four),
that he had slipped through the cracks, at least partly because he
was so good at faking higher abilities than he actually possessed.

Unfortunately, Robert's enthusiasm for his double espresso far
outweighed his enthusiasm for learning to read.

"How much of the *Magic Treehouse* book did you manage to
read last night?" I had given Robert books intended for third graders.

"Didn't have time. Work."

"Okay, let's look at the first page. What does this say?"

"I don't know."

"Sound it out."

"I'm too tired."

Mrs. Clausen—who I had become convinced was a Liz Claiborne–
clad deity—lent me a couple of books about reading strategies and
even sat in on a couple of sessions with Robert. Still, it was painful.
Robert looked downtrodden and unhappy to be in school. If not
for his scones and muffins (oh, those muffins!), I might have just
hit my snooze button and said the heck with him.

We finally took a leap forward, almost by accident. One afternoon, I popped into Jill's office and found her reading *Food & Wine*.
After some initial irritation—I didn't have time for leisure reading at
home, much less at work—I asked to borrow the magazine.

Robert liked it. He couldn't fully understand it, but at least he
wanted to. That was a start. I hit a thrift store and picked up some

old cookbooks and back issues of *Saveur*. At last, Robert had a reason to read.

A couple of weeks after Nicolette and Rodney's elopement (which is to say, a couple of weeks after my weekend with Jonathan—though it seemed so long ago), Jill planned a post-wedding surprise party. It was after school on Friday in the teacher's lounge. Lars even cancelled rehearsal. The entire faculty was invited, though at least half begged off, saying they had to get on the road before rush hour.

When Nicolette walked into the room, she displayed the open mouth and wide, recently mascara-ed eyes of a person who knows darn well she is about to walk into a roomful of people, cake and presents but doesn't want to ruin the moment.

Rodney was there. So were Nicolette's parents, who were shockingly young. One of the laminated tables had been designated for gifts. Jill had arranged them as best as she could, but there was no way to make the take look anything but paltry.

After everyone hugged Nicolette and Rodney, we drank a toast of Welch's sparkling grape juice (Jill had begged Dr. White to allow champagne, to no avail). Nicolette and Rodney cut the three-tiered white cake from Safeway and fed each other pieces. Rodney pretended he was going to smash his piece into Nicolette's face, but he wisely stopped at the first flicker of panic in her eyes.

Once everyone had received a piece of cake on a paper plate, Nicolette sat on a molded plastic chair next to the gift table. She unwrapped slowly, peeling back the tape without ripping the white and silver wrap and folding the paper precisely.

Mrs. Clausen gave them a rice cooker.

Dr. White gave them a set of knives.

Dawna gave them a white Creative Memories album and a plastic bag full of dove, heart and wedding bell stickers.

The rest of us had pitched in for a gift card to Linens 'n Things. Jill had used some of the money to pay for the cake and paper plates, leaving $165 in credit. Nicolette could buy linens or she could buy things, but there was no way she could afford both.

Her eyes welled up as she looked at the card. She smiled as if in gratitude, but I could see she was in deep pain. "Thank you," she whispered. "Thank you all."

We were out of there by three thirty.

Jill said it wasn't too early to start drinking because it was Friday and we'd just been to a party. I wanted to go home to change first; I was wearing the first clean, pressed, matching clothing I had found that morning: my navy blue skirt and a white blouse, without even a scarf or a pair of earrings to jazz things up. I looked like a flight attendant who had forgotten to pin on her wings.

Lars said we should just go because he lived an hour away, so why waste time, and anyway, I looked elegant. Jill said, "Look at me, I don't look any better"—even though she did, in a tight black sweater, straight black skirt and chunky gold jewelry.

We went to the Happy Cactus because they served two-for-one margaritas before six. It had the added advantage of being near Jill's apartment, which meant she got to ditch her car and, as she put it, become the Designated Drunk.

The Happy Cactus was dead—it was just a little after four at this point—and the margaritas were watery: half the booze for half the price.

We complained about the drinks even as we drank them and ordered (free) seconds. A basket of stale chips sat in the middle of the table.

"I didn't think I'd be able to drink tonight," Jill said. "Suicide watch."

"Was the suicide rescheduled?" Lars asked.

"Nope. Girl's been hospitalized. Second time."

"Who is it?" I asked.

"Regina Spitzer. You know that kid Jared you're having problems with? His sister."

"I'm not *having problems* with Jared," I said. "I hate Jared. Jared is the spawn of Satan."

"You shouldn't hate a student," Jill said. "It's a maladaptive coping mechanism."

"Oh, please." Lars reached for a chip. "You only say that because you don't have a hundred and twenty kids assigned to you. Most of them are great, but for a few, hatred is the only reasonable response."

"I met with the whole Spitzer family this week," Jill said. "Majorly dysfunctional. Parents are still married, but they hate each other. Kids aren't getting enough attention, and they're each acting out in their own way. Jared is a very angry child."

"He's the spawn of Satan," I said. And then, with some unwelcome sympathy wiggling into my heart: "What's wrong with the sister? I thought she was bulimic."

"She is. But apparently that wasn't killing her fast enough, so she took a handful of pills this week."

After we drained our second margaritas, Jill asked me, "Feeling any better?"

"No."

"Why, what's wrong, Nat?" Lars asked. Normally, I don't like it when people call me Nat—it makes me think of tiny, itchy bugs—but from Lars, it was okay. I liked the familiarity. "Is this still about that Jared kid?"

"No," I said.

"Natalie had her heart broken," Jill announced.

"The swine," Lars said.

"No," I said. "It was my own stupid fault."

From there, Jill launched into a colorful telling of my romance with Jonathan. Highlights: "So she tells him I'm the prison warden. Do I really look that butch?" And: "He drives a pickup." And: "Guy must be loaded. He dropped a fortune on meals." And: "They had sex in Sedona."

"At least you got to have sex," Lars said.

"That's what I said!" Jill piped in.

By this time, we'd given up on the Happy Cactus and were standing in the parking lot. Lars suggested we head over to The Bunkhouse, an idea I greeted enthusiastically because it was close to my parents' house. I dropped off my car and squeezed into Lars's shiny Prius.

The Prius didn't stay shiny for long. The Bunkhouse is a dusty, Wild West kind of place. The dirt parking lot was already crowded.

"I was thinking," Lars said as we walked inside to the rustic bar to order margaritas and burgers (which was pretty much all they served at The Bunkhouse), "you're better off without that guy. I mean, the story you told, the act you kept up—it's like improv. It's so cool. And if that guy can't appreciate your originality, he's just not worth your time."

We took our plastic cups and burgers to a picnic table outside. There was a bonfire in the middle of the clearing and a little raised stage at the front. Later there would be live country music; for now, it was piped over loudspeakers.

"Should've worn my cowboy boots," Lars said, biting into his burger. Grease dripped onto his paper plate.

"Do you even own a pair?" Jill asked. She picked up her own

burger and pinched it delicately, as if trying to keep the grease from getting on her palms.

"Can't live in Arizona without cowboy boots," Lars said.

"Jonathan wore cowboy boots," I piped in. That's how my mind was working: everything went back to Jonathan. At least I hadn't said, "Jonathan likes his hamburgers well-done," or "Jonathan only drinks Cadillac margaritas"—both of which I'd thought but held in. A broken heart makes for a dull conversationalist.

"Could Jonathan two-step?" Lars asked.

"I have no idea." It bothered me that I didn't know.

"Well, I can. Let me show you."

The dance floor—well, the dance dirt—next to the bonfire was empty.

"There's no one dancing."

"So we'll be trendsetters."

"Let me finish my burger first." I hadn't even started it.

"You're stalling."

"I'm hungry."

But by the time we finished eating, the dance floor was still empty. Lars stood up and held out his hand. I rubbed my greasy hands on a white paper napkin and stood up to join him. I let him pull me toward the dance floor. Behind us, the sun was starting to set, turning Pinnacle Peak a startling purple.

Lars put one hand on my waist; with the other, he held my hand up loosely. I tried not to think about all the people watching us. "Okay," he said. "We're going to count like this: one, two, one-and, two-and . . . just follow my lead."

We started off okay, but when he tried to switch direction, we collided. I broke into a fit of giggles. "It's all I can do to count," I said.

"Guess I should have tried this with a math teacher. You ready? You can do it. One, two, one-and, two-and . . ." I slammed into him again. We held each other, laughing.

"I think I've got it," I said as we broke apart. "Let's try one more time."

We managed to circle halfway around the dance floor before ramming into each other again and admitting defeat. Holding hands, we wound our way back among the picnic tables to find Jill chatting amicably with two very scary-looking bikers, one of whom had a handlebar mustache, the other several missing teeth. The one with the handlebar mustache was sitting very close to Jill; the other guy sat on the other side of the table.

"Hi!" Lars chirped, holding out his hand. "I'm Jed." The bikers blinked at him before half-standing up and shaking his hand. Their arms were meaty. He gestured to me. "And this is Bobbie Sue." I smiled. "And I guess you've met . . ." He looked at Jill.

"Theodora," she said.

"Rudy," said the guy with the missing teeth. The other guy was named Dave. They were both holding bottles of Bud. Rudy had a Harley tattoo on one of his arms. Dave was wearing long sleeves, so it was hard to see if they sported any art.

"Dave is an accountant," Jill said. "From Portland."

Dave smiled. His handlebar mustache framed a set of straight, bleached teeth. "Not what you'd expect, huh?" He inched closer to Jill. She inched away.

"Not really," I said. "I would have guessed hair stylist."

They looked at me uncertainly. I hoped I hadn't pissed them off.

Lars swung his legs over the bench and settled himself next to Jill. He stretched his arm out and curled it around her shoulders. "Thanks for keeping my wife company," he said.

Dave blinked, startled. "Wife?" He inched away from Jill. "I guess I thought—" He looked up at me, leaving the thought unfinished.

I sat down on the bench next to Lars. I reached up to tuck a blond lock behind his ear. "Theodora is Jed's first wife. But I'm his favorite."

Jill swung to face Lars. "Jedediah! You always said you loved me best!"

"Now, now," Lars cooed, swinging his free arm around me. "You know I don't play favorites."

Rudy hooted. "So y'all are divorced, but you still—"

"Divorced!" Lars said.

"We don't believe in divorce," Jill said. "Divorce is a sin. Divorce leads to eternal damnation."

"I'm divorced," Dave said.

"But if y'all aren't divorced—" Rudy said.

"There is room in a man's heart for more than one love. Love makes the heart expand," Lars said calmly.

Rudy's eyes widened with fantasies of girl-on-girl action. I set him straight. "Theodora and I are sister-wives."

"Two wives?" Rudy hooted.

"Shit," Dave said. "I couldn't handle one. But two—?"

"There are four of us," Jill said.

"I'm the third," I said. "Numbers two and four decided to go to a movie instead."

I don't know if they believed we were polygamists on vacation from Colorado City (we told them the La Quinta Inn chain always gave us a special rate). I don't even know if their names were really Rudy and Dave and whether they really were an electrician and an accountant (though I'm inclined to believe it). All I knew was that it felt good to sit next to Lars, and not just because I needed his body heat on this chilly night. I liked being Bobbie Sue: it felt good to be someone else. It felt good to live in a world—even a make-believe one—without a broken heart. It felt good to smile, to laugh, to dance.

When the country band finally started playing, I was the one to suggest a dance. The three of us—Jedediah and his two wives—trouped out to the dance floor. Arms around waists, we two-stepped the night away.

twenty

It would be an exaggeration to say that I looked forward to Monday morning, but I didn't greet my five forty-five alarm with as much despair as usual. I'd hit the outlets over the weekend (trying, not entirely successfully, to forget traveling the same stretch with Jonathan) and scored an assortment of black clothing: a gauzy blouse, a straight skirt with a big slit up the back and a pair of high-heeled mules. The color black is a godsend for those who lack an innate fashion sense. I'd also found a gray suit on sale (it came with a skirt *and* trousers!) and picked up an assortment of clips, as my hair was in that awkward in-between stage.

I'd almost finished my latte by the time Robert ambled in. "You're late."

"Yeah. Whatever." He dropped his books on the desk and collapsed into the chair, immediately assuming the classic bored-teenager slump.

I gave him The Look. Then I handed him his double espresso, which probably dulled my authority somewhat. Robert accepted the cup and opened the lid. He sipped carefully. I waited for him to produce a pastry, maybe another one of those chocolate croissants he'd brought in on Friday. Nothing.

"Okay," I said, trying to ignore the gurgle from my stomach. Good thing I'd started stocking granola bars in my desk; I'd gobble one before first period. "Reading. How much did you do over the weekend?"

He shrugged. Mumbled something into his cup.

"I'm sorry? I didn't catch that."

"I didn't have time."

"Mm." I gave him The Look again. Since he kept his eyes on his desk, it didn't do much good. "I'm not doing this for me, you know. I could have slept another forty-five minutes." (*Look up, darn it.*) I took a deep breath. "I'm trying to help you."

"I *know*," he said, finally meeting my eyes. "And I appreciate it. The thing is, I don't think it's doing any good."

"Of course it is! I can't believe the progress you've made! If you keep it up, you're going to graduate. That's *huge*."

"What difference does it make? I'm still going to be working at the hospital, same as if I didn't graduate. And if that doesn't work out, I'll probably be flipping burgers or doing road work. It's not like a high school diploma gets you anywhere."

"If you try really hard, you can make it into college. Maybe you start off at a two-year, get your feet wet—"

He sat up straight. "I don't *want* to go to college! Don't you get it, Mrs. Q? I *hate* school. I've always hated school. There's no way I'm going for another four years, even another two years. You're a nice lady, and it's nice that you're trying to help, but I really just want to get out of this place. If it weren't for my mom, I'd have left already."

My hands shaking, I reached for my cardboard cup and lifted it to my lips, remembering too late that it was empty. I looked up at the clock; the first bell would ring in twenty-eight minutes. "Well, you're here now. You want to work on reading strategies?"

He shrugged, slid back down in his chair. "Whatever."

Mrs. Clausen pursed her lips when I told her about Robert. "Let me think on it," she said. And then she gave my arm a little squeeze and said, "Think positive thoughts!"

I tried to think positive thoughts as I began my Freshman Honors class. I tried to smile at Jared (it made my face hurt) and see him as the lost, hurt little boy Jill said he was and not as the spawn of Satan.

We had just started reading *Lord of the Flies*, and I was feeling in control, not least because I had read the book. I asked the class for their initial impressions.

Sarah Levine started. "I was thinking—and maybe I'm just reading into it—but the island seems like a kind of microcosm. And that the anarchy . . . I don't know . . . maybe it's about more than just those kids. Maybe it's what happens when there's no structure, no law, and things start to go really bad."

"Why aren't there any girls in the book?" Claudia asked. "It seemed really antifeminist to me. And the thing is, if there were girls, I bet everything would have been different. They wouldn't have been so mean, and maybe they would have thought of a way to get off the island."

Jared raised his hand.

"Yes? You have something to add?"

"That fat kid is just a total loser," he said.

Spawn of Satan.

Jill was sitting at our usual table when I entered the lunchroom. I was almost there, insulated lunch bag in hand, when Mrs. Clausen motioned me over. "Sit!" she commanded. "I've been thinking about Robert. Are you familiar with Neil Weinrich's internship program?"

"Only in a general sense," I said. I had no idea what she was talking about.

"Neil has spearheaded this marvelous program that matches students with local businesses. Please! Don't let me keep you from eating!"

Lars had just walked in carrying an orange tray. He scanned the room and smiled when he saw me. I gave him a little wave and gestured with my head toward Jill's table: I'd be there in a minute.

"It's okay, I'm not really hungry." I was starving. "Tell me more about the program."

"You should really talk to Neil about it." She twisted around until she located him. "Neil! You have a minute?"

Neil Weinrich looked up from his copy of *Scientific American*. He blinked at Mrs. Clausen for a moment before standing up ramrod straight, sticking his magazine under his arm, picking up his tray and marching over to us.

I looked forlornly over at Jill and Lars. They were laughing. I looked back at Mr. Weinrich and tried to smile.

Neil Weinrich is in his early fifties, with greasy dyed black hair (you can see gray at the roots) and a long, acne-scarred face. His breath smells of wintergreen mingled with decay. He is of average height but seems taller because he holds himself so stiff, his chin tilted upwards. Neil Weinrich is the kind of guy who was picked on in high school and has exacted his revenge by dedicating the rest of his natural life to belittling teenagers. If he were a student today, I wouldn't even consider letting him into the building until he had passed through a metal detector. Naked.

"Mrs. Clausen was telling me about your internship program," I said.

He inhaled. I held my breath in anticipation of his exhalation. "As educators, we cannot expect a one-size-fits-all approach to fit every student," he intoned. "Different students have different needs. Different strengths. Different capabilities. Are you going to eat that roll, Margaret?"

Mrs. Clausen blinked. "Excuse me? Oh. Um, I was, actually. I like a roll after my salad. But if you're hungry, I guess—"

"No! No! Only if you're not going to eat it. But as I was saying, as educators we must be the pioneers who forge new paths for our youngsters, and we must provide them with as many paths as they need to succeed. The world is changing. Technology . . . I could go on."

He did go on. I eventually broke down and ate my yogurt, glancing wistfully over at Jill and Lars.

The internship program did sound good, though (once Mr. Weinrich finally got around to talking about it). It allowed students to spend half of their time in the classroom, the other half in a work setting. Each student was paired with a work mentor, who was supposed to ensure that the student actually learned something on the job and wasn't used as an unpaid drone.

The application deadline had passed. "And you missed the orientation meeting. It was a top-notch event, with former participants speaking, along with some of our business partners . . . you know, the program benefits them as much as it does our students, gives them a role in educating the future workforce. As educators, we can only provide our students with so many tools . . ."

Despite missing the deadline, my student was not out of luck, Mr. Weinrich told me. There were a few business partners available for the right applicant. Nicolette had the applications in her desk. "Mr. Weinrich creeps me out," she whispered, handing me a yellow sheet. "I don't like the way he looks at my boobs."

Robert actually looked excited when I told him about the internship program. "I'd get to leave school for half the day?" he asked, looking over the application form and, I hoped, understanding some of it.

"Yes," I said. "But not to go to the mall. To go to a job."

"What if it's a job at the mall?" he asked, his eyes twinkling. Maybe, just maybe, the old Robert was back.

After school, he showed up at the amphitheater and sat down next to me. It was our first dress rehearsal. Katerina was walking around in a negligee having just finished a scene in which Romeo sneaks into her bedroom.

"I filled out as much of the application as I could," Robert said, trying not to disturb the actors. His eyes kept flicking forward, where Katerina commanded the stage.

I looked at the yellow sheet of paper. In careful, spiky writing, he had written his name, address and phone number. Under "career interests," he had written, "hotel or restaurant or cruise."

"Just so you know," I said, "the chances of working on a cruise ship in Arizona? Not so good." I was so proud of him for understanding what "career interests" meant.

He shrugged and grinned. "Can't blame a guy for trying."

"You need to write an essay," I whispered. The application asked, "What would you gain from an internship? What could you offer to employers?"

"I didn't understand that part," he mumbled.

I read the question to him. "Here's what I want you to do tonight. Jot down ideas about two things. First, why do you want to do an internship? And don't say because you'll get out of school early. What will you learn and how will it help you get jobs in the future? Then tell us why you'd be a good intern. You can talk about your personal skills and your job experience."

"That's . . . I don't think I can do that part."

"Of course you can! I'm not asking you to write an essay. Just put down some ideas. In the morning, we'll work together so you can hand it in." He looked dubious. "Don't worry about spelling. Or grammar. You don't even have to use complete sentences. What you'll be making is a kind of outline, just like we went over in class last week. But it doesn't have to be a proper essay with the Roman numerals and the subcategories, and it doesn't have to be consistent in form. Just think of it as a list of your ideas. Then we can work together to organize your thoughts, to give them a kind of structure—"

He was paying absolutely no attention to me.

Katerina walked over and stood in the aisle, a short way from Robert. "Hi," he said, his eyes bugging out.

"Hi." She giggled, blushed and looked down. The negligee was peach silk and hit her at mid-thigh, which still left a vast expanse of her long legs naked. Her feet were bare, her toenails painted fire-engine red. Her long, black hair was up in a messy hairdo, stray tendrils tumbling along her face and neck.

"You look really good up there," Robert said. "I mean, you're a really good actress."

"Thanks," she said, smiling at the ground.

I stood up and climbed over Robert, mumbling something about checking on the props and grinning like a fool as I scurried down the steps.

twenty-one

The next morning Robert was waiting for me at the classroom door, holding a folder and a brown paper bag.

"Muffins?" I asked, eyeing the bag.

"Lemon poppy seed."

I unlocked my door and turned on the fluorescent lights. It was like I was seeing my classroom for the first time. It was deadly. The Shakespeare quotes had to go—especially since I wasn't even teaching Shakespeare this quarter. I'd set up a writing center, I vowed, and post student poetry. Maybe I'd come in one Saturday and paint the walls green or blue.

As instructed, Robert had produced a list:

Ive bin at hospitle for 3 years I work in loundry
I work herd I work lotsof howrs

I want to see wat its lik to work somplace other then school
    or hospital
I want to work in a hotel or restrant somplace wear I dont
    have to sit down all day
Im good with peple I can make them laf

I helped Robert construct a rough outline, basically just dividing his ideas into sections: why internships are a good idea; why I want an internship; my skills and experience. In conclusion, he was to begin his final paragraph with the words, "In conclusion . . ."

He wrote his rough draft during study hall and met me in my classroom after school. He stood over my desk as I read. The essay didn't need nearly as much editing as I'd expected. "I'm so proud of you," I said, gazing at the lined paper.

"You did most of it," he said, scuffing his sneaker on the floor.

"No way. I guided you a little, but this is your own work. I can't believe how far you've come in a month."

"Whatever," he said, trying to hide a smile.

I locked up my classroom—which took awhile; my lock was funny and always took a bit of jiggling before it would catch. We traipsed down to the Media Center, where he typed the essay into a computer. Spell-check was a godsend. The printer actually worked.

"I gotta get to work," he said when the sheets printed out.

"That's okay. I'll run this over to Mr. Weinrich."

Neil Weinrich was sitting as his desk, nibbling sunflower seeds from a crinkly packet. I tried to see him as a bunny, but no: the man was definitely a rodent.

"Hi, Neil!" I chirped, willing the rat image away.

"Yes, Miss Quackenbush." He squinted and shot me a social smile. I glanced at his room: desks in rows, the periodic table of elements plastered on the walls. You can bet students spent a lot of time staring at the clock over the door.

"I have the internship application. From the student I told you about."

"Yes, of course." He picked up eyeglasses from his desk and slid them on. He stared at the application for a moment before handing it back to me. "I'm sorry, but we won't be able to accommodate this student."

"But you said—you said there were still some openings."

"There are openings for the *right* applicants. There are no openings for Robert Baumgartner."

"Robert has excellent work experience," I said. "And he'll try really hard. Academics have been difficult for him because he's got a learning disability, but this internship can really open doors for him, give him some confidence."

Neil Weinrich picked up his half-empty package of sunflower seeds. He twisted the cellophane until it closed out most of the air, opened a desk drawer and dropped it inside. He closed the drawer and looked back up. "What Robert Baumgartner does *not* need is more confidence."

"I stand behind this applicant." My voice was quavering. "I stake my reputation on it."

He pursed his lips. "It is not your reputation that is at stake. I have been running this program for three years now. It has taken a tremendous amount of time and energy to recruit our business partners. I cannot take a chance on a student who has shown himself time and again to be irresponsible, insolent and tardy simply because you think he's cute."

I stared at him, speechless for a moment. My face grew hot. "Excuse me?" I finally sputtered.

"Oh, it's not just you," he said, backing off. "All females find him charming. It's why he gets away with so much. But I think you've been fooled." There it was then: Neil Weinrich was once again taking revenge on all those "cool" boys who teased him in high school. Robert was different. He had a history of tardiness and irresponsibility, it's true, but I'd never seen him be mean, not once. Still, as much as I didn't want to, I could understand Neil Weinrich's reservations. I just couldn't understand why he seemed to enjoy rejecting Robert.

"What if I set something up?" I said suddenly. "If I arranged an internship for him."

"Finding willing business partners is not easy," he said.

"But I can try?"

He pursed his lips, wiggled his nostrils a little. "I could give you till the end of the week," he said finally.

"But that's—three days?"

He shrugged. "I'm sorry, but I have deadlines. I need to finalize paperwork." He smiled. There was a sunflower seed stuck between his two front teeth. "Maybe you'll work something out."

I was tempted to rush out right then and skip play practice, but I'd missed over an hour already, and it was another dress rehearsal.

It took a second to register that the amphitheater stage was empty except for Dr. White, but the concrete benches were full and noisy. My first thought was that something terrible had happened— a student had collapsed, an ambulance called—but there were no emergency workers, no flashing lights.

I spotted Jill down near the front, and I worked my way

down, pushing past wide-eyed students and angry parents. "What happened?"

She had her arms crossed in front of her chest, her mouth in a hard line. "Closed-minded, censor-crazy, naïve jerks," she muttered.

"What!"

"Some mother came by to pick her kid up early yesterday and saw Katerina in her costume."

"The undies?" I asked.

"It's a *nightgown*," Jill hissed. "It covers more than what half these girls wear to school. So the mother has a nervous breakdown, says this is not suitable. Lars thought he'd calmed her down, but then she reads the script and she thinks it obscene because it has these, like, veiled references to sex. So she calls the president of the PTA, the president of the school board and every close-minded, hypocritical parent she can find and they come down, interrupting rehearsal and demanding an explanation for why the school is allowing obscene material to be presented. *Obscene material*! It's based on a Shakespeare play, for God's sake!"

I scanned the crowd for Lars's golden hair. He was surrounded by three women and one man, all of them red-faced, talking and gesturing at the same time. I recognized Lynette Pimpernel, Claudia's mother. The kids from the play huddled on the benches, whispering.

"Can I have your attention, *please*," Dr. White called out from the stage. People quieted. "I understand that many people are upset. We need to have a meeting, a formal forum where we can discuss this matter rationally. May I *suggest*"—here she stopped and glared at everyone: she wasn't suggesting anything; she was telling—"we disband for now and reconvene Friday evening for a measured discussion and resolution of the issues."

"But this is ridiculous!" Lars called out. "This play is based on *Romeo and Juliet*! It has some sexual references, okay, but nothing graphic. Do you know how many of these kids watch *Real Sex* on HBO? How much porn they're looking at on the Internet?"

"We have parental controls on our computer!" A parent called out. "We have a V chip!"

"And what about when they go to their friends' houses? Do they all have V chips, too?"

I checked the students. Some of them were smirking, though trying to hide it. They'd all seen *Real Sex*. And they'd figured out how to bypass their computers' parental controls in junior high school.

"Mr. Hansen!" Dr. White snapped. "*As I said*, we will reconvene Friday. Let's say seven P.M. In the meantime, I will read the play and discuss this matter with the school superintendent. We are finished here." She glared at the crowd. They stayed rooted. "*Go home*," she snapped.

twenty-two

I should have been upset about the commotion surrounding *Romeo and Jules*. No, I should have been incensed. Censorship! Close-mindedness! Hypocricy!

Dr. White told Lars to postpone rehearsals until after Friday's meeting, though, and I was secretly elated to have all that extra time to hunt down an internship for Robert. Besides, the experience seemed to bring Lars and me closer together. He sat down with me at lunch to go over the points he planned to make in Friday's meeting. He called me in the evenings to vent, ending each conversation with a sigh and, "Thanks for listening."

I called my parents to ask for advice on where to look for an internship. My mother named a few of their favorite restaurants.

"You should try the Hacienda Resort," my mother said. "Not too far away, and it's just gorgeous. Spectacular at the holidays."

"Did you ever stay there before moving to Scottsdale? Because it would be nice if I could say you had."

"Are you kidding? Your father would never spring for the Hacienda. We used to stay at a condo. It was great for him, but it meant I got stuck cooking and cleaning."

"Okay, what about the restaurants. Do you know anyone there? Ever get chatting with the owners?"

"No."

"How about the maitre d's? Did you talk to them?"

"Yeeeees," she said. "We said, 'Table for two, please.'"

"Funny."

"You haven't asked about your sister."

"I was about to." There was a pause. "How's my sister?"

"Big. Putting on weight already. She doesn't look pregnant yet, just—well, you know. Puffy. She's under a lot of stress. I think it's helping her out a lot, our being here. She says she can't remember the last time she ate a home-cooked meal."

Now it was my turn to pause, picturing the endless cardboard containers with the AJ's label, until, finally, I got the words out: "You cook for her?"

I started with the Hacienda. After being transferred something like forty-five times, a woman with a Southern accent told me that they only take college interns. I called a couple more hotels. They also, for various reasons, were hesitant to take on a high school student.

The restaurants were more promising. Our conversations were hurried, as they were preparing for the dinner rush, but two maitre d's and a sous chef told me to bring Robert by the following afternoon.

I called Robert to tell him about the interviews. "Dress nicely," I advised.

He was elated, already trying to decide which restaurant he preferred, the upscale Southwestern or the Pacific Rim. (The third place, a "traditional American" was way down on his list.)

"Let's see how you feel after meeting everyone," I said, hoping he owned some clothing other than logo T-shirts and basketball shorts.

The first two restaurants were a bust. The traditional American didn't serve lunch (I should have checked earlier), and the Pacific Rim place clearly aimed to make Robert an unpaid busboy.

"This is a mentoring experience," I explained. "We'd need someone in the restaurant—someone at a managerial level—to take responsibility for educating Robert about the restaurant business."

The woman raised her eyebrows. "If he wants to learn something, he should go to school."

Robert was quiet as we drove to the Southwestern place. "I can make some more calls tonight if I have to," I said, fully aware that I needed to secure a position by the next day.

"Whatever," he mumbled. His chinos and long-sleeved white T-shirt were starting to look rumpled.

And then we hit gold. The Southwestern place, Aji Amarillo, was chaotic and understaffed. The food smelled wonderful.

"When can you start?" the sous chef, Luis, asked thirty seconds after we said hello.

"Just so we're clear," I said. "The purpose of the program is for Robert to learn something. Cooking techniques, management—real-world experience that will broaden him and help prepare him for a career."

"He'll learn more here in a day than he could learn in a year at cooking school," Luis boasted.

Luis happily signed a Mentor Agreement, leaving a tiny spot of grease on the paper. "When can you start?" he asked Robert. "Can you start now?"

Robert looked at me, pleading.

"Robert has another job," I explained firmly. "He'll only be available for three hours in the afternoon. He can start Monday."

I half expected Neil Weinrich to reject the restaurant on some technicality, but he just looked the forms over and said, "Okay."

"Good, then." I smiled at Neil.

"If he lasts a week, I'll be amazed."

But Neil Weinrich couldn't bring me down, nor could the angry mob of parents that convened in the amphitheater at seven o'clock Friday evening. Lars wore khakis, a button-down blue shirt and a blue blazer. If not for his flippy blond hair, he could pass for a delegate at the Republican national convention. "Go get 'em, Tiger," I whispered as he took the stage. As assistant director, I sat next to him in the front row.

His speech was rousing. He started off with "the very real risks to our children:" drugs, easy access to pornography, mindless video game violence. He recited statistics about how many acts of sex and violence appear between the hours of eight and nine o'clock on network TV on any given evening. He moved on to say that "we can't just lock our children in their rooms" but that we should give them "intellectual alternatives." We should give them art. We should give them music. We should give them drama.

He went on a bit more, but I stopped paying attention to what he said and started thinking about how cute he looked, all fired up like that.

"You were brilliant," I whispered when he took his seat next to me. He took my hand and squeezed.

But it was for nothing. That's how Lars looked at it, anyway. After impassioned speeches by Claudia's mother, a member of the school board and some random guy who didn't even have kids at Agave but apparently just liked to hear himself talk, Dr. White, wearing a black suit and a fuchsia blouse, took control of the stage.

She had considered both sides of the argument. Theater was important. The students had worked long hours on the production; it would be wrong to tell them that the show could not go on. At the same time, parents had the right—no, the duty—to protect their children from material they deemed inappropriate. Having read the play and discussed it with the superintendent, she had determined that the students could perform it—under the condition that the offending scenes were eliminated. Further, she would institute a policy whereby any future play intended for a school production would require approval by her and the school board.

The parents seemed placated. Lars was fuming. He didn't say anything until we reached the parking lot, stopping in front of his Prius, which he had parked under a light. "Fucking mind police," he growled.

"At least they didn't cancel the production."

"They might as well have. It's not even going to make sense now."

"It'll make sense. We'll make it make sense."

"And what plays are we going to do after this one? What kind of stilted, soulless stuff will pass the censor board?"

We stood in the parking lot, talking for about twenty minutes. The night air was chilly. Lars lent me his blue blazer.

"I have a frozen pizza at home," I said, clutching the blazer around me. "The self-rising kind. And a bottle of red wine."

"That sounds really good right now."

I got to the house before Lars, who said he'd pick up a salad on the way over. After sticking the pizza in the oven, I turned on the gas fireplace in the great room and shuffled through my CDs, finally popping in some jazz (which I've never particularly enjoyed but seemed sophisticated). I poured some red wine into my parents' Riedel glasses. I considered lighting candles but decided that would be overdoing things.

He brought a bag of lettuce mixed with herbs. "I forgot to get dressing. You have any?"

He took the glass of wine I offered. I held up my glass. "To perseverance."

"To enlightenment," he countered. We drank.

We went into the great room and settled on my mother's camel-back sofa. Flames licked the ceramic logs in the beehive fireplace. "What do you think of the décor?" I asked. "I call it 'Boston Meets *Bonanza*.'" (Yes, okay, so I recycle jokes.)

"I'm really disappointed in Dr. White," Lars said, staring into the fire.

"I think she was worried about a lawsuit."

"I feel like I've completely compromised my artistic integrity. Which makes me a poor role model for the kids. Like, I should show them what it means to stand up for your beliefs, but instead I just sit down and take it."

"No," I said. "You're being pragmatic. If you keep fighting, the play could get canceled altogether. That's not fair to these kids."

Lars turned to me and smiled gently. "You've been great through all this."

"Thanks," I said, drawing in a sharp breath.

The timer rang.

"Oh! The pizza." I popped off the couch and hurried into the kitchen. I set my glass on the counter and poured some more wine. A drop splashed on the counter.

We ate at the kitchen table: not as romantic as outside, but a lot warmer. "You want me to light the candles?" Lars asked.

"Sure." I dimmed the lights slightly.

He had a second glass of wine. He told me about his first year of teaching, how tired he had been. He told me about being a kid in Seattle. He told me about the summer he spent backpacking through Europe.

I finished the wine.

We went back to the great room, sat down on the couch. He winced.

"What?" I asked.

"My back. Probably because I've been so tense."

"Here, let me rub it."

He sat sideways. I rubbed his well-muscled shoulders through his blue dress shirt. Lars had looked so perfectly pressed earlier; now his shirt was covered with creases, and his khakis were rumpled. I worked down to his shoulder blades. "Mm," he murmured. "This feels good."

"I'm glad." I ran my hands down his spine and then back up again. I made fists and kneaded his lower back. Finally, I slid my hands forward, encircling his waist. I leaned against him, my front pressed against his back.

He tensed. I sat back. He turned around, alarmed.

"Sorry," I said. "I guess I thought—"

"No, *I'm* sorry," he said, retreating to the corner of the couch. "I guess I was sending you the wrong signals. I just—my back hurt. But I didn't mean to—well, I guess I thought . . . *you knew*." He blinked at me. He looked so pretty in the firelight. It made his hair glow like a halo.

My eyes widened. "Oh! No! It's okay! Really." I smiled. "I drank too much wine. Don't worry about a thing. Everything's fine."

As soon as he left, I called Jill. "You were right from the beginning," I said. "Lars is a flamer."

twenty-three

Robert arrived at school on Monday wearing black and white checked chef's pants and a tired expression.

"You ready to start your internship?" I asked.

"Started it already." He ran a hand over his bleary eyes. "Luis called me Saturday—said they were swamped."

"You worked on Saturday?"

"And Sunday." He smiled sleepily. "It was fun. Course, I had to work at the hospital, too, so I'm wiped."

When I had a break, I called the restaurant to talk to Luis. He wasn't in yet, so I explained to the hostess that I was Robert's academic advisor for his internship and that I had a few concerns.

"Robert? That the guy who was in over the weekend? Real good-looking?"

Yes, I said. That was him.

"Real good worker," she said. "Totally saved the bartender's ass."

"Excuse me?"

"Cocktail waitress didn't show up. That Robert kid jumped right in, started delivering drinks. Even mixed a couple."

I caught up with Robert near his locker. "Robert."

"Hey, Mrs. Q." He smiled.

I kept my face stern. "Alcohol. Internship. Not a good mix."

"Luis told you?"

"No, some woman. I have a feeling Luis wouldn't want me to know that he was breaking the law by having a minor serve alcohol."

"It's not like I drank any."

"It doesn't matter. You can't serve if you're under nineteen."

"It's just that they were really short-handed."

"Robert. This cannot—*cannot*—happen again."

Later, on the phone, Luis feigned ignorance. "The kid's under nineteen? Oh, man, no way."

"He's a high school student. High school students are generally under nineteen."

"Oh, well, I guess you never told me."

"It was on his application."

"Oh, well, I guess I didn't look it over too careful."

Luis swore Robert would no longer work the bar. I hoped he was telling the truth.

Neil Weinrich was in the lunchroom when I walked in with my insulated lunch bag. I gave him a quick wave and hurried past before he had a chance to ask me about Robert's internship.

Jill and Lars were sitting at our usual table, eating out of matching Tupperware containers.

"What, no mystery meat?" I asked Lars, peering at his farfalle pasta salad. There were chunks of chicken, some herbs, cherry tomatoes and black olives.

"Jill made me lunch," he said.

"What? You never made me lunch."

"You never asked," she said, spearing a bowtie pasta. "Don't get used to it," she warned Lars. "I just had extra, and I wanted to get rid of it before it went bad."

I settled myself into a molded plastic chair and opened my lunch bag, pulling out an orange, a plastic bag of crackers, a hunk of cheddar cheese and a child-size water bottle. "I'm avoiding Neil Weinrich," I announced.

"Why?" Lars asked, twisting open a bottle of iced tea. "He's kind of hot."

"*Eew*," Jill and I said in unison.

"Just *kidding*." Lars rolled his eyes and tossed his blond hair. I couldn't believe I had ever thought he might like girls. "But have you seen Raoul? The new student teacher—I think he's in science. *Yummy*." He took a giant swig of the iced tea and screwed the cap back on.

The next morning, I called Robert's cell phone when I got to my classroom, five minutes before the first bell. "I just wanted to check on your internship. Are you at school yet?"

"Yes." I heard a car horn in the background.

"Then why are there car sounds?"

"I'm in the parking lot."

"How was the internship?"

He was silent for a moment. "Very educating. I got educated about how to rinse glasses and scrape plates."

"Oh, no."

"Dishwasher called in sick. And they were, like, totally short-handed."

At lunch this time, I lingered by Neil Weinrich long enough for him to ask about Robert's internship.

"So far, so good!" I chirped. "Of course, it's still early." Then I ever-so-casually asked if there had ever been a time when an internship didn't work out.

"We check out our business partners as closely as possible," Neil Weinrich said. "But there will always be times when a business mentor does not fulfill his"— here he paused to look me in the eye—"or *her*—part of the bargain. We normally allow a month-long orientation phase, during which students can switch internships, if necessary. The orientation phase is over in a week, however, so if your student requires a switch, it would have to be done pronto."

When I sat down, Lars was just biting into a square piece of cafeteria pizza. "I think you're too hard on Neil," he said after swallowing. "About his looks, I mean. Check out his shoulders. I bet you anything he works out."

I waited until I got home to make the call. It's not like I hadn't thought about calling Jonathan from the beginning. And I suppose I was glad to have any excuse to talk to him, even if my heart felt like it would burst. I used my parent's phone rather than my cell so my name wouldn't come up on caller ID.

He knew it was me, anyway.

"Hi."

"Hi." I took a deep breath. I had rehearsed my speech. "I'm not calling about you and me because I accept that you cannot forgive me." I didn't really accept it, but it sounded mature. "I am calling to see if you might be able to help someone out. A young man, a student. He has a learning disability and reads at a fifth-grade level." Actually, this was progress. When we started, Robert was reading just slightly better than an average third grader. "I told you about him, actually. He's the one who froze up in the play audition."

"I thought you made up the play."

"No!" I felt oddly hurt, like, *Don't you believe anything I say?* "The play was real. It just wasn't at the . . . um, it was at school."

I explained my predicament: Robert would benefit greatly from an internship, but I hadn't found him anything suitable, and time was running out. With all of Jonathan's industry contacts, he could surely find a place for Robert. "I'm not asking you to do this for me," I ended grandly, "I'm asking you to do it for a very deserving young man."

He was quiet for a moment. Then, softly: "I'm sorry. I can't help you."

"Oh. Okay." I was disappointed but not really surprised. It was time to say good-bye. I didn't want to. "How's Krista feeling?"

He paused a little too long. "Fine."

"My sister's really big and really nauseous. That's what my mother said, anyway. My parents went out to her place in Rhode Island. To help out. So I've got the house to myself again."

I waited for Jonathan to say something—anything. He remained silent. But at least he wasn't saying good-bye, at least not yet.

"Jonathan," I said. "I know I've said it a million times and I know it doesn't make everything better, but I'm sorry. I'm so sorry. Maybe if we could just get together, for coffee or something, we could talk this over and—"

"I have to go," he interrupted. "Good-bye."

"Good-bye," I said to the dead air.

twenty-four

Friday was the final dress rehearsal; Saturday was opening night. Lars spent the first hour in a powwow with the kids, trying to explain why they couldn't just perform the play as they'd rehearsed, in its entirety. They sat, Indian-style, in a circle on the amphitheater stage. Arriving late, I squeezed in next to Katerina. The concrete surface felt cold through my gray dress pants.

"What are they going to do? It's not like they're going to stop the play in the middle. I say we just go for it," Claudia said, despite—or perhaps because of—her mother's leading role in the crusade for censorship.

"The cuts ruin it," Katerina said. "It just doesn't resonate the same way." Dr. White had deemed several of Katerina's scenes "inappropriate."

"I know how upset you guys are about this." Lars ran a hand through his golden hair and sighed. "I'm upset, too."

I did my best to look concerned, but, honestly, the play was the last thing on my mind. After school, I arrived at Aji Amarillo unannounced. I was hoping to catch Robert, but he had already left for the hospital.

"Hi, Luis," I said, putting on my happy face, desperate to make the most of an imperfect situation. He took a drag on his cigarette and squinted at me through the smoke. With his other hand, he stirred a pot of pungent-smelling sauce.

I started in with, "I just wanted to be clear about the requirements of Robert's internship," when my nose took off on its own journey, trying to identify the competing smells of Luis's kitchen. Roasted onions. Garlic. Chili powder. Chicken. Chocolate. And something else vaguely sweet that I recognized but couldn't name.

"It's really great that Robert's getting to experience different aspects of the restaurant. I just want to make sure he'll have some exposure to the management side." Exposure. As in: exposure to secondhand smoke. Onions, garlic, chili powder, chicken, chocolate—where was the tobacco smell?

I blinked at Luis. "Are you smoking a *joint*?"

I called Jonathan from the parking lot.

"You've got to stop calling me," he said evenly.

"Please, just hear me out. I just stopped by to see the chef who's supposed to be acting as Robert's mentor, and he was smoking marijuana."

"Robert," Jonathan said. "That would be one of your imaginary friends? Or was he the imaginary student?"

"I never had any imaginary friends. Or students. It was just the job. Everything else was real."

"So your mother really has Alzheimer's."

"Oh. Well, no. But I really have a mother," I added, grasping at straws. "But—Robert. I can't leave him in there. *I can't.*"

"I spend a lot of time with restaurant people," Jonathan said.

"Yes, I know. That's why I—"

"And I'm trying to be shocked about the marijuana. And I'd try to be shocked if you said the guy was doing shots of tequila at noon or even lines of cocaine and that he couldn't say a single sentence without using the F word and that the entire kitchen staff was undocumented. A kid can get an education in a restaurant kitchen—but probably not the kind you had in mind."

The rehearsal ran late—past six o'clock—but I didn't want to go home yet. I didn't want to go home until I was so exhausted that I could collapse into a deep, dreamless sleep. "You doing anything?" I asked Lars. "Want to grab a bite to eat?"

"Um, yeah," he said. "Sure."

I walked to my car while Lars put some props back in his classroom. My cell phone rang: Jill. "Hey," she said. "I'm bored. You doing anything?"

"I've got a hot date with Lars. You want to come?"

After some back-and-forthing, Lars agreed to swing by Jill's house so she wouldn't have to drive. From there, we hit the Happy Cactus, which was considerably more packed than the last time we'd been there. Since the temperature had dropped, the entire Valley of the Sun had become more crowded. I had to allow an extra five minutes to get to work—and an extra seven to navigate the Starbucks line. My hairdresser needed five weeks' notice to schedule a trim. At least the days were sunny and perfect, though

I'd begun carting around a geeky English teacher cardigan; the temperature dropped precipitously the instant the sun went down.

"You got the two-for-one margaritas tonight?" Lars asked the bartender. But no: bargains were just for the off-season.

We snagged a table in the middle of the room. I took off my sweater and arranged it across the back of my chair. "How'd rehearsal go?" Jill asked. She'd changed into black jeans and a stretchy V-neck top that allowed a glimpse of her ample cleavage. On her feet she wore chunky, high-heeled black sandals. Jill is not one of those tall women who embraces ballet slippers and poor posture in an effort to appear smaller.

Lars shook his head, too pained to speak.

"The kids did great," I said. "Not a single line missed."

"I've let them down," Lars said. "I should have stood up to Dr. White." Lars was wearing a pink oxford shirt and khakis. His hair had been recently trimmed. He looked really pretty.

"It's not worth losing your job over," I said, thinking: Hey! If I stand up to someone, can I get fired?

"I don't want to talk about it," Lars said. "Let's just have fun."

The waitress came with our drinks: margaritas for Jill and me, a martini for Lars.

"Excuse me," Lars said, looking wide-eyed at the waitress.

"Yes?"

"How do you get to the beach from here?"

She squinted at him. "What beach?"

"You know—*the beach*."

"You mean Silver Lake? The reservoir?"

"No!" Lars said. "I mean *the beach*. The one with the waves and the surfers."

"Um . . . are you talking about California?" She was keeping her voice neutral, not wanting to jeopardize her tip.

Lars laughed arrogantly. He looked at Jill and me as if to say, Can you help me out, here?

"No, the Arizona beach," Jill said. "You know—it connects to the Pacific by the inland waterway? It's about a half hour from here. Forty minutes, tops. It's not in any guide books—the locals don't want the secret out. Willow's been there. Haven't you?" Everyone was quiet for a moment. Jill poked me. "*Right*, Willow?"

Willow. Geez. I didn't even get to pick my own name.

"It was a while ago," I said.

"But it *was* in Arizona," Lars said.

"I can't swear by it." I picked up my margarita. Everyone was staring at me. "It could have been Utah."

By the second round of drinks (anticipating my drive home, I had moved on to Sprite), Lars and Jill had given up on the irritated waitress, preying on the tourists at the next table, instead. Within twenty minutes, Bill and Marge McCloskey, down for a week from Minnesota, had elaborate driving instructions to "Kokopelli Beach" written on a series of cocktail napkins. Lars advised them to rent wet suits before heading out.

"I'm going to head home," I announced.

"So soon?" Lars asked.

"My head hurts." It did a bit—probably from hunger. I kept suggesting we order appetizers, while Lars and Jill, who had once again eaten enormous, matching lunches, maintained that the free chips and salsa were more than enough. Jill said she'd bring me lunch on Monday. I didn't believe her, somehow.

I had driven ten minutes away from the bar when I realized why I was so cold; I had left my cardigan at the table. I tried calling Jill, then Lars: no answer. I turned around in a strip mall parking lot and headed back. Maybe they'd have broken down and ordered appetizers by now. I'd kill for a plate of heaping nachos.

They weren't at our table, which had been taken over by a lovey-dovey couple sucking face. All I could see from across the crowded room was the woman's long, blond hair. As I crept closer, I spied my black sweater, still draped across the back of my chair. They probably wouldn't even notice me taking it. I tried not to be too obvious looking at them—public displays of affection have always made me squirm—but I couldn't help but glance up just as I reached the table.

"Oh!" I said.

Jill and Lars pulled out of their embrace. Good God, what were they trying to pretend this time?

But then they looked at me, and I knew. How could I have missed it?

"We've been meaning to tell you," Jill said, holding Lars's hand. Lars said nothing.

twenty-five

Jill just didn't get it. "We didn't want you to get hurt," she kept saying, standing at the edge of the amphitheater. It was Saturday—opening night—and I had just arrived, even though the play was due to start in twenty minutes. I was over an hour late, but responsibility be darned: I was determined to avoid Jill and Lars as long as possible. My cell phone had been turned off since the night before.

"You made me look like a fool," I said. "All that stuff about Lars checking out Neil Weinrich's shoulders?"

"Oh, come on. That was funny—you've got to admit it."

"Actually, I don't."

"Natalie, please. We value you as our friend." *Our* friend.

"Friends don't lie to each other," I said.

Cody came rushing over, his face flushed. His black T-shirt read, STAGE CREW. It hung long and loose over his blue jeans. "Miss Quackenbush! Do you have the colored water?"

"The what?"

"The colored water! That we need to use for the beer!"

"I forgot it," I said unapologetically.

"But what are we going to do?" he squeaked. "We don't have time to get anything else!"

"Deal with it!" I snapped. "Just use plain water or Coke—isn't it supposed to be Coke now, anyway?"

"You shouldn't project your anger onto the students," Jill said once Cody had left.

There was a seat reserved for me, front row center, right next to Lars (who was right next to Jill), but I ignored it. I trudged up the amphitheater's hard concrete steps, my eyes darting around for an empty spot.

Mrs. Clausen was there with a stylish-looking older woman. "Natalie!" she said, reaching out to give my hand a squeeze. "You must be so excited for the kids!" She gestured to the older woman. "Mom, I'd like you to meet Natalie Quackenbush, one of our newer teachers. Natalie, this is my mother, Lavinia Schroeder."

Mrs. Schroeder smiled at me. Her teeth were yellow but straight, her lipstick the perfectly bright shade of pink to set off her royal blue suit. Her white hair looked professionally styled. Her faded blue eyes were surrounded by friendly crinkles. Mrs. Clausen would look just like her in twenty-five years.

"My mother is visiting for Thanksgiving," Mrs. Clausen told me.

"Enjoy your stay," I said, feeling as if I had been hit in the stomach. Thanksgiving was next week. I'd planned on spending it with Jill and Lars. Now I had no one.

I finally spotted an empty seat near the top of the amphitheater—behind Robert, no less. "Hey," I said, sliding in.

"Hey." He glanced at his friends, cleared his throat and sat up straighter. His two friends were taking up more than their share of room on the bench. One had iPod buds in his ears and was grooving his head in time to music that I could only hope he had downloaded legally. The other sat hunched over a beeping Game Boy, which emitted gunfire and explosion sounds every ten or fifteen seconds.

"Excuse me," I said, tapping the boy's shoulder.

"Huh?" He sat up and blinked at me, as if I had awakened him from an especially deep slumber.

"Your Game Boy. You're going to have to turn it off once the play starts."

"Oh. Yeah. Sure."

There was no curtain to rise on the amphitheater stage. Instead, the students made their entrances from behind a fake wall that had been set up for the occasion.

Robert's friend with the iPod strained his neck to look at the first scene. "Where's the girl in her underwear?" he whispered, far too loudly (as far as I could tell, he hadn't turned the music off).

"Shhh!" Robert scowled at him and crossed his arms.

I leaned forward. "No girls in underwear tonight. That part's been cut."

The iPod boy did his best to avoid my gaze. Robert blushed and smiled a little, looking relieved; perhaps he didn't want his friends to see a half-dressed Katerina after all.

Watching the play made me more nervous than I expected. I held my breath when Ralph stumbled over a line, finally exhaling when Katerina rescued him. I had seen the play so many times that it took me an instant to realize what was going on when Katerina strode onstage in her negligee. The kids were performing the original, uncensored version of the play.

"That's not underwear. That's just pajamas," Robert's iPod friend said.

"Huh?" The Game Boy friend looked up. (He'd resumed playing but had turned the sound off. I pretended not to notice.)

Katerina tossed back her long hair. "If my mother catches you, she'll kill us both," she told Ralph.

There was murmuring throughout the audience. I half stood in my seat, trying to see Lars's face. All I could see was his flippy blond hair. As angry as I was, I still felt sorry for him. How could the kids go over his head like that?

No one yelled with outrage. Claudia's mother didn't pop up and demand a halt to the action. Dr. White didn't orate. The scene finished with an implication of Jules's deflowering, and the show went on.

After the actors took their bows, they gestured to Lars to join them on stage. He scurried up. I expected him to look nervous, to scan the crowd for Dr. White, but he had such a set, victorious look on his face that I knew: the kids hadn't rebelled on their own. Lars had told them to.

Lars scanned the crowd. A couple of the kids called out, "Miss Quackenbush!" I slid further in my seat, hiding behind tall Robert and his backward baseball cap. The moment passed. The kids on stage forgot about me. They bowed one last time before filing off behind the artificial wall.

I finally turned my cell phone on Sunday morning. As expected, there were a slew of messages from Jill. I deleted them without listening.

There was a voice mail from Jonathan. My heart pounding, I punched in the necessary numbers until I heard his voice filtered through the phone's tinny earpiece.

"Hi. It's me. Jonathan. About that internship. I have this friend, her name is Suzette Doherty, and she's a caterer. She's built up a good business—lots of corporate clients, fund-raisers, she does weddings, the whole deal. Anyway, I talked to her, and she said she could do the internship thing starting Monday." He gave me her business address and phone number. He didn't tell me to call him back.

I called him, anyway. "I got your message. Thank you."

"You're welcome." Silence. "I think I left all the information you'll need on your voice mail."

"Okay, thanks. I-I appreciate your helping me."

"I just wanted to help the kid."

"You are."

"Suzette will be expecting you on Monday. I hope it works out."

After I got off the phone, I spent the next half hour picturing Suzette. Why couldn't her name be Marge? Or Fran?

Suzette.

My only hope was that years of sampling cream sauces had taken their toll.

twenty-six

She looked like a Suzette. She wasn't that much taller than me—maybe five foot six to my five foot two—but she was one of those women who appears taller than she is due to ideal proportions and perfect posture. Her blond hair was slicked back into an artful ballerina bun. Perfectly arched eyebrows framed black-lashed, bright green eyes. She wore simple catering clothes: tailored black pants, a white blouse and a chef's apron, her only adornment tiny pearl earrings set against the backdrop of perfect pink lobes. I snuck a peak at her left hand, hoping in vain for a twinkling diamond and a band of gold. But no: unless she had taken off her rings to knead some dough, Suzette was available.

"I'm Natalie," I said. "And this is Robert."

"Yes, of course!" She held out her hand. Robert blinked for a moment's indecision and then shook hands like a grown up. Suzette smiled. "Jon told me *all* about you."

Jon? Since when did anyone call him Jon?

"We really appreciate your jumping in on such short notice," I said. I should have worn my red shirt, I thought. I look good in red.

"Don't be silly!" Suzette said. "I'd do anything to help Jon. Besides, I could really use the help."

Celebrations by Suzette was housed in a dated strip mall not far from Old Town Scottsdale. From the outside, it could have been a dry cleaner's: dingy stucco, a big, unadorned window, a cracked concrete sidewalk. Step inside, though, and you were transported to Paris. Well, almost. The front room was tiny, with a cluster of marble-topped bistro tables and wrought iron chairs. Tiny vases held Gerber daisies. Along the walls, murals depicted a French street scene: *la boulangerie, la fromagerie, la charcuterie.*

When I told Suzette I had some forms for her to sign, she told us to sit at one of the tables, then she disappeared behind a swinging door. The wrought iron, though pretty, felt hard on my back. The marble tabletop was icy. I opened my bag and fished out the forms. "This is so cool," Robert whispered.

"What?" Oh, right. I was here for Robert. "Yes. Very cool."

"And Suzette seems really nice."

"She does." My pen didn't work. I threw it back into my bag and dug around until I found another one. Purple ink. It would have to do.

Suzette reappeared with a Guy Buffet tray awash in pretty pastries and demitasse cups. "I thought you might be hungry."

"Not really," I said. I was starving. "But I'll try a bite or two."

She delicately unloaded the demitasse cups onto the table. "Do you like espresso?"

"Are you kidding me?" Robert said. "Suzette, you totally rock."

After signing the necessary forms, Suzette gave us a tour of her gleaming chrome kitchen: the giant mixers, the prep counters, the commercial oven. A few staff members bustled about, happily stirring, sautéing and using words like "brochette." Without exception, and even in their drab kitchen attire, the staff looked hipper than I, with creative piercings, whimsical jewelry and colorful hair streaks.

Robert chattered nonstop about Suzette as we drove back to school in my Civic. I did my best to ignore him, but words like "cool," "awesome," and "totally rocking" kept sneaking into my consciousness.

Robert couldn't wait to go back. He couldn't wait to take inventory. He couldn't wait to use the giant mixers. He couldn't wait to spend more time with Suzette. I felt like a divorced mother whose son had developed a crush on his father's new girlfriend.

I dropped Robert at his little orange car; the final bell had just rung. He gave me the biggest smile and a huge wave as he drove away, and I felt, at last, grateful to Suzette. She was exactly what Robert needed. From all appearances, she was responsible, upbeat, successful—everything anyone could want in a mentor. Or in a girlfriend. I thought of Jonathan. Jon.

I hated her.

Nicolette was at my desk. I had asked her to cover for me and had left her my lesson plans. The last class had been Adventures. We were reading *The Red Badge of Courage*. Marisol and a couple of the other girls were still in the classroom, clustered around Nicolette. They never hung around after the bell when I was teaching. When I was teaching, they poised their fingers above their cell phones as the second hand on the clock made its final journey to dismissal time.

Marisol was sitting on my desk, her back to me. "Miss Badanski, this is like, the best class I have ever had. Ever. It was so totally not boring. You should so totally become a teacher."

"Thanks, Marisol." Nicolette spotted me and smiled. "But I'm not half as fab a teacher as Miss Quackenbush. And, by the way, it's not Miss Badanski anymore, it's Mrs. Muntz."

"Oh, right, that's, like, so totally cool that you got married. Can I see your ring?"

As I approached the desk, the girls scattered. I felt like one of those big U-shaped magnets that shoots away oppositely charged filings. "Thanks, Nicolette. *The Red Badge of Courage* worked out okay?"

"Nah." She waved dismissively. "I hated that book in high school. What I read of it, anyway. It's a total guy book. We talked about character and motivation, just like the lesson plan said, but instead of *The Red Badge of Whatever*"—here she paused for dramatic effect—"we talked about *Veronica Mars*."

"I haven't read that."

"It isn't a book, it's a TV show. But it's, like, got so much more character and motivation than that guy book. It was perfect. The class was totally into it."

I took a deep breath: let it go. "Anyway, I hope I didn't get you in any trouble. Or that I didn't get in any trouble," I added as an afterthought.

"We're not the ones in trouble," she murmured. "Staff meeting in the cafeteria. Starting . . ." She paused to look up at the clock. "Now. You'd better get down there. I'll lock up."

Dr. White was wearing her black suit again, this time with a bright yellow shirt. If I wore something like that, I'd look like a bumblebee. The meeting had already begun. As I slipped onto a cafeteria table bench, Dr. White was saying, ". . . one of the most difficult personnel decisions I've ever had to make. Mr. Hansen has proven himself to be a talented teacher, and I'd looked forward to watching him grow both personally and professionally. However, Saturday's action was an act of pure insubordination, not just toward me, but toward the school board, the PTA and the superintendent."

I scanned the room: no Lars. What were they going to do to him, anyway? Take away his drama responsibilities? Stick him with the slow kids? If Lars had tenure, he could perform ritual animal sacrifices without any significant consequence. But, like me, he was a relatively new teacher, and so, while it seemed unlikely, he could be—

"Terminated." Dr. White's voice broke through my fog. I gasped. No one else did—but then, they'd been here all afternoon, so maybe this wasn't news.

I heard the cafeteria door swing shut and turned just in time to see Jill's blond hair as she scurried out.

Mrs. Clausen came over to me after the meeting. "Such a loss," she said, shaking her head.

"Lars was a really good teacher. His students will miss him." Talking about him like this made him sound like he was dead. Still, deep within me I felt a hint of selfish relief: I'd still have to face Jill at school, but I wouldn't have to live with Lars's smirky blond presence anymore.

As we walked out of the cafeteria, Mrs. Clausen talked about the impact Lars's dismissal would have on the English department. When we reached our cars, she reopened a wound. "Do you have any plans for Thanksgiving?"

"Thanksgiving? Oh, right. That's coming up, isn't it? It'll be nice to have the time off, to catch up on work and everything."

"But what about dinner? If you don't have any plans, Alan and I would love to have you join us."

I blinked up at Mrs. Clausen, awed by her generosity of spirit.

"Can I make a pie?" I asked.

twenty-seven

Robert made the pie. It was pumpkin mousse in a gingersnap crust. He wanted to top it with meringue, but I told him that would be gilding the lily—at which point I had to explain what "gilding the lily" meant.

He gave it to me on Wednesday afternoon, when I stopped off at Celebrations by Suzette. The little vases in the front room held marigolds. Suzette wore a burgundy shirt under her chef's apron. Her blond hair was mussed in an oddly sexy way, little tendrils escaping down the back of her neck, as if she had just snuck off for an afternoon romp.

"You must be busy," I said.

"I *am*, but I *love* it." She smoothed her hair, to no avail. A flour smudge sat below her right eye, making it seem even greener. "Robert has been amazing. He made eleven pies today!"

He grinned at her. "Twelve." (The twelfth was mine, I guessed.)

"The apples are mine, though," she said. "Old family recipe. It's Jon's absolute favorite."

I felt like I'd been punched in the stomach. "So . . . are you, will you be seeing Jonathan tomorrow?"

"Of course! Jon, Jack, Krista—the whole crew. You've heard about Krista, haven't you?" She shook her head. "Poor thing."

"Um, no." I didn't want to hear about Krista. I wanted to hear about "Jon." Then again, maybe I didn't. "What happened?"

"She lost the baby. Breaks your heart."

As I rang the doorbell to the Clausens' tidy ranch house, I tried not to think about Suzette. Or about Krista. But mostly, I tried not to think about Jonathan and his love of apple pies.

The Clausens lived in Arcadia, a little slice of Southern California at the base of Camelback Mountain. Instead of cactus and gravel, orange groves and bright green lawns softened the winding streets and gentrified older homes. ("Older" being a relative term; in Arizona, anything built before 1980 was considered "older," while anyone born after 1960 was considered young.) The Clausens' house was beige with cranberry trim. A harvest wreath graced the front door.

Mr. Clausen opened the door. He was tall and wiry, with a shiny pate and gold-rimmed glasses. I couldn't remember his first name.

"Happy Thanksgiving, Mr. Clausen. Thank you for inviting me." The air smelled of roasting turkey and slow-cooked vegetables. Suddenly, I missed my parents.

"Happy Thanksgiving to you, Natalie! But please, call me Alan." He held out his hands for Robert's pie. "Have you met Paul?"

Paul and I stared at each other. He had on the same black silk shirt he'd worn on our aborted date. His hair was a little longer. He was better looking than I remembered. My face grew warm.

Suddenly, he smiled. "We've met a couple of times, actually." He held out his hand, and we shook like business acquaintances. Rethinking mid-shake, he squeezed my hand and leaned forward for a brief, friendly hug. "I've been meaning to call you," he said as we walked into the living room. "To apologize."

"I'm the one who should apologize. I never should have said those things to Michelle. They weren't true, anyway."

He waved it off. "Don't worry about it. I was taking myself way too seriously. It was funny, in a way."

At times, the future can flash before your eyes. And in that moment, my future looked something like this: Paul and I would sit next to each other at the dinner table and reminisce about Boston. After a glass of wine, we would tell the Clausens about our two blind dates. Everyone would laugh. Tomorrow—no, later that same evening—Paul would call to say he'd really enjoyed talking to me. Perhaps he could take me out for dinner sometime soon?

We would go to that Asian fusion place on Scottsdale Road. I would order the miso-marinated Chilean sea bass.

From then on, we would go out a few times a week. I would try the sushi at the Asian fusion place. It would be really good. I would start spending nights at Paul's tastefully furnished, centrally located apartment. Paul would turn out to be a wonderful cook. On Sundays, he would bring me breakfast in bed: bagels with cream cheese and smoked salmon.

When we'd been going out a year—no, make that six months—Paul would present me with a velvet box. As I smiled at the gleaming diamond inside (which would be a respectable one carat) and then at Paul (who was really, truly wild about me), my face would hurt and I'd feel sad, though I wasn't sure why.

I would slip the ring onto my finger. We would call our parents. My mother would say, "You know we like Paul. But are you sure he's *the one*?"

I would look across the room at Paul's steady, trustworthy face, blink, and say, "Yes, Mom. I'm sure."

A week or so later, when I'd grown used to wearing the ring (but before I'd received any engagement gifts that I'd have to ultimately return), I'd bump into Jonathan while buying organic produce at the Trader Joe's on Frank Lloyd Wright Boulevard. We'd stare at each other. He'd notice the ring, and his face would fall.

"I guess I always thought . . . never mind."

I'd touch his cheek, make him look me in the eyes. "What?"

"That you would never love another man the way you loved me."

"I never did," I'd whisper. My eyes would fill at the thought of hurting Paul. "I never could."

The jeweler would give Paul a full refund on the diamond.

The girlfriend ruined everything. "I don't think we've met," she said, joining us next to the Clausens' camelback sofa. She held out her right hand. Her left hand she planted firmly on the small of Paul's back. She couldn't have marked her territory more clearly if she'd peed on him.

Her name was Janet, and she was an accountant. She and Paul had met through their running club. She was originally from Minnesota and had one of those funny accents that over-emphasize the o's. Her straight brown hair angled down her face, resting at her collar. She was really, really skinny, with a long neck and a visible

Adam's apple. She started most of her sentences with: "Paul and I like to . . ."

"Paul and I like to run up there," she said when I told her I lived in North Scottsdale. "Some of the developments have nice running paths."

When Mr. Clausen—Alan—announced that dinner would be a little later than planned, Janet said, "Paul and I like to eat on the later side, anyway."

I wandered into the kitchen to say hello to Mrs. Clausen. The kitchen had sunny yellow walls and white appliances. Countless bowls, platters and cutting boards covered the blue-and-white tile countertop. Mrs. Clausen wore a flowered apron over a rust turtleneck and tan slacks. Her hair and makeup were perfect, of course, but her expression was worried. "I turned the oven off by mistake when I went to use the timer. Now the bird's going to be out an hour later than planned."

"Don't worry about it," I said. "Everyone's nibbling on the veggies and dip. Can I peel the potatoes?"

She rummaged through a drawer until she found a peeler. "That would be really helpful."

Dinner was served an hour and a half later than planned—at six-thirty rather than five. Outside the window, the orange trees looked black against the night sky. For dinner, in addition to the turkey and stuffing, there were mashed potatoes, rolls, broccoli, candied carrots and cranberry sauce. Janet had brought a yam casserole topped with marshmallows. "Would you like a roll?" I asked her, passing the basket.

"No, thank you. Paul and I are trying to limit our glutens."

Elderly Mrs. Schroeder sat on the other side of me. "Will you be staying in Phoenix for long?" I asked her.

"Oh, no, I hate Arizona!" she chuckled. "Never go there if I can help it. My husband, Larry, keeps trying to get me to move to Sun City, but I'm not budging. Have you met Larry?"

"No, I haven't."

"He'll be here any minute. He went out to get milk." I did a quick scan of the table. I wondered where Larry was going to sit.

Across from me, Paul was saying to Jeff, one of the Clausens' sons, "The trick is to bring twice as much water as you think you need. And to turn around before the sun starts getting hot." Jeff was in his last year of college, applying to medical schools. The Clausens' other son, who taught history to underprivileged seventh graders in Washington, D.C., was spending the holiday with his wife's family.

"Paul and I like to put in at least six miles on weekdays," Janet piped in. "More on the weekends. Last Sunday morning we were out of the house before five." So much for breakfast in bed.

"Janet hasn't run one marathon," Paul announced.

"We won't hold that against you," Jeff laughed.

Janet leaned forward and grinned. "That's true. I haven't run one marathon—I've run *three*. Paul, you are *so bad*."

"Aargh!" Mrs. Schroeder shrieked. Conversation stopped dead. "There's something wrong with the yam casserole! The marshmallows taste like dirt!" We all stared at the orange mound on her plate.

"Those aren't marshmallows," Janet said, blinking furiously. "It's tofu."

"*Why*? Why would you do that?" Mrs. Schroeder's eyes bugged out. Her hands shook.

"Paul and I like to limit our sugar intake," Janet murmured.

Mrs. Clausen stood up. "The casserole is delicious," she said firmly. "If you'll excuse me, I'm going to put the pies in the oven."

I snuck a peek at Mrs. Schroeder. She looked calmer, though her hands were still shaking a bit. I took a tiny bite of the yam casserole. She was right. It needed sugar.

"Are you from California?" Mrs. Schroeder asked me.

I checked her face. She was smiling pleasantly, all traces of irritation gone. "No, Massachusetts, actually."

She picked up her wineglass, took a tiny sip and put the glass carefully back in place. "How do you like California?"

"California? It's, um, nice, I guess. I've only been once."

"But you're here now!" She picked up her fork and took a delicate bite of the yam casserole. "Tasty," she said.

When we'd all finished eating, I ignored Mrs. Clausen's admonition to stay seated and started carting dirty china into the kitchen. Soon, the counter was covered with half-empty serving bowls, sticky wineglasses and china plates coated with large portions of uneaten yam casserole. "I'll deal with this mess later," Mrs. Clausen said once the table was clear. "Let's just serve the pies and get this over with." I'd never imagined Mrs. Clausen could be anything but composed. Tonight she looked downright twitchy.

"It's too bad your father couldn't be here tonight," I said, picking up a stack of dessert plates.

She stopped moving for a minute. "Natalie, my father couldn't be anywhere tonight. My father died thirteen years ago."

I took a deep breath. At some level, I'd known this. "Oh, I'm so sorry."

She sighed. "Don't be. My mother told you he'd gone out to get milk, didn't she?" I nodded. "Most of the time, she's okay. Or, at least not too bad. The medicines they've got these days—they're amazing. But the minute the sun goes down . . ." She shook her head. "She used to be so sharp. So charming. This disease—it takes the person away but leaves the body behind. It's cruel."

"I'm so sorry," I said again, overwhelmed by the inadequacy of my response.

She shrugged with resignation and then smiled sadly. "My mother had a lot of good years. I'm thankful for that." Then she drew herself up. "How are your parents doing? Are they holding up okay?"

"Yes," I said, swallowing hard. "They're healthy. Perfectly healthy."

"Good. Then appreciate them while you can. Now, let's get this dessert out there before my mother really loses it." Oven mitts on her hands, she picked up the pumpkin pie. "Robert didn't sneak any tofu in here, did he?"

Mrs. Clausen sent me home with a brown bag of leftovers: a bag of turkey, some rolls, and the last two pieces of pumpkin pie. "Let me help you with that," Paul said, taking the bag and walking me to my car. Janet had gone to "freshen up" before heading back to Ahwatukee. I unlocked my car doors and took the bag from Paul, placing it carefully on the front passenger seat and strapping it in.

He laughed. "Do seat belt laws apply to turkeys?"

I smiled back. "I don't know, but I'll be living off that food for days. I don't want it falling on the floor."

He stuck his hands in his pockets. "It was nice to see you again."

"You, too." I wrapped my arms around myself and shivered. It had been warm during the day, so I hadn't brought a jacket.

Paul tilted his head to the side. "Can I call you some time?"

"Um, sure," I said, trying to figure what he'd ever need to call about. "Why?"

He laughed nervously. "To, you know, see you."

"You mean, like—on a date?"

"Well, yeah."

I squinted at him. "You have a girlfriend."

His eyes flickered involuntarily back to the house. "Not really. We're just . . . friends. Well, more than friends. But we're just dating. It's not exclusive or anything."

"Does she know that?" I asked.

He was quiet for a minute. Then he sighed in irritation. "Just forget it," he said. "I thought you might be lonely. I was just trying to be nice." He turned and started back up the Clausens' front walk.

"Paul!" I called out. "Wait." He stopped and turned. I spoke clearly but not so loud that the neighbors would hear. "Just so you don't think I'm talking about you behind your back, I want you to know something. I think you're a jerk. And since you've probably found the only woman in the world who finds you interesting, you should probably stick with her."

My heart thudding, I strode around to the driver's side door and got in, shutting the door with a satisfying thud. As I drove away, I snuck a peek at the house, but Paul had disappeared inside. In the front window, though, the curtains were drawn back, and a pale face peered out at me. I wasn't sure, but I think I saw Mrs. Schroeder smile.

twenty-eight

I'd been awake for at least twenty minutes when Jill called. "Oh, sorry—did I wake you?"

"No, I was up." My froggy voice cracked a little.

"Go back to sleep—I'll call you later."

"*I was up*." I cleared some morning phlegm from my throat. I should never answer the phone before my first cup of coffee. I'd turn off the ringer in my room—but what if there was an emergency? What if Jonathan called?

Jill kept her voice light. "I just wanted to see if you had any interest in shopping. The day-after-Thanksgiving sales and all. I was thinking about checking out Fashion Place, though parking could be tough. There's always Nordstrom Rack if that doesn't work."

I checked the clock next to my bed: nine twenty. "No, thanks," I said.

"It would just be the two of us."

"*No, thanks.*"

Two cups of coffee later, I almost wished I'd said yes. Four days away from school had sounded like such bliss. I would watch movies, soak in the spa, sip my coffee at leisure. The problem was, I'd watched three movies since Wednesday, and if I drank any more coffee, my stomach would start to hurt. A few days ago, the idea of soaking in a spa alone had seemed indulgent, but now the reality struck me as pathetic.

I did some laundry, changed my bed, read *The Arizona Republic*. That took me almost to lunch. Finally, I came up with a plan. During the remaining three days away from work, I would, well—work. I was behind on my grading. I was behind on my planning. If I couldn't be happy, at least I could be productive. Unfortunately, I'd left a pile of ungraded essays in my classroom, along with my grade book. I had a key to my classroom, though; with any luck, the building would be open.

The road to school was almost eerily empty. Everybody must be at the mall. Maybe when my parents came back to town my mother and I would spend an afternoon at Fashion Place. I would splurge on cosmetics at whatever counter was offering a free gift. For lunch, we'd eat at Café Nordstrom.

At the first traffic light, I fished my cell phone out of my purse and dialed Shelly's number. My mother answered.

"Happy Thanksgiving plus one," I said. (My parents and I had traded messages the day before, but we'd never had a chance to talk.)

"Are you driving?" my mother asked. "You shouldn't use your cell phone when you're driving."

The light turned green. I pressed the accelerator. "There's hardly any traffic."

"There's always traffic in Scottsdale. It's getting to be like L.A."

"When have you ever been in L.A.?" I flicked on my blinker and began to change lanes. An SUV sped up to block me. "Jerk," I muttered, swerving back into my lane.

"What did you just say?"

"Nothing."

"Do you want to call me later? When we can talk?"

"I can talk now." The SUV passed me on the right. I slid in behind him.

"I have something to tell you." Her voice sounded serious.

Adrenaline flooded my head. I thought of Mrs. Schroeder. I thought of irony. Of cruel justice. "Is everything okay? You're not sick, are you?"

"Of course not. I'm fine. Your father's fine. It's Shelly we're worried about."

I thought of Krista. "Is something wrong with the baby?"

"No, the baby's fine. *He's* fine, I should say—we found out on Wednesday."

"A boy. Wow." The thought of a tiny penis growing inside my sister's womb seemed intimate and beautiful and grotesque all at once.

"But Frederick's not coming back," my mother continued, "and we don't think Shelly is up to doing this alone."

"Doing what? Giving birth?"

"Not just giving birth. Giving birth is the easy part. Taking care of a baby—feeding it, making a home. Natalie, your father and I have decided to move to Rhode Island."

A car horn blared. I realized too late that I had run a red light. I checked my mirrors frantically: no sign of a police car. My heart thudded in my chest and up through my throat.

"Natalie? Are you there?"

"I'm here," I said. "I'm still here."

I sat in the faculty parking lot for a good fifteen minutes. There were only two other cars in the lot, one of which I recognized as Dr. White's silver Ford Taurus. The other was a beat-up two-door sedan that probably belonged to a janitor. In front of me, the school building loomed blocky and anonymous, the spiky succulents in the landscaping making it seem even more forbidding. If I moved away, would I miss the school? Would I miss the woodpeckers in the saguaros, the lizards on the stones? Would I miss anyone? Would anyone miss me?

Moving was my mother's solution. "There are plenty of teaching jobs in Rhode Island." I couldn't see living in Rhode Island, but I could always go back to Boston. I still had some friends there, though others, like me, had moved away to start their "real lives." I had followed my parents West. I could follow them back East. At what time, though, would I stop following my parents and start leading my own life?

The front door was locked, but it didn't take long to find an open side door. Ahead of me, the corridor loomed long and empty. It looked like the setup for a slasher movie. If someone jumped out of a doorway and slit my throat, no one would hear me scream.

But there were no slashers at school today. Presumably, they had gone to the mall like everyone else.

The knob to my classroom turned before I'd even put in the key. Darn it. Nicolette had locked up; I should have told her to jiggle the knob. A glance through the glass panel told me that the room had been undisturbed, however: my stack of papers was in place, as were my tape dispenser and stapler. Really, there wasn't much in here worth stealing.

I pushed open the door. The smell hit me immediately. I stuck a hand over my nose. I stepped back into the corridor and stared at my classroom. Nothing seemed amiss. I crept in slowly, my hand still over my nose, my eyes darting around for the source of the odor. It seemed to be coming from my desk.

He'd left it on my chair: a Ziploc bag filled with feces, the top unzipped. The bag was one of those special holiday kind, a design of orange and yellow maple leaves trailing across the front. A perfect bag for holding pumpkin cookies or sunflower seeds. Or shit.

I had to get it out of there. I rummaged through my drawers until I found a plastic Safeway bag. I managed to get the Ziploc bag inside without touching it. I scurried down the hall and out the door, flinging the bag in a Dumpster. I stood there for a moment, just staring at the blue Dumpster, until I realized that I had left the door to my classroom open. Anyone could go in. Who knows: maybe someone was waiting in there now, had been waiting there since Wednesday. I flung open the school door and ran down the hall, breathing hard. The door to my room as still open. My tote bag lay untouched on my desk. Aside from the fluorescent lights buzzing overhead, the room was quiet. It stank.

The windows were sealed shut, eliminating any possibility of a cross breeze. There was some disinfectant cleaner and a rag in my desk. I doused the chair and rubbed furiously, even though nothing from the bag had spilled. Had the perpetrator spared me on purpose, or had he simply run out of time?

The perpetrator. I stared at the student desk in front of me, front row center. The perpetrator had a name.

I couldn't be expected to like all of my students equally. Or, to like some of them at all. Professionalism, however, dictated that I treat each student with respect.

Unless a student crossed a line.

I walked over to Jared's desk and stood there for a moment, as if I could conjure up his image. With a hissing noise, I spat. My saliva landed on the edge of his chair. The spit looked like venom to me. Like hatred. Like desperation. Without warning, my eyes filled. One tear, then another, dropped on Jared's desk like those first fat raindrops that fall seconds before a monsoon hits.

I wiped my eyes angrily on my sleeve. I grabbed the disinfectant and sprayed Jared's desk and chair. With the rag, I rubbed and rubbed until my tears were gone—along with my spit and any lingering essence of Jared. I rubbed and rubbed until the desk was just a piece of metal and wood.

twenty-nine

Monday morning I wore my charcoal gray suit and arrived at school five minutes before the first bell. That would allow me enough time to ensure there were no more surprises waiting in my classroom without forcing me to spend too much time thinking about what had happened on Friday.

Robert was sitting on the floor outside my room, talking on his cell phone. He glanced up at me, said, "Gotta go," folded up the phone and stuck it in his pocket. He scowled.

"What?" I said. I yanked on the doorknob. It didn't give. I relaxed somewhat, fished keys out of my bag and stuck them in the lock.

"I've been here twenty-five minutes."

"Did we have an appointment?" I did a quick scan of the room. It looked fine. More important, it smelled fine.

Robert heaved himself off the floor. "It's *Monday*."

I looked up at him—way up. He must've grown an inch since

the school year began. "Last Monday you said you didn't have time to meet before school," I said evenly. "Same with Tuesday and Wednesday."

"But I didn't say it about *today*." He shoved his hands into his pockets and trailed me into the room. Now that the weather had turned cooler, Robert had traded his basketball shorts for athletic pants that made *whooshing* noises when he walked. "Over the weekend, you know, when I was working and stuff, Suzette and me were talking about school and stuff, and she said it's really important that I graduate."

"*Suzette and I*," I interrupted.

Robert rolled his eyes. "Right. Whatever. Anyway, Suzette said maybe I could go to cooking school someday, but they're gonna want to see how I did in high school. Plus, she said it's important when talking to clients to sound, you know, educated. And to be able to write notes and letters without making any mistakes."

"Those are all good points," I said, not adding that I'd made them countless times before he'd ever even met Suzette.

"So, anyway, I got up extra early today, and I remembered my notebook and everything, and you weren't even *here*."

I dropped my bag on my desk. "Look, Robert. I have over a hundred students. I have no personal life and I hardly ever sleep. If you want to come in for extra help, great—let's set a time, and I'll be here. But I'm not going to get up an hour early and drag myself over here on the off chance you might show up."

"Forget it," he said, heading back out the door. "I'll just hire a tutor."

"You don't have to do that," I said.

"I wouldn't want to take up any more of your precious time," he said, slapping the door frame on the way out.

* * *

The day didn't get much better. My first class was Freshman Honors. Over the break, they had finished *Lord of the Flies*. Jared sat in his assigned seat, front row center, and stared at me with his reptilian eyes. I stood next to my desk, wondering which was worse: to sit in the chair, knowing what Jared had placed there, or to stand up the whole time and give Jared the satisfaction of knowing that he had frightened me.

I pulled the chair out from behind my desk and dragged it to the front of the classroom, creating a shrieking sound that caused several students to moan and cover their ears. "How about we do something a little different today," I said. "You're probably sick of hearing me talk." I smiled. Claudia smiled back, even laughed a little. Claudia's suck-up reflex was flawless. "I'd like to give someone else a chance to lead the discussion." I glared at Jared. He glared back. "Jared. Why don't you take a seat up here? In my chair."

He pulled himself out of his seat and slithered over to my chair, slipping onto it without hesitation. He was nothing if not cold-blooded.

"Jared. Tell us this. What part of the book did you find most compelling?" I kept my voice even, unemotional.

"You mean, what part did I like?"

"Sure. Or what you found the most interesting." I'd be shocked if Jared had even finished the book. I expected him to comment on the cover or to proclaim total ignorance with a sick kind of pride.

"I liked the part where they kill the fat kid."

"Piggy?" I said.

"Yeah. Where the boulder hits him and stuff. That part was really funny."

The palms of my hands were sweaty. My armpits, too. "Most people," I said, "most people don't find that part funny." After three months of talking to the kids about the subjective nature of literature, I had backed myself into a corner. Jared's opinion wasn't wrong; it was simply unusual. Which meant that Jared wasn't a raging sociopath; he was just an original thinker.

"Cody," I said, abandoning the idea of letting Jared lead the discussion. "What about you? What was your favorite part of the book?"

"I didn't . . ." He mumbled something I couldn't hear.

"Excuse me?"

"I didn't read it."

I blinked at him. "Why not?"

"I just didn't."

"None of it?"

"No."

I closed my eyes for a moment and sighed in exasperation. "Okay. Cody, you get a zero for today and for every day until you finish your reading. Let's move on. Sarah? What were your thoughts on *Lord of the Flies*?"

"I had an orchestra concert," she mumbled.

"Excuse me?"

She kept her eyes on her desk, her voice low. "I had an orchestra concert. I play the clarinet, and I had a solo, so I had to practice. But I'll finish the book tonight, I promise."

I snatched my grade book off my desk. "And a zero for Sarah, too. Anyone else?"

* * *

During my first free period, I went to talk to Dr. White about Jared. She was on the phone when I knocked on her door, but she held up a finger to let me know she'd be off in a moment, finally ending the conversation with, "Yes, yes, I understand your concerns." Dr. White had a knack for understanding people's concerns without actually agreeing with them.

I sat down in one of the two chairs on the far side of Dr. White's desk. Like Jill, Dr. White had enough chairs for one (truant, anti-social, drug-addicted or otherwise self-destructive) student and for his or her (failed) parent. The principal's office was surprisingly stylish for a school: black laminate desk, stainless steel chairs, potted succulents. Student art framed on broad white mats hung on pumpkin-colored walls.

When she hung up the phone (which was silver and looked really cool on her black desk), she smiled and leaned forward. "I'm glad you're here. I need to talk to you."

"You do?" Was she going to fire me? Effective when? What kind of unemployment check could I hope to draw?

"You know about Lars, of course." She stopped smiling.

"I do."

"It was a shame. And we're going to miss him. But we have to move on."

I nodded. I had no idea what she was getting at.

She looked me straight in the eye. "I'd like you to take over the drama program."

"Me? I'm—I'm honored, but the truth is, I don't know anything about drama."

She shrugged. "Neither does anyone else around here. At least you have some experience from the last play."

"Lars did everything, really. I mean, I helped the kids run their lines, rounded up some props—that's about it. I couldn't direct or anything."

"Natalie." She sat back in her chair. "I understand how you feel. But this isn't Broadway. This isn't even off-off-off-Broadway. You'll be fine."

I opened my mouth to protest further, but then I shut it. That was that, and I knew it. Dr. White wasn't asking me to take over the drama program. She was telling me to. At Agave, each teacher had to take responsibility for at least one extracurricular program. Drama was intimidating, but it could be worse. I could get hit with detention duty, parking lot patrol or the knitting club.

"Now that we've got that settled, what did you want to talk to me about?"

I blinked at her. Oh, right. The bag o' poop.

"It's about Jared Spitzer," I said. "There was—an incident. Over the weekend." I took a deep breath. "I came in on Friday to pick up some work, and I found a bag of feces on my desk chair."

She stared at me. "Human feces?"

"I don't know. I didn't look that closely."

"In a paper bag?"

"Plastic. A baggie. The zipper kind, with a holiday decoration—maple leaves." She looked at me, awaiting more information. "It was a freezer bag. One quart." There. I'd said it. Now the security crew could go find Jared and haul his butt off to reform school.

She asked how he had gotten into the room. I explained that the lock was a little funny, that you had to pull on it a certain way or it didn't catch. I didn't mention that Nicolette had locked up for me. I didn't want to get her in trouble. Besides, I wasn't really supposed to ask Nicolette to take over my class. I was supposed to go through the "approved channels," which basically meant talking to the vice principal, who would then talk to Dr. White, who would then talk to Dawna, who would then tell Nicolette to take over my class.

"How do you know it was Jared?" she asked.

"I just know," I said after a pause. "I can tell by the way he looks at me. Like, like he hates me."

"We need something more than that," she said softly. "What did you do with the bag? If we give it to the police, they can probably get some fingerprints off it."

"I threw it away."

She stared at me. "Why?"

Why? Because it repulsed me. Because it mocked me. Because it made me feel despised, like a failure. I cleared my throat. "I didn't think we'd need it."

She fluttered her eyes in exasperation. "Don't you ever watch *CSI*?"

My throat hurt from withholding a sob. "Is that a TV show?"

She laughed, a deep, rich sound. "Oh, Natalie, you're working too hard. I'm sorry this happened, and if we could catch the kid who did it, he'd be in deep—well, you know." She smiled wryly. "But without any kind of evidence, we can't just assume it was Jared. Keep your eyes open. If he does something again, we'll be ready."

"Does something again?" My heart sped up. The possibility hadn't even occurred to me.

I ate lunch with Neil Weinrich. As if that weren't pathetic enough, I was actually glad to have his companionship. He caught my eye when I walked into the faculty dining room. Jill was sitting with a couple of the history teachers. She looked up when I walked in the door; I looked away. I felt so pathetic, standing there alone with my insulated lunch bag while all the voices around me echoed off the cinderblock walls and the cold tile floors. There were kids who felt like that, kids for whom lunchtime was a daily torture. There's something peculiar about working with adolescents. Even as you have to be more mature than the average adult—more dignified, less easily amused, a better role model—you can't help but fall into adolescent patterns. Who's cool? Who's not? Where do I fit in? Maybe it's a case of osmosis. All those hormones. All those insecurities. You can't help but be affected.

Neil Weinrich was sitting with a few other math teachers. Generally, math and English teachers don't mix much, but Neil flashed me a yellow-toothed smile. I smiled back, questioningly, until he motioned for me to join him.

"Hello, Miss Quackenbush," he said as I placed my lunch bag across from him. "Do you know Miss Rothstein and Mr. Smith?"

"Call me Natalie." They smiled but didn't tell me to call them by their first names. Miss Rothstein was about my age, with a plain face and a pear-shaped body. She wore a pale pink blouse with navy, pleated trousers, demonstrating even less fashion sense than I had. A small diamond sparkled on her left hand.

"Pretty ring," I said. "Congratulations."

"Thanks." She didn't smile.

"When's your wedding?"

"June eleventh. We wanted April, but we couldn't get the hall until then."

"Hotel rooms will be cheaper," Mr. Smith said. "Your guests will thank you." He picked up a tiny carton of milk and took a swig. A line of white liquid dribbled down his chin. He wiped it off with the back of his hand.

Miss Rothstein scowled. "Nobody's thanking me. Everybody keeps saying, why can't you just do it when it's cool outside? Why can't you get married someplace with normal weather? Brad— that's my fiancé—said his brother's wife told him she isn't even coming. She said she can't take the heat. Brad says you just have to let people do what they're going to do and not let it get to you." With a plastic fork, Miss Rothstein stabbed at her Tupperware bowl full of salad: lettuce, cucumber, radish, tomato. No meat. No cheese. No dressing. Miss Rothstein had a wedding dress to fit into. I pitied her students. As a rule, hungry women are not nice people.

I asked a few more questions about Miss Rothstein's wedding. ("Just one attendant—my sister;" "Maui;" "Pachelbel's Canon;" "chicken, salmon or portobello mushrooms in case someone's a vegetarian. But the only vegetarian I know of is Brad's brother's wife, and now she says she's not even coming.") The men chewed their lunches without expression—unless "complete and utter boredom" can be considered an expression. Finally, Neil interrupted a discussion of shoe-dying (which Miss Rothstein and I agreed was so twentieth century) to say, "Miss Quackenbush, have you performed your student's on-site evaluation yet?"

"Huh?" I articulated. Then, remembering (oh, yeah) Neil had once said something (that I had ignored) about observing Robert at work and providing an evaluation. "I've performed the site visit," I said (I had stopped by Suzette's to pick up the pumpkin pie, after all), "but I haven't filled out the form." (Where had I put that stinkin' form, anyway?)

"So, you've been on a catering assignment?"

"Uh, no. But I've seen him working in the kitchen. The boy can make a mean pie, I'll tell you that much."

Neil scrunched up his face, pretending to think, pretending to consider letting me get away with my half-assed evaluation, until—no. That wouldn't do. He had standards, after all. "I'm sooooorry, Miss Quackenbush," he said, looking genuinely pained. Or at least like he was trying to look genuinely pained. "But I must insist that you visit your student on site."

"On . . . what site?"

"Well, he's working for a caterer, isn't he? So you should observe him at a catering site."

"Oh. Okay." That meant I'd have to call Suzette.

"We couldn't get the caterer we wanted," Miss Rothstein interjected. "For our wedding."

"No?"

"She was booked until August."

thirty

As luck would have it, Robert was working a party later that week—a holiday cookie exchange, Suzette informed me when I called her. I paused, trying to figure out where a caterer would fit into such an event. "But I thought the point of a cookie exchange was for people to bake."

Suzette laughed. "In our mothers' day, people had time for that sort of thing. Most of my clients, though, they lead such busy lives—juggling family, careers and volunteer work—that they no longer have time to bake. This way, they can enjoy an afternoon among friends and leave with an assortment of home-baked goods without having to waste a day slaving in the kitchen."

Suzette sounded like she was reading from a brochure. Perhaps she was.

To reach the party, I had to bypass a gatehouse. Unlike Robert's, this one wasn't just for show. "And what is the name of the family you are visiting?" the security attendant asked, his eyes narrowing at my dusty Civic.

"Um, I don't actually know. I just have the address." The wrought iron gate ahead of me remained firmly closed. I shifted in my seat. I really had to pee.

He picked up a phone, his eyes never leaving my face, and punched in some numbers. "A Miss . . . Quackenbush is here to see you?" After a pause, he covered the mouthpiece. "I'm sorry, but they're not expecting you," he told me.

I sighed in exasperation. "Just tell them I'm with the caterer."

His face lit up. "Why didn't you say so in the first place?"

The house was big. No, that's not right. My parents' house was big. This house was huge. Looming. Impressive. It was taupe stucco with a coral-colored tile roof. The yard was landscaped with pink gravel, mesquite and paloverde trees, cacti and succulents. In short, it looked like every other house in the Valley of the Sun, only bigger.

The woman who answered the door was neatly dressed in a white polo shirt and khaki pants. Her hair was black and shiny, her skin a light brown. A small child clung to her legs. "Mrs. Meyers?" I asked (the gatekeeper had told me her name once he'd established I was part of "the help").

She smiled shyly and shook her head. "No, missus. She back there." She motioned beyond the vast living room with its mile-high ceilings. "In the *cucina*."

"*Gracias*," I said, following the warm, sweet, buttery smells.

The kitchen was bigger than any apartment I had ever lived in. It had one of those built-in fridges that blends in with the cabinets, all done in a distressed red finish (which was a lot more attractive than it sounds). The countertops and islands (there were two, one of which held a commercial-grade stove) were brown granite, the floors a wide-plank wood that was as handsome as it was impractical. Around the kitchen—in the display nooks, on the shelves, on top of the cabinets (which allowed plenty of room due to yet another towering ceiling)—were brightly colored Mexican objects: enormous vases, donkey statues, woven baskets.

Jill would kill for this kitchen, I thought involuntarily. Instead, it belonged to a woman who didn't even bake her own cookies.

The women were congregated on the far end of the kitchen—in what would be called a great room if there weren't an acre-sized living room on one side and, most likely, a family room somewhere beyond. The women were blond beyond statistical probability, mostly thin, clad in skirts and trousers that draped just so. They favored short-sleeved, form-fitting turtlenecks and gold jewelry.

I spotted Robert immediately (not hard, since he was the only male there). He wore a crisp white shirt and black trousers. He was taking a cookie sheet out of one of the ovens (there were three). "Mm," I said, walking over and gazing at the treats. "What are they?"

"White chocolate macadamia nut. With cranberries." He set the tray down on the countertop and pulled off his oven mitts. "It was my idea to bake them here. Suzette was going to just have me bring over the trays and pass them out. I've got ten different kinds of dough here." A timer dinged. He stuck the mitts back on and headed for another oven.

"No, it's much better to bake them here." I was already writing his evaluation in my mind. Innovative thinker. Entrepreneurial spark. "The smells are heavenly." I was sucking up, perhaps too obviously. Robert and I had been cordial since our spat on Monday, but we hadn't really made up, even though I had twice offered to come in early. Maybe next week, he'd said.

Robert set the second cookie sheet on the countertop. "Mexican wedding cookies?" I asked.

"Close," he said. "Pecan sandies. The Mexican wedding cookies are out already."

"Where's Suzette?"

"At the office. She said she might stop by later. Bella is here." I looked back at the women clustered on and around the overstuffed sofas in the great-ish room. A twenty-something woman with dark, slicked-back hair flitted among them bearing a tray of cookie samples. She was dressed like Robert, in black slacks and a white shirt. I recognized her from Suzette's kitchen, but she had wisely removed her eyebrow stud for today's event.

A tall, slim woman with bright red hair came over. She wore a green velvet top and cream-colored trousers. "You must be Mrs. Quackenbush. I'm sorry I didn't know your name when they called from the gatehouse." She smiled warmly and held out her perfectly manicured hand. "I'm Belinda Meyers."

"Call me Natalie," I said, thinking: since you're, like, my age. "Thanks for letting me stop by." The doorbell rang. "Um, is there a bathroom I can use?"

The bathroom Belinda Meyers directed me to was occupied, so I wandered beyond the kitchen; in a house this size another bathroom couldn't be far. The room just beyond the kitchen was what a real estate agent would probably call a Billiards Room: a space entirely devoted to holding a pool table. A mounted television loomed in an upper corner; a slider led out to the backyard. I could see a boulder-rimmed swimming pool and spa, a built-in barbecue, a beehive fireplace, and views of the golf course. Of course, golf course views meant that golfers had corresponding views of the Meyerses in their bathing suits. No wonder Belinda stayed so thin.

Failing to discover a toilet off the game room, I continued down the hall past the office (his) and craft room (hers) until I hit the theater room. In the great-ish room there had been a big screen TV. Here there was a huge screen TV flanked by bookshelves. The carpet was oatmeal-colored and spotless. The tan sectional couch was so huge and hugged the curved walls so perfectly that it had to have been custom-made.

There were no books on the bookshelves, at least not that anyone would read (*Phoenix: A Pictoral History*; *A Day in the Life of Russia*; *Southwest Gardens*—you get the picture). This was where they kept their family photos, presumably so that they could gaze at them during commercials. Here was Belinda Meyers smiling on her wedding day, her red hair glowing against her veil, her older but still-handsome husband squeezing her shoulders and looking far too relaxed. Here was the small child I had seen earlier, leaning over a white picket fence. Here was the child during the same studio session, laughing on a rocking horse. Here were the three Meyerses dipping their toes in the ocean during some tropical vacation. And here, on a lower shelf, in a little frame, were two other children, older, guarded, not quite so cute. They were standing outside, the light glaring off their faces. They were squinting, their smiles forced. The girl looked to be on the verge of adolescence. Her sandy hair was long and falling in her face. Her legs looked too long for her body. The boy was a couple of years younger, his hair the same color—as if it couldn't decide to be brown or blond. He had a bit of roundness left to his cheeks. He leaned toward his sister as if looking for comfort.

Is this how it was for Jonathan, I wondered, a stray snapshot of him serving as the only regular presence in his father's life?

When I returned to the kitchen, Robert was cutting sugar

cookies into tiny, mouse-bite-sized pieces. "The ladies don't like to eat whole cookies," he explained.

"I'm proud of you," I blurted. "For how hard you're working. For the job you're doing."

He looked up at me, colored slightly, and smiled.

"Natalie?"

I turned around, and there she was, even blonder, thinner and better dressed than the other women in the room. "Krista?"

"How do you know Belinda?" she asked.

"I don't," I said. "I'm here for Robert." He flashed one of his luminous smiles and held out a cookie tray.

"No, thank you," she said, patting her concave tummy. I thought about her miscarriage. Robert whisked the tray off to the sofas.

"Robert is one of my students," I explained. "Doing a catering internship. I have to write an evaluation."

Krista's eyes widened. "Does Suzette know?"

"Of course." Then realization dawned. "He's not a prisoner, he's a high school student."

"You left the prison?"

I tried to think fast. I opened my mouth to say something about being scared off by the possibility of a riot, and then I shut it again. I shook my head. Stop, I thought. Stop. "I was never at the prison. It was just a story I made up. I'm a high school teacher."

"Ah," she said, leaving her mouth open for a moment as she let this information sink in.

"I thought Jonathan would have told you."

"Jonathan doesn't tell me much."

"I can't blame him for being angry," I said. "My friend and I— well, sort of my ex-friend—we did this thing where we'd meet guys in bars and make up stories. It was incredibly juvenile and twisted."

She laughed. "I used to do that."

"Really?"

"Everybody did. I mean, you've had a few cosmopolitans, you're feeling bored . . . I used to say I was a flight attendant. Or in the FBI Witness Protection Program because I'd ratted out a mob boss."

"One time we pretended to be polygamists."

She laughed. "If a guy's drunk enough, he'll believe anything."

My smile faded. "Jonathan wasn't even drunk, though. And I let it go on way too long."

She shrugged. "Yeah, you did. But Jonathan . . . I don't know. He's dated a lot of women, but with you, he was different . . . the way he looked at you, the way he talked about you." She smiled gently. "Jack and I thought you were a keeper."

"He's got Suzette now, though," I said miserably.

"Suzette? They dated a long time ago, but I don't think there's anything going on now."

"She came to Thanksgiving dinner," I whimpered.

"Thanksgiving? She didn't *come* to dinner—she *cooked* the dinner. Though I must admit, she lingered a little longer than was necessary."

"You mean, she was just there delivering the food?"

Krista's nose twitched. "Okay, it's pathetic, but I've never learned to cook a turkey. Or anything, for that matter."

"No, no—it's okay!" I brightened. "It's just, the way she's been talking about him, I thought there was something going on."

She shook her head. "As far as I know, there hasn't been anybody since you." She tilted her head to one side. "Maybe it'll still work out."

My shoulders sagged. "I lied to him. Repeatedly. That's no way to start a relationship."

Krista plucked a green bottle of Evian from a row on the counter and twisted it open. She took a swig and replaced the cap. "When I met Jonathan's father, I told him I'd only been married once." She wrenched the bottle cap off again and downed some more water.

"Was he angry when he found out?"

Her mouth still full of mineral water, she flicked her eyebrows in an approximation of a shrug and swallowed. "He didn't have the right to be. You see, he told me he'd never been married at all." She smiled wryly.

"So you were even."

"I suppose." She looked me straight in the eye. "Though you're right. It wasn't any way to start a relationship."

"I'm sorry about the baby," I blurted out.

Her eyes widened, and I instantly regretted bringing it up. But then her face softened, and she said, "Me, too. Though maybe it's for the best, at least as far as our marriage is concerned. Jack pretended to be thrilled, but he wasn't. He was just going along with it because he knew how much I wanted a baby."

"Was it because of his age that he was unhappy?" I asked indelicately. "Maybe he didn't want to be starting over when he already had a grown son."

"Oh, no—actually, I think he would have been happy to start over if it meant spreading his seed and buying a kind of genetic immortality. The thing was"—here she lowered her voice—"we had to use a donor."

"A donor?"

"Jack's boys don't swim the way they used to. The fertility specialist tried a few things, but I didn't want to waste any more time. I'm not getting any younger, you know. So I made a trip to the sperm bank, felt an immediate connection with donor one seventy three, and spent a romantic evening with a turkey baster."

"Did Jonathan know?"

"I don't think so. I certainly didn't tell him anything."

I plucked my own Evian bottle from the counter and twisted off the cap with a satisfying hiss. A turkey baster, I thought. "It's probably just as well you have your Thanksgivings catered," I said.

thirty-one

I didn't have to go in early to help Robert anymore because he had hired a tutor named Ladd. Ladd was twenty-two, one of Suzette's regular bartenders and, according to Robert, "one smart dude."

"I'd do it for free," I said.

"Yeah, but sometimes you get what you pay for," he said casually. I tried to take it as a joke, but it stung.

"Ladd knows everything about everything," Robert said. "History, philosophy, Scientology . . ."

"You mean science?"

He considered for a moment. "Yeah, maybe."

Maybe it was just the time of year, with everyone counting the days until Christmas vacation, but my students were uniformly apathetic and unreliable. I began to give my college prep kids five minutes at the end of every class to begin their homework because it seemed to increase the odds that they'd finish it later at home—or at the mall or at Starbucks or wherever they went after school. (Dogs no longer ate homework; now students showed up empty-handed because "my frappuccino spilled.") My honors students weren't much better. Even Claudia missed an assignment—though she did make it up a day later, employing an especially lovely font and attaching a note that said, "Sorry this is late! ☺ It won't happen again! ☺ Please don't mark me down!!! ☺ ☺ ☺"

Cody seemed to ignore his homework more often than not. "Is the work too hard for you?" I asked him after class one day, though he'd always been a capable student.

"Nuh-oh," he said in that way that teenagers do, as if "no" were a multi-syllabic word and you were a complete moron for asking a question in the first place.

Jared remained his usual disturbing, distracting, sociopathic self.

"Did you do your homework?"

"I don't know."

"You *don't know?*"

"I don't remember."

"Okay, then, you get a zero for the day." I leaned over my grade book and wrote a zero in the appropriate column.

"Oh, wait—now I remember. I did it." He smiled slowly, meanly—one of those mouth-only smiles that doesn't affect the eyes.

"Show me."

He opened up his blue binder, flipped to a tabbed section and pointed to his completed work. We held each other's gaze. He didn't blink. Around us, several students covered their mouths in a vain attempt to suppress laughter.

"Okay, then." Ballpoint pen in my sweaty hand, I wrote a check over the zero. I smiled at Jared (mouth only; no eyes). "Keep it up."

Jared was the only kid I knew who could piss me off by doing his homework.

Home was no refuge. In the garage was an enormous white real estate sign: MARJORIE WAMSLEY, FRYE REALTORS, WE WORK FOR YOU! The sign sported an enormous picture of Marjorie that had to be fifteen years old. She still wore her hair in the same lacquered blond pageboy, but her mouth had begun to droop around the corners, and her eye shadow lodged in the creases on her eyelids. She possessed a seemingly endless wardrobe of black blazers in various lengths, all intended to cover her late middle-aged spread. Marjorie had helped my parents buy this house. Now she would help them sell it. From a real estate agent's standpoint, my parents' geographic indecision was a dream come true.

The house wouldn't go on the market until January. Marjorie said nobody buys houses during the holidays. She also said that homes sell best when they exhibit a "neutral yet inviting décor." In other words, Boston-meets-*Bonanza* had to go.

When I got home from work that day, Marjorie was in the living room, sitting on the couch with a scrawny blond woman in tight white pants and a white turtleneck. "Natalie, I'd like you to meet Kim Standish. Kim is our stager."

Kim stood up and held out a hand. She looked like an egret. "Your parents have some lovely antiques."

"We're going to have to put them in storage," Marjorie said.

"The couches can stay," Kim assured me. "And all of the kitchen furniture. But the log bed in the guest room . . ." Here she paused, trying to find just the right word.

I shrugged off my jacket. "I think it's hideous."

Kim brightened. "So we're on the same page."

Not really. My page was entitled "Ditch the Kitsch," while Kim's read, "Remove Half the Furniture and Put the Other Stuff at Weird Angles." That was after packing away all of the family pictures and my mother's Hummels.

At my request, Kim didn't take any furniture out of my room, though I obligingly stashed my hairbrush, cosmetics and papers out of sight. There wasn't a lot to remove, anyway, just the matching blond wood bed, nightstand and dresser that I'd had since high school. In the sixteen months that I'd lived here, I had neglected to hang a single picture. Doing so would have seemed too permanent, somehow, like living with my parents wasn't just a pit stop on the way to my own life but rather a declaration of permanent dependence.

Kim changed all that. First she moved my bed to the corner, so it stuck out diagonally into the room. Then she transformed the space into a child's room. A boy child. She covered my bed with a stiff black-and-white spread that looked like cowhide. She stuck a black cowboy hat on the back of my bedroom door and plastered the walls with framed movie posters of cowboys and Indians atop speeding horses. A lasso affixed to one of the diagonal walls near the headboard struck me as unforgivably kinky.

Worst of all were the "special touches" Kim scattered throughout the house. In the master bath, perched next to the Jacuzzi tub, sat a champagne bottle, two flutes and a selection of bubble bath. An enormous bowl of oranges—propped next to a retro juicer and an empty glass pitcher—dominated the kitchen counter, while a half-completed game of backgammon sat on the coffee table. I felt like ghosts inhabited the house—clean, citrusy, game-playing ghosts.

* * *

Since I had no weekend plans, I ended the school week by assigning a rash of in-class essays. I would spend Saturday and Sunday thoughtfully critiquing the load, perhaps while soaking in a bubbly tub. The college prep kids had to compare and contrast any two characters from *Great Expectations*. The Adventures students were to write a persuasive essay on one of the following topics: 1. Why books are better than television; 2. Why chocolate is better than vanilla (or vice versa); or 3. Why the dress code should (or shouldn't) be abolished. I was reasonably certain they'd all choose the third topic (once I explained the meaning of the word "abolished"), but I threw in the others for good measure.

As for Freshman Honors, the in-class essay served as a final test for their *Lord of the Flies* unit. With a flash of unoriginality, I instructed the students to choose one character and explain how he dealt with the Three Big Conflicts: man versus man, man versus nature, and the crowd favorite, man versus himself. I was free during the period before honors. I spent it on a couch in the English office, attacking the Adventures essays.

I think we shoudnt have a dress code becuz we all have good close at home that we cant where. Like I have this really cool shirt its brite pink with some sparkles and I reelly want to where it but I cant becuz its straps are to skinny. If I wor it I woud get sent down to Dr. Whites office but I think I shoud be able to where it becuz I bowt it with my own money.

I got to my classroom a few minutes before the bell rang and began sticking the blue essay books on each of the students' desks. I was about halfway through when my in-class phone rang.

I hate the in-class phone. No one ever just calls to say hello.

Dawna calls to remind me about lunchroom duty. Dr. White calls when she wants me to fill out a report about an underperforming student. Or—

"Mrs. Quackenbush? This is Lynette Pimpernel. Claudia's mother." As if I didn't know. As if I didn't remember her endless e-mails, not to mention the *Romeo and Jules* protest meeting.

"Yes, Mrs. Pimpernel." I glanced at the clock on the wall. One minute till the bell.

"I wanted to talk to you about Claudia's recent assignment. The vocabulary words? Claudia tells me you marked her down a grade because she handed it in a day late."

I rolled my eyes but kept my sigh inaudible. "Yes, that's my policy, as Claudia knows. Students lose a full grade for every day an assignment is late."

"Yes, and I completely support you in this. Students must learn responsibility. And Claudia has always been a diligent student."

"She certainly is, Mrs. Pimpernel. And I doubt that one B will have much effect on her final grade."

"Can you guarantee that?"

The bell rang. "No, I can't guarantee anything. I won't know the grades until I do my final calculations at the end of the quarter. But a single homework assignment doesn't have a huge bearing on a student's final mark." Sarah Levine entered the class. I caught her eye and handed her the blue books, motioning her to pass them out. "Mrs. Pimpernel, I'm sorry, but I'm going to have to go now. Claudia's class is just beginning."

"Oh? Claudia told me you were free this period."

"No, I was free last period. It's different every day." The kids were coming in a stream now, shoving their books under their chairs, fishing out pencils and erasers and positioning them on their desks just so. There was an air of tension in the room. These kids took tests seriously.

"Could you call me after school then? I'd really like to talk a little more about how the grades are calculated."

I closed my eyes briefly, trying to gather strength. I was not going to launch my weekend—my pathetic, work-and-bubble-bath-centered-weekend—with a phone call to Claudia's mother. "The students are doing an in-class essay today."

"On *Lord of the Flies*. I know, Claudia told me." Claudia told her. Yes. At which point Lynette Pimpernel probably began drafting an essay for Claudia to memorize.

"At any rate, I need to get them started. Then I can call you from the department office."

Three minutes later, after sticking the essay topic on the overhead projector, I trotted down the hall and dialed the Pimpernels' home number. Using my cell phone was out of the question. The Pimpernels probably had caller ID; no way was I going to end up on their speed dial. As for leaving the kids unattended, it was hard to cheat on an essay test. Besides, with the glaring exception of Jared, these were good kids with a deep fear of getting in trouble.

"I'd like to explain why Claudia's assignment was late," Mrs. Pimpernel began, having gotten her second wind. Before I could find a polite way to say I didn't care, she explained that her husband had received a community award that night, and that it was a very special night for him and a very special night for the whole family. And Claudia is extremely close to her father, he's her role model, really, which is why she is so intent on attending Harvard in a few years, just like her dad. Has Claudia ever mentioned that her father went to Harvard? And that she hopes to follow in his footsteps? At any rate, after this important, special, role-model-worthy night, the family got home extremely late and Claudia, committed student that she is, was prepared to stay up until the wee hours doing her vocabulary homework, but we all know how important sleep is for growing bodies, and her mother and father agreed that she had to go to bed. Besides, Claudia has an exceptional vocabulary for a fourteen-year-old—she spoke her first words at eight months; the doctor said he'd never seen anything like it—and she probably knew all of the words on the list anyway. In light of all that and in light of Claudia's exemplary performance, couldn't I award her full credit for that homework assignment?

"No," I said.

"But—"

"No."

When I returned, the room was deathly quiet except for the hum of the heaters (on this December day, it was a brisk sixty-two degrees outside) and the scratch of the pencils. The students barely glanced up when I tiptoed over to my desk. I pulled the chair out as quietly as I could and was about to sit down when I saw something long and thin slip from the chair onto the floor: a snake.

I jumped back and screamed. The students' heads popped up, eyes wide with shock. A couple of the girls shrieked when they saw the creature. One boy said, "Is it alive?" Another said, "That's a baby gopher snake. It's not poisonous."

It was dead. I registered that information in my brain, but my primal reflexes remained on high alert, my heart pounding, my head buzzing. It was beige with black marks and less than two feet long—smaller than plenty of snakes I'd seen slithering across the street. Its head was rounded, not angular. There was no rattle on its tail.

Jared laughed.

I gawked at him, blood rushing in my ears. His eyes were squeezed almost completely shut. He was that amused.

"*You little shit.*"

He stopped laughing. The other kids stopped looking at the snake and stared at me instead.

"Pick it up," I commanded.

His eyes darted from side to side. "No way. I don't like snakes."

"*Pick it up.*"

He rose slowly from his chair and approached the snake. "What am I supposed to pick it up with?"

"The same thing you brought it in with. Your hands."

"I don't like snakes." He was growing pale.

"You're coming with me. And you're bringing the snake."

Dawna screamed when we walked in the front office, her pudgy hand flying to her mouth.

"What the—" Nicolette began, catching herself just in time.

"I need to see Dr. White," I said, my voice quavering. "Is she in?"

thirty-two

If not for Lars, Dr. White probably would have fired me. She was struggling to fill one position, though, and if she sacked two teachers in one month, the union would have her head (although, like Lars, I was untenured and thus officially expendable). She called my behavior rash, cruel and unprofessional, and she expressed fear that Jared's parents might bring a lawsuit.

"But he did it!" I said. "He left a dead snake on my chair!"

"You have no proof."

"I have the snake. You can bet it's got Jared's fingerprints all over it."

"Of course it does. You made him carry it."

"Oh." I stopped short and blinked at my own stupidity. I really had to start watching *CSI*.

At least there were no snakes at my house. Instead, there was a tanned, older couple sitting at the kitchen island with Marjorie Wamsley.

"Natalie! I hope we didn't scare you." They didn't. I'd seen Marjorie's white Lexus SUV out front but had assumed she had dropped by to check on the staging. Marjorie slid off her stool and straightened her black blazer. Today's was hip-length. "Meet Rob and Betty Sandler."

"Hi." I forced a smile.

"Natalie is house-sitting until her parents sell the property."

Rob and Betty Sandler blinked at me, then smiled. They wore matching periwinkle blue polo shirts. Mr. Sandler wore khaki shorts, while his wife sported a white golf skirt. I, meanwhile, was dressed for an entirely different season in a black turtleneck and a gray skirt.

Most likely, Marjorie hadn't told the Sandlers that anyone was living in the house. As Kim the stager had explained, house sellers should remove all of their personal touches so that potential buyers can project their lives onto the home's blank, stylish canvas. An inhabitant was the ultimate personal touch. Suddenly, I was embarrassed. I hadn't made my bed this morning. Even worse, the Sandlers were going to think I stocked my bathrooms with champagne.

"The house isn't on the market yet, is it?" I asked Marjorie, keeping my voice as casual as possible even as I wondered where I was going to live should Rob and Betty Sandler ask for a quick closing.

"No! Of course not!" Rob and Betty's eyes dropped to the granite countertop. Marjorie tilted her head to the side. Her blond hair didn't move. "Rob and Betty are active seniors looking for a home in North Scottsdale. I am committed to putting them in their dream house. Your parents said it would be all right to give them a sneak preview." She smiled, holding my gaze. This was not my house, and we both knew it.

"The property won't go on the MLS until January," Marjorie continued. "Of course, if Mr. and Mrs. Sandler fall in love with the house . . ." She raised her eyebrows. I could practically see the numbers whirling in her head: both sides of the commission! On top of the sum she made last time around! "Wouldn't a quick sale be a wonderful Christmas present for your parents?"

"Now, now!" Mr. Sandler laughed. "We haven't even made an offer yet!"

"The great room is spectacular," Mrs. Sandler murmured.

Once they left, I drank the champagne while soaking in my parents' oversized bathtub. Vanilla-scented candles burned. Piano music flowed from my portable CD player. I pushed a button with my big toe, and the Jacuzzi jets began to whir. The water churned and swirled, foaming the bubble bath like a meringue. Internally, I chanted the home spa mantras. *Pamper yourself. Relax.* Jets pounded water between my shoulder blades and against my hips. *Breathe deeply. Let the tension fall away.*

This was pathetic. But the champagne was surprisingly good. I poured another glass. And then another. The glass was tiny.

Jonathan answered his phone on the first ring. "I was just drinking champagne in the bathtub," I blurted into the phone on my mother's nightstand. "My parents are moving. They hired a stager, and she put champagne in the bathroom, and I just drank it. Do you know what a stager is? How are you?"

He paused for so long, I began to think he'd hung up. "I'm okay," he said finally. "I don't know what a stager is."

"A stager is someone who makes a house look good so it will sell. But it's more than that. She sets the house up so people can imagine themselves living there and having this perfect, make-believe life. Like, they're going to squeeze fresh orange juice every morning and drink champagne in the bathtub. And they're going to play backgammon in the living room instead of watching the big TV. Have you ever seen *CSI*?"

"What? Um, no."

"Me, neither. I thought I was the only one." Nervously, I rubbed my parents' scratchy bedspread. Kim had covered my parents' king-sized bed with some burlap-like fabric. I couldn't imagine sleeping under something so rough. "I saw Krista last week. At a party. Except I wasn't really at the party. I mean I *was* at the party, but I wasn't *at* the party. I was just there to see how Robert was doing on his internship. He's doing great. And I really appreciate that you set the whole thing up. Did Krista tell you she had seen me?"

"No."

"It was good to see her. I mean, I enjoyed talking to her. She said—this is kind of funny—she said she thought I was a keeper. For you. I told her it was my fault things didn't work out. But she said maybe they still would."

I waited for Jonathan to say something. He didn't.

"But I guess she didn't tell you any of this," I said.

"Krista left my father."

Now it was my turn to be speechless. "What?" I finally gasped.

"Over the weekend."

"But I just saw her!" I said, the way you do when someone dies suddenly. "But—why? They seemed happy."

He sighed. "They always seem happy. My father and whoever he's married to at any given time. Usually he does the leaving.

Maybe Krista just beat him to the punch. Or maybe he's just getting older."

"Do you want to talk about it? I mean, maybe we could get together. And talk about it. You could come over. You should see my room. It's all done up in cowboy stuff."

"I don't think so."

"When I said you should see my room, I didn't mean—what I meant was, I'd just like to see you. To talk to you. And, maybe, help you. With your father, I mean."

"I don't need help with my father. I'm not upset. I'm not even surprised. With my father, breakups aren't a case of if, they're a case of when."

"Like father, like son?" I said before my inebriated internal censors had a chance to stop me.

"That's one way to look at it."

I didn't make any more phone calls that weekend, nor did I drink any more champagne. I left the empty bottle in the ice bucket; no one would notice.

I resolved to stop thinking about Jonathan and simply concentrate on my work, but it wasn't easy. On Sunday night, with my stack of student papers graded, my lesson plans prepared, I allowed myself a moment's weakness and Googled Jonathan, even as I recognized that this was where all of my problems had started. Had they, though? All along, I had assumed that things would have been fine if, after our first meeting, I confessed to Jonathan that I'd been putting him on at Route 66. He would have laughed it off. Right? Then again, maybe not. Maybe if I had come clean at the beginning, our affair would have been cut that much shorter.

Online, there were no new mentions of Jonathan. I found the old picture of him and Krista at the benefit. How could I ever have thought they were married? She is all glamour, shining in the camera's flash. He stands apart from her, shoulders angled slightly away, hands in his pockets: the lonely stepchild.

Once I'd exhausted all of the references to Jonathan Pomeroy, I indulged in a bit of cyber-narcissism. "Natalie Quackenbush," I typed into the search line.

The first listing was for my neglected school Web page. There were a couple more mentions of me in relation to Agave: an old PTA newsletter introducing new faculty, a dated school e-newspaper (there was no print version) announcing audition details for *Romeo and Jules*. My name popped up on my college alumni site; I'd sent in a letter when I'd moved to Arizona on the off chance some of my old friends might want to get in touch with me (as yet, they hadn't).

And then I saw it: *i hate ms quackenbush.* I blinked at the screen. Surely there was another Ms. Quackenbush. A sloppy accountant who caused an audit. A careless hairdresser who left the peroxide on too long.

I double-clicked.

i hate ms quackenbush. she is the biggest bitch in school. she is mean and stupid. i hope she gets fired, i hope her house burns down, i hope she gets bitten by a snake.

i wish i had another teacher. i wish i had mr. hansen, but i can't because he got fired even though he was a much better teacher than ms quackenbush.

i hate ms quackenbush i hate ms quackenbush i hate ms quackenbush.

she can eat shit.

i hope she dies.

thirty-three

There would be no hysteria this time. No name-calling. No reptiles.

Monday morning I put on my charcoal gray suit (with the pants) and stopped by the front office. After checking Dr. White's schedule, I had Dawna assign an appointment slot during my free period.

There would be no unfounded accusations. No lawsuit fears. My behavior would be above reproach.

"I think we can catch him this time," I said, clutching the sheet I had printed from my computer.

"Catch who?" Dr. White asked.

"Jared." I passed her the paper and stood on the far side of her chrome desk, trying to read her expression. My heart was racing. My face felt warm.

Finally, she put the paper down. She looked up slowly. "Goodness."

"If we can trace the computer—isn't there some way to do that? If we can figure out where Jared's blogging from, we can catch him."

Dr. White held my gaze. "This is a very serious offense. You have every right to be frightened. And angry. But we don't know that Jared did this."

"Of course he did! He's evil! Nobody else would write these things about me!" I burst into tears. So much for no hysteria.

She came around from the other side of her desk. She was at least six inches taller than me. I thought she was going to chastise me, tell me to get a grip, to be more professional.

Instead, she hugged me. I hugged her back, soaking her green silk jacket with my tears. She was softer than she looked, almost squishy. "This is so hard," I blubbered. "Why is this so hard?"

Dr. White patted my back gently. "My first year of teaching, I used to go home from school every day and cry."

"But this is my second year of teaching."

"True. By my second year, I was down to only two or three good cries a week."

"Does it ever get easy?"

"Easy? No. But it gets easier. And it gets to be joyful. And incredibly rewarding. Believe me, Natalie, you'll never find a job half as fun as teaching."

I nodded through my tears and pretended to believe her.

There were no computer geniuses on staff at Agave. There were, however, a few students who had been suspended for "illegal systems entry." According to Dr. White, Tyler Farrell was the most talented hacker by far.

"How good can he be if you caught him?" I asked. By now Dr. White had retreated to the far side of her desk, while I sat on a chair opposite.

"A friend ratted him out after he bragged about changing his grades. Like all tragic heroes, Tyler had a fatal flaw—his ego." She paused for a minute, tapping her pen on her desk. "Or maybe his fatal flaw would be his utter lack of conscience."

"No," I said, dabbing my nose. Dr. White kept a tissue box on her desk. I wasn't the first person to fall apart in here. I cleared the phlegm from my throat. "A fatal flaw, by definition, is what destroys the hero. Tyler's amorality didn't get in the way of his computer hacking. In fact, it probably helped. What brought him down was the bragging. So, his ego's the flaw."

"You're right," she sighed, leaning back. "I'm rusty." Dr. White had been an English teacher for fifteen years before going into administration.

Tyler Farrell was well over six feet tall, pear-shaped and slack-muscled. He wore gray nylon shorts that fell below his knees and a black T-shirt that read, BYTE ME. His hair was carrot orange, his skin luminescent white dotted here and there with bright red pimples. Stick this kid in the sun for ten minutes and he'd burn. No wonder he spent his time in shuttered rooms, preferring the cyber world to reality. The real world could give him melanoma. Had Tyler grown up in Seattle instead of Scottsdale, his whole life might have been different.

Ignoring the chair Dr. White offered, Tyler stood hunched over the computer behind her desk. If he wasn't careful, he'd have serious back problems in twenty years. With fingers so fast they blurred, Tyler typed my name into a search engine and pulled up the awful entry. I held my breath, afraid that he would laugh.

Instead, he moaned in disgust. "Oh, man, this is pathetic."

"It is." I smiled cautiously, encouraged by the affirmation. Tyler understood that I was a nice teacher.

He grunted. "I mean—*Xanga*? Man. This kid's on the boards with the girls eating laxatives and writing bad poetry about their boyfriends. You ever read that crap? Pathetic. He could've set up his own Web page, had a free-standing blog at least. It only takes a few minutes to get it going. Who's gonna dig through Xanga?"

There was a knock on the door: Jill. Dr. White had left a message on her voice mail. I had hoped she wouldn't get it until after I'd left; the bell would ring in five minutes.

"What's up?" she said. Then, spying Tyler: "Wow. It must be serious if Dr. White let you on her machine."

Tyler's shoulders tightened. He didn't turn around. Jill caught my eye. "*Passive aggressive*," she mouthed. I smiled in spite of myself.

Dr. White said, "Natalie looked herself up on the computer." She motioned to her machine. "She found this."

Jill's mouth twitched. "You Googled yourself?"

I rolled my eyes. "Just wanted to see where I lived, what I was doing. We've been out of touch."

"Oh, my God," Jill said, peering at the computer screen. Tyler edged away from her. "This kid's got serious problems. You think it's—" Her eyes flicked over to Tyler. "You think it's the kid who you'd think it would be? The kid with the dysfunctional family who has a history of emotional aggression?"

"Yeah," I said. "I think it's Jared."

"We've asked Tyler to help us identify the blogger," Dr. White said. "Until we have any further information, we're not going to make any assumptions. Natalie has over a hundred students. It could be anyone."

"No, it couldn't." I shook my head. "The whole no-capitals

thing is misleading. Look at the comma usage. This kid knows his punctuation. That rules out at least two-thirds of my students."

Jill put her hand on Tyler's arm. He edged even closer to the corner of the room. If she pushed him much farther, he'd have no place left to go. "I'm proud of you, Tyler," Jill said. "This time you're on the side of the angels."

"Dr. White said that if I help her out, she'll reduce my school probation," Tyler mumbled.

For the rest of the day, I scanned the eyes of all of my students who had mastered comma usage. I failed to detect any hatred. It's not that these kids thought I was the greatest thing since iPod phones; they just didn't think much about me at all. I was *She Who Assigns Homework*; *She Who Gives a Final Grade*; *She Who Makes Me Read Boring Books.*

Due to the schedule rotation, I didn't have my honors class, which was a relief. I felt oddly frightened of seeing Jared, of discovering the depths of his cruelty.

I ate lunch at my new usual spot, with the math department. I'd become friends—or at least friendly—with Miss Rothstein. We were so tight that she asked me to call her by her first name, Stacey. Today she was showing me a printout of her Macy's gift registry. She had requested white towels, white sheets and white dishes. She had even requested a white bath accessories set.

"I hope it's not too much white," she said

"You could pick an accent color," I said. "Eggplant, maybe."

"You mean, like, purple? I don't think so." She sighed. "I could never pull off purple."

"Nicolette was going to do a lot of eggplant," I said. "You know Nicolette in the office? But then she eloped, so she never got to register."

Stacey picked up her tiny milk carton and took a drink. "I heard Nicolette was getting a divorce." She grimaced at her carton. "I hate skim milk. The day after my wedding, I'm going back to whole."

Jill was sitting at her desk, eating her lunch: some sandwich on focaccia. She smiled when she saw me. "Is Nicolette getting a divorce?" I whispered.

She motioned for me to shut the door and sit down. "Big blowup," she said once the door was closed. "They'd been saving money for a party in the spring—a kind of post-wedding reception."

"But I thought she didn't want that," I said. I was still whispering even though no one could hear us through the door.

"That's what she said at first. But then we talked about it. I explained the real purpose of ceremonies: they mark a transition. One part of our life ends, another begins." She gestured as she spoke. Her fingers were perfectly manicured a ruby red. Her clothes, as usual, were black. "Without a wedding," she continued, "Nicolette felt like she and Rodney weren't really married."

"Plus she missed out on all the presents."

"That, too. So anyway, they had this pile of money building up." She leaned forward for emphasis. "And then, without discussing it, Rodney used the cash to make a down payment on a new truck."

"No!"

She settled back in her chair. "He's exhibited poor impulse control from the beginning."

"Is Nicolette very upset?"

"I'll say. She keeps saying that she loves him but she can't trust him. Nicolette has a completely idealized view of romantic love. Cognitively and emotionally, she hasn't quite made the leap from adolescence to adulthood."

"So maybe it's for the best," I said. "The breakup."

She scrunched up her face. "I don't know. Even though they're both emotionally immature, they seemed really . . ."

"In love?"

"Yeah." She took a big bite of her sandwich.

"What've you got on the focaccia? Roasted eggplant?"

She shook her head and then swallowed. "Portobello mushroom. With a red pepper aioli. You want a bite?"

"No, thanks." I stood up.

She put her sandwich down on its sheet of waxed paper and stood up. She towered over me. She slumped a bit, perhaps trying to bridge the gap. "I'm glad you stopped by."

I looked at the floor. "Yeah, well, I just wanted to see what was going on with Nicolette."

"Lars said to say hi."

"Did he find a job yet?"

She shook her head. "No, but he has a promising lead. Charter school in Glendale. Nicolette says Dr. White's about to fill his position. She's got two good candidates—she just has to decide which she likes better."

I nodded. I'd heard this, too. "So it's working out?" I said casually. "You and Lars?"

"I guess." She paused. "You know how immaculate he always looks? How clean? You should see his apartment. Total pig sty. He's got these two roommates from Arizona State—he completely regresses around them. Between the beer and the farts, I can't stand to be in that place for more than ten minutes at a time. It's like being in a frat house."

"So you should stick to your place."

"I know. But of course, I've got a roommate, too." She sighed. "I don't know. I like him. I really do. And, weirdly enough, he likes me. But I always seem to attract guys who want to be dominated, and I'm afraid Lars is another Peter Pan." She shrugged and tried to smile. "I don't want to be his mother."

I tilted my head to one side. "You could be his Wendy instead."

She smiled. "That's one way to look at it. I've missed you, you know." I didn't respond. "Would you come out with us sometime soon?" she asked. "I mean, with Lars and me. It would be like old times."

I was quiet for a minute. "I'm not sure I want it to be like old times."

"It'll be like new times, then," she said. "Think about it?"

"I'll think about it." I eyed her sandwich and weakened. "You know, I wouldn't mind just a little taste of the sandwich."

thirty-four

No one ever tells you to sit down for good news, so when Dr. White offered me a visitor chair the next morning, I held my breath. Tyler had gotten there ahead of me. Today's T-shirt, gray this time, was emblazoned with a computer code, which, for all I knew, translated into something like, "I know your American Express account number and your mother's maiden name."

Ten minutes into my first period class (Freshman Honors), Nicolette had clicked into my classroom on the painfully high heels that she wore with her excruciatingly tight white jeans. "Dr. White needs to see you," she said. "I'll take over."

I practically ran out of there. Knowing that honors was my first class of the day, I'd arrived early to make sure my room was clear of feces, reptiles, bugs, bombs, or any other surprises. Once the bell rang, I poured all of my energy into not meeting Jared's eyes. I was afraid I would start crying.

"Did Tyler catch him?" I asked Dr. White once I was seated. She nodded. "It's Jared, isn't it?"

She shook her head.

I looked at Tyler, who, for once, had turned away from the computer to face us, though one hand still trailed on the keys, as if for comfort. "Was he hard to find?" I asked. "It is a he, isn't it?"

Tyler rolled his eyes. "Took me, like, five minutes to get his name. If that. He registered under his real name, as if no one could ever get past his screen name. *Pathetic*."

"But you used only legal methods to find this information, right, Tyler?" Dr. White said casually.

He grunted in the affirmative—I think it was the affirmative—without making eye contact.

Dr. White thanked Tyler and sent him to class with a yellow pass. Then she closed her door and sat down behind her desk. She clasped her hands in front of her, leaned forward, and looked at me with concern. "It was Cody Gold."

For an instant, I thought she was kidding. Cody wouldn't write those things about me! Cody was like a puppy dog. Cody loved me! "But—why?"

She shook her head slightly. "I have no idea. Have you had any problems with him?"

"No! He's always—well, I always thought he liked me."

"Your students don't have to like you," she said gently. "They just have to respect you."

"I *know*. But Cody . . . he had a little crush on me, I think. It seemed sweet at the time. But now—" I stopped. If I talked any more, I'd start crying. To maintain self respect, I could allow myself no more than one breakdown a week in Dr. White's office. No, make that one breakdown a career.

"I've called Cody's parents," Dr. White continued. "They'll be here for a meeting at three o'clock. I'd like you to join us."

I nodded and stood up. Suddenly, I wanted to get out of there.

My classroom was no more appealing, though. As I approached, I could hear Claudia's voice: "How can you tell the difference between genuine love and infatuation?"

I was trying to figure out how that would figure into a discussion of *A Separate Peace*, when Nicolette answered, "Ya know, I still don't know. I mean, when I met Rodney, I thought: this is it. He was so not like the other guys I'd gone out with."

I was about to march in and end the discussion before Nicolette started comparing and contrasting Rodney's sexual proclivities with the countless partners who'd gone before when I caught a glance at Cody's face. I recoiled, as if I'd seen a snake. Or a bag of crap. Or the face of someone who had betrayed me.

My eyes filled with tears. I envisioned Cody finding a dead snake in his yard (surely he didn't hate me enough to kill something), smuggling it into his backpack and leaving it on my chair in anticipation of my fear and humiliation. I envisioned him finding some dog poo in his backyard (surely he didn't hate me enough to hoard his own shit) and stinking up his locker for an entire day until he had the chance to unload it.

I was a failure. Anyone who could inspire such venom should be doing something else.

I fled to the teacher's bathroom and shut myself in a stall until the bell rang.

Next was one of my college prep classes. I had the students take turns reading aloud. They were quiet, expressionless, slumped over their desks.

Next came Adventures. Five minutes into a lesson on semicolons,

I thought: this is ridiculous. These kids haven't mastered commas; why bother with semicolons? Only three kids handed in homework. (Robert's excuse: "I worked a party for Suzette last night—you know I quit my job at the hospital? And anyway, I got home really late.")

Robert lingered after class. I felt a little better. Robert liked me. He was still borderline illiterate, but at least he liked me. I asked him how Ladd's tutoring was going without pointing out that his work had slipped off since he'd stopped coming in for extra help in the mornings. Robert considered his paid tutor for a moment. "He's—he's bending my mind. An interesting dude."

Katerina sauntered in. Robert beamed. He hadn't hung around to talk to me. Of course not.

Katerina said, "Ms. Quackenbush, is it true that you're directing the winter play?"

It was true, I said, though I didn't think I could do as good a job as Mr. Hansen.

Her smile fell. "Yeah, Mr. Hansen was really cool."

Jill caught me as I was sneaking out the door at lunchtime. "I forgot my lunch," I lied. "I was just going to grab a burrito."

She came with me even though she probably had a plastic container filled with something wonderful waiting for her in the faculty fridge.

"I talked to Cody's mother this morning. She and her husband separated last month," she told me as we sat in a booth at a Taco Bell, sipping giant Diet Pepsis and waiting for our gorditas. "Most likely, Cody's transferring his feelings of anger onto you."

The acoustics in this place were terrible. Shrieking chairs, slurping sodas, rustling paper: the sounds bounced off the walls and ceiling. People talked too loud, trying to be heard over the noise, making the din even worse. At the tables around us sat men in various matching shirts. One table had burly white guys wearing royal blue T-shirts that read, VALLEY PLUMBING. Another table had short, solid Mexican guys. Their T-shirts were purple and read, GOODMAN'S LANDSCAPING.

Everyone looked happier than me, the plumbers, the landscapers, the moms with toddlers trying to claw their way out of strollers. Me with my save-the-world attitude and my eighteen years of schooling. The plumbers probably out-earned me by a good twenty thousand dollars a year.

My cell phone rang. I fished it out of my bag. "Hot date?" Jill asked.

I checked the display number. "My mother." I let it go to voice mail.

A group of familiar-looking teenagers walked in, two skinny girls and a boy with bad acne and squinty eyes. I smiled. They ignored me. Jill waved. They ignored her, too. "Two bulimics and a chronic liar," she murmured. "If you have to use the bathroom, I'd do it now."

I didn't smile.

"Oh, come on, Natalie!" she said. "So one kid doesn't like you. It's not the end of the world. Cody Gold has problems that have nothing to do with you."

"Has he been acting out with any of his other teachers?"

"Well, no," she admitted. "But that doesn't mean anything."

"Of course it does," I said. A girl at the counter called our number. I glanced at my watch. "We've got five minutes to eat," I said. "Let's get moving."

* * *

I didn't go to the meeting with Mr. and Mrs. Gold. When the final bell rang, I packed up my bag, locked up my classroom and hurried off to my car before anyone could stop me.

I was a coward, true, but it was more than that. It hit me during my third college prep class of the day, with a third group of students reading the same Dickens passages aloud, their bodies slumped just so, sneakered feet splayed out, elbows on the desks, eyes glazed, hands holding up faces that would topple over without the support. I didn't want to be here anymore than they did. I wasn't saving the world. I was boring the world.

Dr. White had two good candidates for Lars's job. Why turn one away?

I felt oddly free and jubilant. If I hadn't wasted the bathtub champagne, I'd pop it now. No matter. When I got home, I'd turn on the spa, slip into my bathing suit and soak away the tensions from the last year and a half.

Marjorie Wamsley ruined everything. "Shoot," I said when I saw her white SUV parked out front. Then, remembering that my role-model days were numbered, I amended my exclamation to, "Shit." Saying a bad word felt so good, I said it again. "Shit, shit, shit."

Marjorie and the Sandlers were standing out by the spa. *My* spa. I stuck a smile on my face and strode outside.

"Oh, hello, Natalie! Did your mother reach you?"

"What?" Oh, right. I'd never returned my mother's call. "I was just going to call her back."

"We have some exciting news!" Marjorie said. Mr. and Mrs. Sandler smiled shyly behind her. "The Sandlers have made a very nice offer on the home."

"On this home?" I said stupidly.

"This very one!" Marjorie chirped.

By the time they left, two hours later, I didn't really want to go in the spa anymore but I did anyway, recognizing that my backyard-as-resort days were numbered. The sun was just starting to fade, and the air was chilly. The flagstones iced my feet; I should have worn flip-flops. As I slipped into the spa, I had one of those cold-to-hot, agony-to-ecstacy moments. The steamy water thawed my feet and stung my legs. I halted halfway into the water, my bottom half too hot, my top half too cold, until, with a squeal, I plunged myself up to my chin in the Pebble Tec cauldron, settling at last into the blood-warming brew.

I left the jets off, immersing myself in the dusk sounds of the desert. Mourning doves cooed, their voices soothing rather than sad. Owls hooted in the distance. My heart thudded in my ears. Above the stucco wall that surrounded the yard, jagged mountains rose brown and purple against a dusty pink and blue sky, while the majestic saguaros held their prickly green arms aloft.

This is "When I Lived in Arizona," I told myself, as the clouds darkened and the present faded into the past.

thirty-five

Dear Dr. White:

It is with great sadness that I announce my resignation, effective December 21, as a secondary school English Teacher at Agave High School. My decision to leave is personal and is not in any way a reflection on you or any of the other staff members at Agave High School.

Please know that I have nothing but the greatest respect for you, and I thank you for all of the efforts you have made on my behalf.

Sincerely,
Natalie Quackenbush

"No," she said, placing the letter on her desk.

"Excuse me?" I stood across from her, one foot pointing toward the door, poised to make my exit.

Dr. White crossed her arms across her chest. She was wearing a new suit today: Christmas red. Her blouse was white and had a wide, pointy collar. Her glossy lipstick matched the suit. Her skin shone dark and brown. Dr. White had the right complexion for Arizona. "You're upset about Cody Gold. You're being impulsive."

I shook my head. "I'm not. I've been thinking about this for a long time. This was just the thing that pushed me over the edge. The tipping point. The final straw."

She smiled, just a little. "Have you started your writing unit yet? The part about avoiding clichés?"

"No, that's next quarter. Or, it would have been."

She held the letter out to me. "Finish out the year. Then decide."

I left the sheet in her hand. "I've already decided. This is the right thing to do."

She put the letter back on her desk. "The first two years are the hardest. You're a good teacher, Natalie. Don't give up."

I backed away. "I'm sorry, Dr. White. I hate to disappoint you. But I can't do this anymore."

She didn't give up. First she sicced Mrs. Clausen on me. "We don't want to lose you from teaching, Natalie. You're incredibly talented."

Then she moved on to Jill.

"Cody Gold's parents are separating just as he is hitting puberty. He felt a kind of Oedipal attraction for you. It's only natural he would lash out."

She even had the vice principal, some guy named Mr. Flynn, talk to me. "Dr. White tells me you're one of our finest history teachers."

"I teach English."

"Oh, right. Well, best of luck to you."

When I had a free period, I stayed in my classroom to avoid any more ambushes. I shut the door and called my parents. We had spoken last night. I told them the Sandlers seemed like nice people, that my parents' house was going to a good home, as it were. I didn't tell them I was going to quit my job; I thought I should tell Dr. White first.

My sister answered the phone. "Aren't you supposed to be at work?" I said.

"I have a cold."

"Bad one?"

"Not really. But Mom made this big deal, says I have to be especially careful because of the baby, and God forbid I should get pneumonia, blah, blah, blah." Shelly sighed. "She's driving me crazy. She's completely taking over my life. She treats me like I'm twelve."

"A pregnant twelve-year-old, no less."

She moaned. "My life is so fucked up."

I rolled my eyes. "Is Mom around?"

"She went to the store. She's buying chicken soup and ginger ale."

"What about Dad?"

"He went with Mom. He's driving me crazy, too. He keeps saying if he were in Scottsdale, he could be playing golf."

I took a deep breath. "I'm moving back East."

"What?"

"I've quit my job. I'm moving home. Or, home-ish. I'll probably go back to Boston."

"But—why? You have a job, friends . . . Mom said you have a boyfriend." Her voice dropped. I think I heard her sniffle, whether from her cold or the memory of Frederick, I wasn't sure.

302   carol snow

"I hate my job, and I don't have any real friends," I said as evenly as I could manage. "There's no boyfriend. That's over."

"Men are assholes," Shelly said.

The kids made it harder. Katerina stayed after class to talk about the winter play. "I've got this idea, and, like, tell me if you don't think it's going to work. But you know how you said you were, like, not feeling confident about directing? Well, the thing is, I've always wanted to direct. So, I was wondering—would you consider taking me on as your student director? It would be, like, the biggest thrill of my life."

Sarah Levine lent me a poetry anthology she had read at home. "I love Keats, especially. Sometimes I start reading him, and an hour goes by and I don't even notice." She smiled shyly. "I waste so much time that way."

Even Claudia got to me. "Mrs. Quackenbush, do you think you could read this short story I wrote? It's about this girl, nobody really understands her, so she runs away to New York to be a dancer. Everybody thinks she's dead, but then she gets to be really famous, and they realize who it is. And there's this guy, she loved him when they were young, but when he drives to see her dance, there's this snowstorm and his car crashes and he dies." She took a breath. "Anyway, I think it could be better, but I've taken it as far as I know how."

Cody wasn't in class. Jared and I ignored each other.

Robert handed in his homework, a short descriptive paragraph. So did Marisol. Actually, over half of the other Adventures students did the work. I glanced at Robert's paper and managed to catch him before he walked out the door. "Did Ladd help you with this?"

He shook his head sheepishly. "The thing with Ladd is, well—he's not really a good tutor. He's not even that good a cook."

"You got all your punctuation correct," I said. "Everything! Even the quotation marks."

"It took a long time," he admitted. "I spent a lot of time looking at the stuff we worked on together. The comma exercises and stuff."

"Keep it up," I said.

He looked at the ground. "If you have any time, well . . . could we go back to meeting in the mornings?"

"Of course!" I said without thinking. "At least until the holiday break." He looked at me quizzically. "I just can't schedule anything after that."

It went on like that for the rest of the week. Every day, Dr. White asked me if I'd changed my mind. Every day, I told her no.

I took to eating lunch with Jill again. Miss Rothstein (Stacey) ate with us one day; the next day, having heard that I'd handed in my resignation, she was back at the math table. I couldn't blame her. I had one foot out the door; there was no point investing in a friendship.

My parents had already bought me plane tickets to Providence for Christmas. Maybe they could get a refund on the return flight.

In a week I'd be gone.

On Friday afternoon, I made a final visit to Dr. White's office. "I've thought it over," I told her for the fourth and final time. "I'm going to tell my students on Monday."

She nodded. I waited for her to say something. She didn't. She looked sad.

Jill caught up with me as I left the office. "I was just calling your cell phone. You've got to come out with me tomorrow night. A last hurrah."

"Another night at the Happy Cactus?"

She shook her head. "Something nicer. It's a surprise."

thirty-six

Lars pulled up in front of my house—my parents' house; the Sandlers' house—in his Prius. Jill hadn't told me that he was coming. I immediately vowed to act like I didn't care—only to realize that I really didn't.

"Nicolette's going to meet us over there," Jill told me.

"Over where?"

"You'll see."

"You look pretty," Lars said.

"You do," Jill echoed.

"Thanks." I was wearing a new filmy black shirt and skirt.

"Your hair has grown," Lars said.

"Yes." I touched it without thinking. Portions fell below my chin, but it would take months to get rid of all the layers.

"You have any hair gel?" Lars asked, reaching out to tuck a strand behind my ear. "Or some pomade?"

"I don't even know what pomade is."

He reached out to smooth the hair on the other side of my head, squinting intently. "It's kind of like mousse, only thicker. Like a paste."

I looked at Jill. "Are you sure he's straight?"

She shrugged. "That's what he tells me."

Jill reapplied my makeup and changed my jewelry ("Bold!" she said. "Go bold!") and Lars pouffed up my hair using an assortment of salon products he kept in his car.

"Do your roommates know you buy this crap?" Jill asked Lars, holding up a thirty-dollar jar of hair gunk. "That you drive around with it? Because they might stop buying you beer. They might start stocking the fridge with wine coolers and Zima."

Lars stepped back to survey his work. My hair was beginning to defy the laws of gravity. "I'm not worried," he said. "Jeff gets manicures."

"Jeff?" Jill shrieked. "You mean Jeff the belcher? Jeff who never flushes? You're kidding me."

"Where have all the cowboys gone?" I said.

Jill raised her eyebrows. "Where, indeed?"

Driving through the neighborhood, we admired the green Christmas lights wound around towering saguaros. White icicle lights hung above doors like shiny bangs, while giant red balls dangled from paloverde trees.

Last Christmas, my father bought a fake, pre-lit tree for our living room; cut evergreens don't last long in the desert. My mother and I found chili pepper lights at Target, and my father strung them around the windows. We hung an evergreen wreath on the front door. Within days, the dry needles fell to the ground at the slightest touch.

Shelly and Frederick came for a few days. My mother, wearing her red reindeer sweater, cooked—well, heated—a Christmas ham and served side dishes from AJ's: whole cranberry sauce, baked apples, duchess potatoes, green bean casserole. Frederick ate the corn bread stuffing with chorizo and jalapenos; the rest of us took one bite and left the rest on our plates. We ate on the patio; next to us, the spa's waterfall gurgled into the pool. My father, in a green reindeer sweater, served margaritas and asked, "Can you believe we're eating Christmas dinner outside?" at ten-minute intervals. It hadn't felt like Christmas at all. It felt like a magical, once-in-a-lifetime party.

This year, I hadn't even bothered to hang a wreath on the front door. I wondered where the chili pepper lights had been stored. Could we hang them up in Rhode Island, or would that look completely ridiculous?

"I can't believe you're leaving," Jill said, twisting around from the front passenger seat to make eye contact.

"I never intended to stay forever." I sat in the backseat, my hands clasped in my lap, and gazed out the window.

"Aren't you going to miss it?"

We were about to turn onto Scottsdale Road now, passing the pretty shopping center where I got my hair cut. I'd miss Angelo, my hairdresser, who was doing everything in his power to ease me through the awkward in-between stage as I grew out my layers.

The traffic was so backed up that we missed the light. Lars's Prius crept forward, waiting for the light to turn green again.

"It's too crowded," I said. "It's getting to be like L.A."

We made it through the intersection and drove down the wide expanse of Scottsdale Road. We passed new neighborhoods, constructed in the past six months, and older ones, which had been around since the nineties. Arizona possessed an overriding sense of newness, of promise, of reinvention. But were the six-month-old houses any different, any better, than the ten-year-old houses? And what of my own reinvention, my new beginning? After a year and a half in this place, I was just me—plain old Natalie.

It's funny: when you're moving, the littlest details seem significant. There was The Great Indoors, where I'd helped my parents pick out a (really cool) faucet after the one in my bathroom sink gave out. There was Nordstrom Rack, where Jill talked me into buying the only sexy pair of shoes I've ever owned—stiletto heeled, strappy, studded with rhinestones. I had yet to wear them but loved them for their promise of adventure. A bit farther down the road, we passed the Jiffy Lube where I got my oil changed. I had at least three coupons that I'd never get to use. There was the Asian fusion place with the incomparable Chilean sea bass. There was the bar where Jonathan met Jill and Nicolette.

Lars pulled up in front of the Hyatt. A valet opened the doors, and I stepped out. "Pretty swish," I said. "Who's paying?"

"We are," Jill said. Lars looked stricken.

We walked through the high-ceilinged lobby and down some steps to the lounge. Nicolette sat in an overstuffed chair, her pink cocktail glimmering in the candlelight. Across from her sat a young businessman with a small, straight nose and neatly trimmed brown hair. He wore wire-rimmed glasses and a well-cut suit. He'd look good in a tux.

Jill leaned close to my ear. "I'm thinking Lenox for the china, Fiestaware for everyday."

"And a good set of knives," I whispered back. "Wüsthoff or Henckels. Can you register a second time around, though? Or would that be gauche?"

Jill raised her eyebrows. "I'm thinking a full registry, twenty bridesmaids and a ten-foot train on the dress. The word of the day, my dear, is *annulment*." When we approached the table, Jill raised her voice. "Well, hello!" Just to be safe, she didn't use Nicolette's name.

The young man stood up and brightened. "You must be Nicolette's friends."

She'd used her real name. This was serious.

Nicolette looked up and shifted in the overstuffed arm chair. "Hey," she said. She forced a smile. She was looking practically demure tonight, in a black tank top that revealed only a discreet peek of cleavage, a cropped turquoise sweater, and a white miniskirt. Her mass of blond hair was pulled back in a clip. She blinked when she saw me and then smiled. "Your hair looks awesome, Mrs. Quackenbush."

"Call me—"

"I mean Natalie."

I softened. "Thanks. You look nice, too."

"We should get out there," Lars said, checking his watch.

"Out where?"

Lars and Jill exchanged a look. Jill cleared her throat and then announced, "To the gondolas. Natalie, for your going away present, we're giving you a gondola ride."

"Awesome!" said the young businessman. "I'm Ryan, by the way." Nicolette sipped her pink drink and gazed off in the distance. "I'm here on business from Sheboygan."

Lars scrunched his nose, trying to remember his geography. "Michigan?"

"Wisconsin."

"Ah, yes." Lars nodded. And then, lacking any other association: "Good cheese."

"The *best*," Ryan said, a touch too loud. "You can forget about that California cheese. That's not even really cheese." He smiled at Lars and then looked back at Nicolette. Well, he looked at her breasts.

"Nice to meet you," Jill said. "Nic, you ready?"

Nicolette sprang out of her chair and downed her cocktail in one motion. She put the glass on the table and nodded.

"I'm a financial analyst," Ryan said. "Well, in training." His eyes sparkled in the candlelight. He put a proprietary hand on Nicolette's shoulder. She flinched slightly.

"I'm not sure there's room for you in the boat, Ryan," Lars said, edging closer.

Ryan leaned into Nicolette. "So we can make room! Cozy up, if you know what I mean."

Jill shot Lars a look: *do something*.

I tilted my head at what I hoped was a coquettish angle. "So, Ryan, you're . . . okay about Nic?" I looked at Nicolette. "You *did* tell him, didn't you?"

She looked from side to side. "Well, not exactly." She checked my face, trying to see where this was going. "Well, not at all."

"Oh, Nic!" I shook my head. "I'm *sure* Ryan won't mind." I beamed at him.

"Mind what?" he asked.

I opened my mouth as if to speak and then closed it again. I gave Nicolette a quick once-over before turning back to Ryan. "Can't you tell just by looking at her?"

He took a step back and surveyed Nicolette. His mouth twitched. "I don't have any problem with, uh, enhancements." He stared openly at Nicolette's breasts.

Nicolette opened her mouth to protest—they were real, after all—when I said, "The implants are the least of it! You see, Ryan."

Here I paused for effect. "A few short months ago, our pretty little Nicolette was, well . . . our pretty little Nicholas."

Jill clapped her hand over her mouth. Lars picked up the routine immediately. "Natalie! That's for Nicky to share!"

Ryan was frozen in shock.

"I just . . . I believe in honesty," I said. "Okay, in a couple of months, when she's had her—his—no, her . . ."—I lowered my voice—"*equipment* removed, there will be less of an issue. But for now . . ." I gave Nicolette The Look. "You should have told him."

Jill, Lars and Nicolette laughed as we walked down the grand steps and past the various pools. "Natalie, that was brilliant!" Lars said.

"A triumph," Jill said. She looked at me. I wasn't smiling. "What's wrong?"

I shrugged. "I told myself I wasn't going to do that anymore. Make up stuff."

"It was just for fun," Lars said.

"This time it was. But sometimes people get hurt. Besides, I'm going to be thirty in a few months. I'm getting too old for this kind of thing."

"Thirty is the new sixteen," Lars quipped. "We can act like adolescents till we're forty."

"And then what? What happens when we're forty?"

"That's when we become young adults. We'll quit our jobs and backpack through Europe."

"I've already quit my job," I sighed.

Nicolette looped her arm into mine. "Well, I think you did an awesome thing back there. I didn't think I'd ever get rid of that guy."

"What was wrong with him?" Lars asked.

I was trying to find a nice way to say that Ryan was a drunk yuppie looking for a one-night stand when Nicolette burst into tears. "I miss Rodney!" she sobbed.

Jill took her in her arms. "It's okay! You're experiencing a sense of loss, and that's completely normal. You made the right decision. Remember how you said you were enabling Rodney's impulse control problems? And that you feared falling into a pattern of codependence?"

Nicolette took a step back. "*I* never said that. *You* said that. I don't even know what that means!"

Lars retrieved a tissue from his pocket and handed it to Nicolette. "She means that Rodney would do things without thinking—get married, buy a truck he couldn't afford—and you just got kind of sucked into it."

"And codependence basically means that you need him and he needs you," I said.

Nicolette rolled the tissue into a point and wiped carefully under her eyes. "I didn't know that was a bad thing. I thought that was love."

I heard him before I saw him: ". . . excited about this opportunity," and ". . . brought along the numbers of some of my customers who'd be happy to talk to you." I kept walking forward, slowly now, staring as we got closer, certain that any minute I'd see that it wasn't Jonathan but just some look-alike.

He was talking to Lars. Once we'd passed the lighted swimming pools, Lars had hurried ahead, saying, "We don't want to miss the boat—you guys can catch up with me."

They were standing next to a fire pit. Jonathan was wearing a black fleece pullover, jeans and black cowboy boots. He pulled some papers from a dark portfolio and handed them to Lars. The gondolier, in a straw hat and red-and-white striped shirt, stood on the dock nearby, obviously not in any hurry.

"Jonathan?" It came out like a whisper.

He turned to me and stopped talking immediately. He stared at me for a moment and then looked at Lars. "You don't really work for the Hyatt, do you?"

Lars grinned angelically.

"Oh, no," I said. "Lars, you didn't—Lars, what did you do?"

Jill and Nicolette caught up with us. Jill was looking at the ground. Nicolette peered around frantically. "Is Rodney here, too?"

"Who's Rodney?" Jonathan asked.

"Rodney's not here, Nicolette," Lars said. "Sorry."

She bit her lip and nodded. She sunk into an Adirondack chair and stared into the fire.

"I don't know what Lars told you . . ." I began.

Jonathan crossed his arms. "He told me he was Hyatt's food and beverage manager. He asked me to meet him here to discuss taking me on as a supplier. Which I thought was weird since I'd never heard of him and I don't do a lot of business on gondolas. But this account would have doubled my business."

Lars ran a hand through his blond hair. "I wasn't sure you'd come if I told you the real reason we wanted you here." When Jonathan didn't respond, he added, "I work with Natalie. Well, I used to. I got fired." He grinned sheepishly.

Jonathan narrowed his eyes. "Are you people completely incapable of telling the truth?"

"They're teachers," Jill piped in. "As role models, they are constantly faced with unrealistic expectations. To retain any sense of emotional balance, they have to find ways to let off steam."

"You're not a teacher," Jonathan replied. "What's your excuse?"

Jill's mouth twitched. "I just like to mess with people."

"I had nothing to do with this!" I said. "Jonathan, I'm sorry. *So* sorry. I realize now how hurtful making up stories can be." Involuntarily, I glanced at Lars. Lars-who-was-not-gay. "I will never, ever lie again."

"She means it," Nicolette said from her perch by the fire pit. "She was just saying that, like five minutes ago, after I met this loser guy in the lounge and—"

"*The important thing to remember here is*—" Jill interrupted. She stalled out. She had nothing to add, I suddenly realized; she was just trying to save me from Nicolette.

"Look, Jonathan," I said. "I'm really sorry Lars tricked you. I understand you don't want to see me anymore. I'm moving in a week, anyway, so you don't have to worry about it." I swallowed hard, mentally congratulating myself on keeping my voice steady.

"So how about a gondola ride?" Lars said. "I've already paid for it, so you might as well go."

"Actually, I paid for it," Jill murmured.

"Me and Rodney had our first kiss on the gondola," Nicolette whimpered, hugging herself by the fire.

"I don't think Jonathan wants to—" I began, just as Jonathan said, "Sure."

"Really?" I whispered.

He shrugged. "Why not?"

"You changed your hair," Jonathan said once we'd left the launch. He'd chosen to face me rather than sit next to me. The gondolier had handed us plaid blankets when we sat down. I spread mine across my lap, wishing Jonathan were under it with me. He left his folded on the bench next to him.

I touched my hair. It felt gluey. "Lars and Jill styled it. Usually it's flat like always, just longer. But I guess that's an improvement."

He shrugged. "It always looked nice."

I swallowed. "Thanks."

"So—you're moving?"

I nodded. "In a week. My parents sold the house. I guess I told you that. I was going to find another place to live, but then I realized, I might as well just leave."

"What about your job?"

I took a deep breath. "I quit. I was a lousy teacher, anyway."

"That's not what Robert says."

"You've talked to Robert?"

"A couple of times. When I've been over at Suzette's. Robert says you're his favorite teacher."

I pictured Robert's easy grin, his muffins, his basketball shorts. "That's just because I go easy on him."

He shook his head. "He said that he would have dropped out of school if it weren't for you. And that all the other kids like you, too." He smiled a little. "I think what he said was, 'She's not as boring as most of the other teachers.'"

I smiled. "I guess that's a compliment. But—that's just one kid's opinion. Not everyone feels that way. Trust me." We were gliding past blocky modern houses with enormous plate glass windows. Through one, I could see a man slouched on a sofa, hypnotized by the flicker of the television. "So, you're over there a lot?" I asked. "At Suzette's?"

He shrugged. "Every now and then. To make deliveries." The gondolier made little splashing noises with his pole. Above us, a cloud glided past the moon, dimming the shine.

"So, are you and Suzette," I began. "I mean, Krista said you used to be—together. A while ago. But every time I talked to Suzette, she made it sound like, well, like you and she . . ."

"What?"

I pictured Suzette: the perfect blond hair, the regal bearing. "Like you were a couple."

He closed his eyes for a moment. I could hardly breathe. "You don't know who Suzette is, do you?"

I shook my head.

He looked me in the eye. "Suzette is The Stalker."

"*What?*"

"She'd finally stopped calling me. I thought she'd moved on, found somebody else. I figured it would be okay to ask her about the internship." He shrugged. "I'm on the verge of changing my phone number."

"Then, why?" I asked. "Why did you call her about Robert?"

"I wanted to help you out. Help your student. And I'm glad I did. Robert's a good kid."

I smiled at him. I expected him to smile back. Instead, he gazed off into the distance. I pulled my plaid blanket up to my neck.

The gondolier broke our silence. "May I sing to you?"

His mournful aria floated out into the night as he continued to pole down the meandering, man-made lake. I peeked at Jonathan's face just as the cloud slid past the moon. He looked sad, but maybe it was just a response to the haunting music. The gondolier's voice lifted and rose, finally ending on a long, high, warbling note. "Would you like me to sing another song?" he asked.

Jonathan's mouth twitched. "You know any country and western?"

I laughed. I held Jonathan's gaze. "I've missed you," I said.

He looked down. My heart pumped violently. Finally, he looked up. "I'm just—I can't . . ." He shook his head. He looked up at the gondolier. "Can you take us back to the dock?"

I bit my lip, holding back tears.

"Can't," the gondolier said.

"Excuse me?"

"The guy at the launch, your friend—" He twisted around to look back at the shore, where Jill, Lars and Nicolette waited. I could see the glow from the fire pit. "Your friend said I couldn't bring you back until you'd kissed."

"You don't have to," I said. I looked at the gondolier. "Just take us back. Please."

"It's okay," Jonathan said. He leaned forward and kissed me, briefly, gently, touching me only with his lips. My mouth tingled as he pulled away. We sat opposite each other, staring.

The gondolier stopped the boat but didn't turn it around. "Yeah, um, that wasn't long enough."

"Excuse me?"

"Your friend said it had to be at least twenty seconds. He told me to time it." He shrugged. "That was a second and a half."

I stayed quiet. Jonathan and I held each other's eyes. Finally, he moved over to the seat next to me. He looked up at the gondolier. "Okay, start the clock."

He put his arms around me this time, loosely at first and then tighter. His kiss grew harder, hungrier. I put my hands on his neck and then on the back of his head, drinking him in. From a distance, I heard the gondolier say, "Eighteen, nineteen, twenty." We ignored him. The gondolier broke into a Patsy Cline song.

"That's more like it," Jonathan murmured.

I covered his mouth with mine before he had a chance to reconsider the kiss. It was more leisurely than before, less desperate. Finally, we pulled apart, resting forehead to forehead. "I don't know if I can ever trust you," Jonathan murmured. "I'm afraid you'll lie to me again."

I kissed his eyebrows, his eyelids, his nose. I rested my forehead back against his. "I'm afraid you'll run away from me," I whispered. "That you'll leave me all alone."

"So I guess we're even," he said.

"I guess we are."

The gondolier began to turn the boat around. "I can take you back now."

"Just a few more minutes," Jonathan said. He tilted his head and kissed me lightly.

"Sorry, but your time's almost up," the gondolier said. "If we're not back in five minutes, I'll have to charge you for another ride."

"Give us another half hour," I said, running my hands through Jonathan's hair. "The guy on the dock will pay for it."

epilogue

The wedding was held in my parents' backyard on a brisk but
sunny Saturday in late January. The movers had finished carting
away the furniture two days earlier; the cleaners would come on
Monday. By the end of the following week, the high-ceilinged
stucco house would belong to the Sandlers, and Marjorie Wamsley
would be tooling around Scottsdale's gated communities in yet another new luxury SUV.

"Always a bridesmaid," Jill muttered, sucking in her breath and
yanking up a side zipper. I thought I heard something rip, but I
knew better than to say anything.

"You never know," I said, zipping up my own, identical dress.
It was ice blue with silver beads, a scandalous leg slit and a plunging neckline. Mine sagged at the top. "I'm thinking of sticking
some socks in my bra."

Jill narrowed her eyes. "Not a bad idea." Her ample cleavage was busting out of the top. The dress didn't come in Jill's size; she had to make do with the largest one in stock. "I'm never going to make it through the day," she grumbled. "This thing is cutting off my circulation." The dress was supposed to be ankle length, but mine dragged on the floor, while Jill's ended at mid-calf. Only a couple of the bridesmaids (there were eleven) could carry off the dress. As maid of honor, plump little Dawna pulled rank and wore something else entirely: a midnight blue, drop-waist beaded number. She looked like the mother of the bride—assuming she'd given birth when she was two.

We used my former bedroom—now empty—as the bridesmaids' dressing room, leaving the master suite to Nicolette. Secretly, I was relieved that the furniture was gone. I couldn't bear the thought of Nicolette and Rodney having sex on my parents' bed.

Nicolette looked stunning in a surprisingly simple strapless white satin gown, her hair swept up and studded with white roses and tiny rhinestones. In her arms she cradled a bouquet of white flowers loosely tied with a thick organza ribbon.

"You look like something out of a magazine," I told her, sneaking into my parents' old bedroom shortly before Nicolette was to make her grand entrance.

"You think so?" She scurried over to a pile in the corner. She grabbed a worn copy of *Modern Bride* and flipped hastily through. "My inspiration." She held the page up for me to see.

And there she was: Nicolette. Or, rather, some girl who looked just like Nicolette, right down to the flower and rhinestone placement in her blond hair.

"You look prettier," I said. She did. "Besides, this girl's just a model. You've got a real groom waiting for you downstairs."

As for the groom, Rodney looked, like, well . . . like Rodney in white tails and a top hat. The coat strained at his biceps. His cologne was spicy citrus and could be smelled from half a yard away. He waited next to the spa while Nicolette made her grand, slow entrance. His face was flushed, his eyes shiny. At first I thought: oh, no—Rodney's drunk! And then it hit me: he was simply a man in love. (Who, okay, may have had a couple of beers to calm his nerves, but who could blame him?)

Jill and Lars never had to trick Rodney into taking a gondola ride with Nicolette. Rather, the day after my reconciliation with Jonathan, Nicolette did the obvious thing: she called Rodney. She told him she loved him. He said he loved her, too. She said she wanted a real wedding. He said okay. They figured out a way to make it work on a limited budget. If only all of life's dilemmas were resolved this easily.

The ceremony was short. Nicolette said something about how much she loved Rodney, then Rodney said something about how much he loved Nicolette—most of which we all missed because Nicolette had insisted I turn on the pool filter, the resulting water-fall being exotic, romantic . . . and noisy. Then some guy named Jim who may or may not have had any legal authority (they were already married, after all) proclaimed them "joined in front of God, their friends, family and community." Then Rodney kissed Nicolette so sloppily I could hear it over the waterfall and past nine bridesmaids. We were arranged by height; I was second to shortest, beating out Nicolette's eleven-year-old sister, Daniella, by an inch. Since there was not enough room for us on the flagstones, Daniella and I had been relegated to a gravel patch that was difficult to navigate in my silver stiletto heels.

Not everything had gone according to Nicolette's glossy magazine dreams. The invitations weren't engraved. They weren't even printed. Two weeks earlier, she'd sent a mass e-mail that read:

Nicolette and Rodney invite you to attend their wedding—the real one!—a week from Saturday at Miss Natalie Quackenbush's parents' house (they're moving but it's still their house) at 1:00 in the afternoon until . . . ?

The bride and groom are registered at Macy's, Linens 'n Things, The Great Indoors, Williams Sonoma, Target, Nordstrom, JC Penney, Sears, Bed, Bath & Beyond, Ross-Simons, Robinsons-May and Sports Authority.

There was no sit-down dinner. Hors d'oeuvres were all that Robert and his crew—Katerina, a few kids from Adventures, and the boys I'd seen him with at the play, all attired in black trousers and white shirts—could handle. Besides, my parents' backyard, big as it was, couldn't possibly handle enough tables to seat all of the guests. There had to be three hundred people there.

There was no live band. Rather, Nicolette brought her iPod along with a set of Bose speakers. After a while, I managed to block out the hip hop music. Rodney brought a karaoke machine.

There was no professional photographer. However, Dawna assured Nicolette she would make "the most awesomest wedding memory book ever." Since Dawna was in the wedding, her husband used one hand to hold onto little Chenille (who we all worried would fall into the pool) and the other to snap pictures with the family camera. Nicolette's mother (who looked way too young to have a married daughter) snapped compulsively, too, as did at least thirty other guests, including eleven-year-old, eyeshadow-wearing Daniella, though she mostly took pictures of Robert.

None of it mattered. Jonathan, who looked staggeringly handsome in a dark suit, crisp white shirt and red tie, called in a favor from a party supply business. They supplied wine, highball and martini glasses, plenty of folding chairs, and several long tables to hold the mountains of gifts. Since Rodney hadn't had time to round up attendants—or, perhaps, this being his fourth time down the aisle, he had simply exhausted the patience of his nearest and dearest—Jonathan served as a kind of de facto usher, guiding the guests to the rows of borrowed chairs.

Lars manned a bar stocked mainly by the teachers, who, in a merry affront to their chronic respectability, came bearing jugs of vodka, six packs of beer and boxes of wine. Lars served drinks like a professional. Actually, having been turned down by the charter school, he was a professional—he'd taken a job at the Happy Cactus to hold him over until he could find another teaching position.

"Good to see you, Lars," Dr. White said, approaching the bar. She wore a pale pink suit, the skirt calf-length and slit, and a ruffled blouse. Dr. White made pink look like a power color. She ordered a Cape Codder—"Make it weak, please"—and asked Lars about his job hunt.

"I'm evaluating several possibilities," he said. "Weighing my options."

"We all miss you at Agave, you know. And we wish you well." Dr. White smiled at me. I'd come by for a soda (there were an awful lot of my students here, after all). "I'm glad you came to your senses, Natalie," she said. I'd withdrawn my resignation hours before Dr. White was going to offer the job to someone else.

His back blocking Dr. White's vision, Lars dumped a liver-threatening amount of vodka into a highball glass, added a splash of cranberry juice for color and garnished with a lime. "Here you go." He smiled.

Dr. White reached for the glass. "Oh, my—that's a bit bigger than I expected."

Lars smiled angelically. "It's mostly juice."

Within an hour, Dr. White had commandeered the karaoke machine. She looked like Aretha Franklin. She sounded like a drunk
high school principal.

Finally, Nicolette and Rodney piled their gifts into the back of
Rodney's new truck. "Good thing I got the new truck," he re-
marked. "The gifts wouldn'ta fit in my old truck."

Nicolette didn't respond. Instead, she picked up an especially
pretty box and shook it lightly next to her ear.

The guests left soon after; it was approaching dinner time, and
the hors d'oeuvres and cake, while delicious, had been a bit sparse.
Robert and his crew picked up the abandoned napkins and put the
dirty glasses back into their plastic crates. Well, the crew did most
of the work; on my way to the bathroom, I practically tripped over
Robert and Katerina, who were clutching each other next to the
kitchen island. They both turned bright red (as did I) and scurried
off to wipe the counters.

Finally, it was down to Lars, Jill, Jonathan and me. Lars dug out
a bottle of chardonnay he'd squirreled away under the bar and
poured us each a glass. We trudged over to the spa. Jill and I hiked
up our shimmering dresses (we'd long since abandoned our panty-
hose and heels), settled onto the flagstones and dipped our feet into
the water. I had just turned on the heat; the water was still chilly.
The men joined us, taking off their shoes and socks and rolling up
their trousers.

"Brr," Lars said.

"It'll warm up soon."

Lars splashed the water with his toes. "So, Nat, how's the new
place working out?" I had just moved into Jill's old apartment; she
and Lars had rented something together near Old Town.

"I'm not there very much," I said, shooting a glance at Jonathan. He smiled. "And what about the two of you?" I asked. "How's living in sin?"

"When I leave my clothes on the floor, Jill says I am being passive aggressive," Lars said.

"You are," Jill said.

"And she says I suffer from narcissistic tendencies."

"You do."

He took her hand. "But I think she likes me anyway."

The water grew warmer and warmer until my toes began to glow. In the giant saguaro, a woodpecker *rat-tat-tatted* away. On the far side of the yard, a rabbit hopped into view and nibbled on some sprinkler-sustained plants.

"It was twenty degrees when I was at my sister's," I said. I'd planned to stay two weeks. I lasted five days. "My father kept checking the weather on the computer and announcing the temperature in Scottsdale. He and my mother are making noises about buying a condo out here, something little that they can lock up and leave for months at a time." I gazed at the purple mountains. "It won't be anything like this, though."

"I'm going to miss this place," Jill sighed. "We'll never have such a nice spot to hang out in."

Jonathan picked up his wineglass and held it up to the light. The yellow liquid reflected splotches of pink from the desert sunset. "Not necessarily," he said. "Wait till you see my father's new house."

Carol Snow has a master's degree in education from Boston College and is a former contributor to Salon.com. Visit her website at carolsnow.com.